BEYOND THE COMFORT ZONE: THE WAR THAT NEVER ENDS

FRANK WILKINS

Beyond The Comfort Zone
The War That Never Ends
Copyright © 2021 by Frank Wilkins
Revised Version of the 2015 Run

Library of Congress Control Number:	2020917427
ISBN-13: Paperback:	978-1-64749-560-2
Epub:	978-1-64749-238-0

All rights reserved. No part of this publication may be reproduced, distributed, or transmitted in any form or by any means, including photocopying, recording, or other electronic or mechanical methods, without the prior written permission of the publisher or author, except in the case of brief quotations embodied in critical reviews and certain other noncommercial uses permitted by copyright law.

Although every precaution has been taken to verify the accuracy of the information contained herein, the author and publisher assume no responsibility for any errors or omissions.No liability is assumed for damages that may result from the use of information contained within.

Printed in the United States of America

GoToPublish LLC
1-888-337-1724
www.gotopublish.com
info@gotopublish.com

Contents

FOREWORD v
FOONOTES viii

Chapter 1 1
Chapter 2 14
Chapter 3 28
Chapter 4 33
Chapter 5 38
Chapter 6 67
Chapter 7 110
Chapter 8 119
Chapter 9 126
Chapter 10 143
Chapter 11 148
Chapter 12 157
Chapter 13 165
Chapter 14 174
Chapter 15 183
Chapter 16 191
Chapter 17 203
Chapter 18 207
Chapter 19 215
Chapter 20 237

GLOSSARY 247
BIBLIOGRAPHY 254

This book is dedicated to my mother, who may have been the greatest cook in all of human history, and to my father, who fought for his country in two wars. Without them, I wouldn't be the man I am today.

F.W.

FOREWORD

In case you haven't noticed, you're living in the middle of a battlefield. Your state, this nation— Western civilization itself— is in the middle of a war.

I'm not talking about any war fought with guns and missiles. This war is being waged in people's minds. In this war each one of us is an objective, a target and a prize.

Does that sound far-fetched? Think about it. Daily, we're bombarded with commercials, news bulletins, political statements, entertainments, and other items designed to capture our attention. We have advice columnists telling us what to do, ads telling us what to buy, and TV commentators telling us what to think. And we have only one really reliable person to help us make sense out of it all— ourself.

Our minds are important. Everything begins there. Every idea, every perception, every decision comes out of our own thinking. So it stands to reason, when each of us finds a higher truth to believe in, that's important too. Because just about every major decision we make in our life will be affected by what we believe in.

This type of war for people's minds is not new.[1] Before the pyramids were built, ancient Egypt was a battleground between various local deities. In the 2nd Dynasty (27th century BC), followers of the gods Horus and Seth were struggling for control of the country. That was at the dawn of recorded history— and it's a safe bet that such conflicts were taking place long before the invention of the written word.

---

[1] Although such conflicts had been known since ancient times, the term "culture war" was coined in the 19th century. In the 1870s, the government of Bismarck's Germany launched a campaign to repress the Catholic Church. This quickly developed into a church vs. state conflict, which German writers of the time described as a *kulturkampf*, or a "struggle for civilization." [9:Vol. 7:30]

This same type of conflict is what we're seeing today, right in this country.

Since the earliest colonial times, American society has been grounded in Judeo-Christian culture. There have been many denominations of churches and synagogues, but essentially this has been the character of our society. Of course, there have been people of other religions, too, such as Buddhism and Islam. And there've been atheists, people who don't believe in God at all. But only since the 1960s have we seen something entirely new in this country— the appearance of a militant brand of atheism.

The followers of this new atheism promote their ideas vigorously. They do so at times by attacking traditional faiths such as Christianity. Of course, this is a free country. They have a perfect right to state their beliefs, and to criticize other beliefs. I support this freedom, and I respect their rights.

But there's another side to that coin. Just as they have a right to attack Christianity, men and women of faith have a right to answer those charges. And it's a legitimate response. That First Amendment was written for everyone, not just for atheists.

As a former agnostic, I can understand the thinking of atheists. I used to be immersed in the same basic mindset. I also understand that both sides can't be right. There either is a God, or there isn't.

By reading this book, you are showing a type of courage that not everybody has. As I said, we're living in a battlefield. This book isn't an exhortation to join in the battle. It's simply to help you see a clearer picture of what's happening. Its purpose is to get people to think.

Believe it or not, a lot of people would rather do anything than think. And a multi-billion dollar entertainment industry— offering everything from comic books to cable TV— is proof of it. It's a simple process called escapism.

And we all need a little escapism. We all have our comfort zones, where music, television and countless other amusements give our minds refuge from the pressures of everyday life. That's why it's grown into a major industry.

People will pay big bucks to stay in that beloved comfort zone. It takes courage to look beyond that. And— just as important— it takes honesty.

This book is designed to take you beyond the comfort zone.

FOONOTES

Just a word here about the footnotes. Some books use all those Latin abbreviations, such as "ibid.," and "op. cit." I prefer to use English. At the end of this book, you will find a bibliography listing my sources. Each of these sources is numbered. As an example, if you find a footnote which says [12:150], it simply means "Source No. 12, page 150." (The two sources from *Encyclopedia Britannica* also list the volume number in the footnote.) Where I've referenced quotes from the Bible, the sources are shown like this: {John 20:23}. This means, of course, that the quote refers to the Gospel of John, chapter 20, verse 23. It can then be looked up in any Bible of your choosing. I hope that this system will be simple to follow, as well as convenient.

Chapter 1

THE BIG QUESTION

"Is there a God?" This is the eternal question which, sooner or later, is asked by every functioning human mind.

The question is so simple— and yet the answer to it (or the way that we choose to answer it) carries tremendous influence over our thinking, our world-view, and even our very lives.

We live in a culture that questions everything, and teaches us to demand proof with every answer. Yet the personal belief in God is largely a matter of faith. Anyone can talk to the God he believes in, simply by praying. But how rare it is, that someone actually hears God say something back. I've certainly never had any two-way conversations with Him, and I've never met anyone who claims they have.

Our society doesn't make it easy to believe in God. Instead, it teaches us to put our faith in things like science, technology, even in the meanderings of our own hearts. When I mention the heart, of course, I'm referring mainly to love. Love is big in our culture. And in a way, there's nothing wrong with that. After all, romantic love is often a catalyst which transforms our lives in many ways— many of them wholesome, beneficial and beautiful.

On the other side of love (I don't like calling it the "dark" side, because in an ideal world love should have no dark side), we have the spectacle of our society *marketing* love. It may not be very romantic to say it, but all you have to do is look around: love sells. Weddings, engagement rings, honeymoon vacation packages, anniversaries— even such minor things as floral bouquets and boxed candy— are all part of a major American industry. If romantic love were eliminated from our culture, I'd guess that probably a fifth of our national economy would vanish.

This doesn't include sex. If sex suddenly disappeared— not in the real world, but in our culture— from places like the movies, daytime television, magazines and billboards, I'd estimate that would probably destroy *half* the economy. What would we ever do without those scenes of bed play that spice up our entertainment? Not only do they sell many valuable products, but every day it's there on TV for our children to watch while they're at home. (Nothing like a free education for the kiddies, eh?)

Just by taking a look around us, we can see how our culture— even our society itself— is geared towards drawing us away from faith in God, not reinforcing it.

But in every human mind, the question is still there. Does God exist? If so, what kind of God is He? If God doesn't exist, what is life all about? What is its purpose? What is our *own* purpose?

These are abstract questions, but there's nothing abstract about the way they affect our lives. I know. I've been an agnostic, a non-denominational Christian, and finally a Roman Catholic. Each one of these states of being has affected my life tremendously.

Now, faith hasn't made me "perfect," and I'm sure it never will. But if God had wanted us to be perfect, He could have made us out of stainless steel. Obviously He had a different plan in mind. Even so, I'm glad to say that faith has given me far more purpose— and strength— than I ever had without it. If I can't have "perfect," I'll be glad to settle for "better, and still improving."

I've learned many things along the way— but I'm saying one thing right now, and I'm not going to whisper it or tremble with fear over it: The best thing I ever learned is that God is real.

It's not always a smooth ride, going from agnosticism to faith. In fact, it can be a pretty bumpy road. But you can trust me on this: It's worth it.

Think of it like this. By telling yourself, "There's no proof, so there's no God," you're not only making a huge leap of faith right there, but you're putting blinders on yourself— restraints of pride, cynicism, and false logic. From that moment on, everything you *choose* to disbelieve is going to lose all relevance for you. And over time, you'll do whatever is necessary to reinforce your personal doctrine of non-belief.

You will close your mind to all historical evidence of God's existence. You'll automatically scoff at the idea of miracles. You'll start to look at organized religion as a collection of greedy pastors feeding off a bunch of "superstitious" fools.

Atheism is an insidious mental process. As lack of faith grows, so does animosity towards faith. Disdain for "greedy" pastors and priests easily morphs into resentment and hostility. Pity for the poor "deluded" faithful transforms into contempt. What do hostility and contempt have in common? They are both forms of hatred.

But the irony of this is amazing. While rejecting God, the same person who closes his mind to this one thing finds it necessary to open the door to another. Like it or not, the human psyche requires us to believe in *something*. Something in our psychological make-up *compels* us to have some type of faith. There is just no other explanation for the way people think. At some point in his life, every individual simply *has* to reconcile himself to metaphysical issues.

THE WORLD OF ILLUSIONS VS. THE NEED FOR REALITY

It's as if some part of our psyche can sense that there's more to existence than what we see each day. Somehow, we perceive that this daily world is like a darkened, underground mine. We know that light exists, because something deep within us tells us so. But while we're bombarded with music, video images and commercials daily, we can sense that these are illusions— like part of some artificial "light show" in the underground tunnels. (Music, in itself, can uplift us and sometimes even help us spiritually. But the way it's being commercialized has turned it into just another money-making product.)

Deep inside the mine, we know that there is genuine light somewhere— real truth. The videos and music cannot be that truth. Their only purpose is to grab our attention, tranquilize us, and get us to spend money. But somewhere outside the mine there is light, which is truth. Because we can sense this, we know that we must find our way through the maze. For some reason we want to find the light which is real. The Greek philosopher Plato once drew an analogy of this world being like a cave. In many ways, we can see that this applies to our own society, just as it did in his time.

Occasionally, this yearning for truth has moved many people to settle for artificial, man-made sources of light. For several generations, a large part of the world's population believed in Marxist communism. Marxism is an ideology; however, it's also a religion— complete with its own world-view, its own set of morals and its own prophecy. Any good Marxist (if you can still find one), will tell you it's the most "scientific" belief system that's ever sprung from the mind of man. The fact that it's been used to justify dictatorships, oppression and mass murder is merely incidental. And this is an historical fact which any good Marxist will cheerfully ignore, if you let him.

Of course, if you look back in history, there are tyrants who have also used Christianity to justify crimes. But Christianity itself has never advocated murder and oppression. Marxist communism has always taught that the end justifies the means.

Another ideology, still popular in our own society, is feminism. Standard feminist ideology demands that women should have the power of life and death over their children, even up to the day of birth. The baby in the womb is deemed subhuman (nothing but a "fetus"), unworthy of any right to draw his or her first breath. You can forget about the scientific proof that each baby is genetically complete from the moment of fertilization— scientific fact is of no importance to anyone trying to justify the slaughter of unborn children. Considering the tens of millions of babies aborted since the *Roe v. Wade* decision in 1973, we can see that the body count racked up by feminism will soon surpass the deaths generated by communism and Nazism combined— if it hasn't already.

Ideologies aside, this country has countless religions operating, many of which are in direct opposition to the Judeo-Christian God. Just look at all the followers of Wicca, mother-goddess worship, even a few who claim to believe in the ancient pagan gods.

In the last half-century (a mere two generations), we've seen religions like pyramid worship, "New Age," and outright Satanism springing up. Even dyed-in-the-wool atheists have to believe in something. There are always the abstract gods of Mammon (money) and technology to put one's faith in. Madalyn Murray O'Hair was a world-famous atheist who sued to have all prayers banned from public schools back in 1962. [43:917] Apparently she put her faith in gold, until she (along with a son and granddaughter) were all murdered in 1995, for a half-million-dollar pile of it which they'd accumulated.

So, part of the Big Question is not whether we'll have any faith, but what exactly do we choose to put our faith in? If not God, then who (or what) else?

Don't kid yourself— faith is important. And having once lived without it, I can tell you why. Just look at a daily paper. Any typical newspaper from any day of the week will make at least one thing obvious: As the old cliché goes, "No man is an island." We live in a big world, and that world doesn't just start at our doorstep— it even wants to invade our home.

Every day most of us must step outside, knowing that we'll have to deal with whatever comes our way. There are a few people who are exceptions to this. But even they depend in part on what's happening in the world around us. Someone who's independently rich will still have to monitor the markets to protect their money. Anyone who's an invalid will depend on the availability of medical coverage and the politics which govern it. Whether we like it or not, we are all part of that big world outside our door.

And that world is not geared toward benevolence. If we have cable TV, we're saturated with commercials on nearly every channel, telling us how to think and what to buy. And, of course, there's daytime TV with its soap operas, striving to bring as much treachery, deceit, violence and extramarital sex into our homes as the law allows. (All that stuff sells.)

As soon as we step outside we have ultraviolet light, polluted air, and an urban society littered with petty criminals to welcome us. Once we're in the car or on that bus, we're surrounded by countless other vehicles being driven by people who are themselves driven to "be on time."

For the vast majority of us who get through the day without becoming a statistic, we have fellow employees and supervisors to deal with. If we're employees we have to bring home paychecks, and if we're employers we have to worry about payrolls. Both company and employee are vulnerable to that vast, amorphous entity called "the economy," which can change the lives of millions with very little warning and not much delay.

Once we look beyond our national borders, life gets even more interesting. There was a time when Americans believed the oceans protected us. That myth was shattered at Pearl Harbor. Much later, a lot of people thought we could afford to ignore things like airplane hijackings in Beirut and embassy bombings in Africa, and just keep going back to "business as usual." Then those Middle Eastern terrorists launched the attacks of 9/11. The result was a serious, long-running war which— in reality— may continue for many more years. It's a situation where every country is a potential front.

One of those fronts is right here at home. The United States hasn't been in a position like this since the Cold War. We've still got terrorist organizations out there just chomping at the bit to get their hands on the materials for an atomic bomb, and at least two hostile states (Iran and North Korea) which are in production. These are not alarmist outcries; they're facts. Sometimes, looking at such facts, it's impossible not to wonder just how long it'll take for the mix to be complete.

All this might sound like excessive worry, or even paranoia, but if anyone in August 2001 had predicted that the U.S. would be attacked and the World Trade Center destroyed, what would others have said about that? The ancient plagues of envy, hatred and conflict have not disappeared from the Earth. The future still holds plenty of uncertainties.

So, the question is: What do we put our faith in?

No one wants to put his faith in something phony. We all have to deal with a life filled with realities, and there should be something real for us to believe in. Can God be real?

THE INCREDIBLE DIFFICULTY OF BELIEVING

As a former agnostic, I honestly know how difficult it can be to believe in a God. And it's not hard to see that others can find it just as difficult.

The ancient Greeks developed the idea of *philosophy*. The word "philosophy" is itself Greek, and it means simply the love of wisdom. There were many Greek philosophers, including Socrates and his famous student Plato.

Nowadays, we have quite a few modern schools of philosophy, such as Existentialism. There are also theoretical physicists, who work at explaining the dynamics of the physical universe. Some of these philosophies and theories are like structures. They are built for one purpose: to help people to understand the meaning of life, and/or the universe around us.

But there's more to it. Many of them appear to be constructed not only to explain these questions about human existence, but also to give people some of life's answers— and something to live for— *without God*.

Think about it. Some of the greatest minds in Western civilization have devoted themselves to building a view of the universe which has some *purpose,* but no God. It's as if the most important goal in life is to find answers to every question— except that one.

In many of these theoretical constructs, God is the one thing that cannot be entered into the equation. The very question of God's existence is generally avoided, because it isn't "logical." To many of these great thinkers, it appears that God is simply too irrational, too simplistic, too primitive to be taken seriously. So by dismissing (or ignoring) the possibility of God, they can invent their own answers to life's great questions.

As an example, there's one very brilliant theoretical physicist who is currently active. His name is Garrett Lisi, Ph.D. On a popular science TV show called "Through the Wormhole," presented in 2010, Dr. Lisi discussed his theory of universal physics. Based on a geometric structure of his own design, which has been named "the E8 Lie (pronounced lee) Group," Dr. Lisi described his idea as "an Exceptionally Simple Theory of Everything." During his presentation, he made the following statement:

"It's much more satisfying to me that this bit of geometry could have come into existence than to imagine [that] some complicated Creator with some sort of personality and complex structure brought this simple thing into existence." [Source No. 41]

In other words, his brilliantly conceived theory was far easier for him to believe in, than any Creator God. And his 248-layered E8 Lie Group diagram (which is challenging to comprehend, even when shown in three dimensions) is much simpler for him, than any God who has "some sort of personality and complex structure".

Dr. Lisi is without doubt a scientific genius, and I am definitely not passing any kind of judgment on him. After all, I used to be an agnostic myself. On the contrary, I think he should be respected for his honesty. He has openly stated that one of his own favorite aspects of his theory, is that it explains the structure of the universe without requiring any reference to God.

This idea actually sums up the essence of many philosophies and theories. Once great thinkers have deleted God from the equation, they've opened all other possibilities. Now they're free to pursue their own answers, which will be as good (or better) than those of any other mortal man. They're soaring into the intellectual stratosphere which only the chosen few can conquer.

They're visionaries, with no higher power to contradict them. They're pioneers, blazing a trail for others to follow. They're looking straight ahead. They're confident in their course. They're comfortable with their blinders on.

One must admit, it's an attractive idea. After all, we're Americans. We're taught to believe in democracy, in freedom of thought, in pluralism. How can we reconcile all this with the concept of a God who is supreme over everything? Not just any god, but a God who is unique, sharing the turf of His universe with no other god? Not only that, but (most incredible of all) a *personal* God, who actually loves each of us individually and cares for us. This idea of a "Creator with some sort of personality" was precisely what Dr. Lisi felt was too "complex." And this is understandable.

Who could have imagined such a God? For at least the first 700 years of recorded history (and countless centuries of prehistory) no one knew there was a God like that. The people of ancient times had almost no concept of such a deity. Some cultures had vague ideas of a benevolent creator god— sometimes seen as a father of the other gods— but that was as far as it went.

Nearly every ancient civilization known to history had *armies* of gods. They invented separate gods of creation, love, fate and war— everything they could think of. Most countries had gods of drunkenness, fertility, healing, and even humor. In ancient Egypt and Hatti (the nation of the Hittites), it was stated with pride that each country worshiped a thousand gods. In the world today, the best parallel we can see would be the Hindu religion of India, where many gods are still worshiped.

Only two major cultures of the ancient world had any experience with monotheism. One was in Egypt. One pharaoh of the 18th Dynasty (Akhenaten) tried to suppress the worship of the traditional Egyptian gods, replacing them with a single deity, a sun god. The other, of course, was the ancient Hebrews, who put their faith in the God whom they knew as Yahweh.

It's stunning to realize that this same Hebrew deity, the God of a few tribes of desert nomads who once labored as slaves in Egypt, is now recognized as the true God whom most of the world worships today. The three great revealed faiths of modern times— Judaism, Christianity and Islam— all trace their theological roots to the God of those nomadic Hebrews.

But does that make Him real? Just because a single God has been worshiped throughout the last 4,000 years of human history, and is now worshiped (in one form or another) by most of the world's population, does that make Him real?

No. What makes Him real is the actuality of His existence— the very fact that He is there.

As a former agnostic, and one who was strong in my disbelief, I can tell you that the only way to find satisfactory proof of His existence is to look for it. You don't have to look very far. There's incredibly strong evidence in almost every direction. There are even some outright miracles which provide actual physical proof— some of them readily observable today, for anyone to see.

You can look back in history— not only biblical history, but more recent history— and find numerous examples of God's intervention in human events. You can investigate various religions, some of which have their origin in the beginnings of Christianity itself. You can even try communicating with God (praying once in a while) and asking Him to show you proof. It isn't necessary to tell anyone about it. Your search for the truth can be strictly between you and Him.

Some people pride themselves on the idea that they don't "need" a God. But pride isn't named as one of the Seven Deadly Sins for nothing. Sometimes it can do more damage than ignorance.

There was a certain world-famous billionaire in the 20th century. His name was Howard Hughes. (A fairly recent movie about him was *The Aviator,* starring Leonardo DiCaprio.) This Mr. Hughes was a very interesting billionaire. He never smoked and his health was generally good. He was as rich as Croesus and he could buy just about anything he wanted.

Hughes made quite a name for himself. In 1947 he took the world's biggest plane (which he had ordered built) and flew it for a short distance, to prove it was airworthy. When the U.S. government wanted to dredge up a Soviet submarine with nuclear weapons which had sunk in 1968, Hughes actually paid to have a special salvage ship, called the *Glomar Explorer,* built. Then he made it available to the government to secretly retrieve the sub. In other words, Hughes was a man who could get things done.

Here's the point: For all his wealth and fame— for all his apparent power— Howard Hughes was still one of the world's great losers. His only legal wife, a beautiful Hollywood actress, left him. He was so terrified of germs that he locked himself up in one penthouse or another, with only his servants for company. It was said that he was even afraid of things like scissors, and so he let his hair grow wild.

Here was a guy who evidently didn't need any God. It was as if he was his own god— he had power, wealth, and a self-made business empire. But he retreated into isolation and he died in isolation, while taking a private jet back to Texas in 1976. He thought he had it all. He thought he owned it all, or could at least buy it all. But in reality he wound up with nothing but his fears, his bank statements and his self-imposed prison. Even a billionaire can end up in his own private hell.

The only trouble with the notion of "not needing God" is, sooner or later you're going to suffer. Nobody goes through life without trials and suffering. And those who think they're above it are only fooling themselves.

Sooner or later, we all have troubles to deal with. This world isn't geared for ease and perfection. But with God helping us, we can get through everything and even prevail. I'm not just talking about faith— I'm talking about miracles. I'm talking about direct intercession in people's lives. I'm talking about real help, with all of life's real problems.

And the answers are so simple. During the years I was an agnostic, I wouldn't believe in anything I could not see proved. On that solitary premise, I closed my mind to any God and I closed my eyes to any proof. It's amazing, how little stupidity it takes to change one's life. And it never changes it for the better.

I have to admit, I do have an advantage over many. I finally opened my eyes and started searching. And when I started looking for answers, they were given to me. God gave me the proof I wanted. In this book I'm going to describe some of the things He showed me.

I guess it's an unfair advantage, that I've seen the things I have. I don't simply have faith in God; now I *know* He's there. But if I hadn't finally stopped closing my mind, I'm sure He wouldn't have shown me anything. I think it's very rare, that God will force someone to open their mind to Him. The reason for this is a thing called "free will." We can all choose our own beliefs, our own path in life. And we can make those choices because God gave us the gift of free will.

But what's the best way to use this gift to our advantage? Is someone better off simply telling himself there's no God, and then closing his mind to it? Does putting blinders on ourselves help us in life? Or is it more intelligent to look for the answers? And this brings us to the most astounding part of the Big Question. It's astounding, because faith isn't just a matter of abstract thinking— it's also a question of simple practicality.

For those who have the courage and honesty to look for the answers, the result carries limitless rewards. *Once we discover that God really exists, the discoveries have just begun.*

Because then we find out that this God is not some cold, distant deity. He's actually a loving, caring, personal God who looks after every one of us individually. And it follows that He can do amazing things for us— things that can change our lives for the better.

One of the great benefits of faith is an inner strength that transcends all human weakness. We're all human beings, burdened with worries, fears, self-doubts, and a slew of other emotional handicaps. This is how we all start out; it's what we call the human condition.

And there's good reason for having some of those fears and self-doubts. No one knows our weaknesses and shortcomings better than we do. Even if we try to laugh off the truth, we know it's still there inside us. And at times we tend to magnify our faults. It's been said that "each of us is our own worst critic." I think that's true for all of us, at one time or another.

But just knowing that God is real infuses us with another, greater truth— not a truth based on blind faith, but a truth set in the solid rock of reality. With God, we have someone to turn to, someone to lean on, and someone to help us. And all that's necessary is for us to reach out to Him, and *know* that He's listening.

As a former agnostic, I know that just saying this won't convince any dedicated disbeliever. Some people go through life glued to their TV sets. Nothing is more important than their favorite sitcoms, or those treasured sports events. Some spend their time catering to other little addictions. Some people may actually think their time is too valuable to be spent thinking about little things like God. Maybe they think they've "heard it all before."

But I'm going to say some things you haven't heard before. If you have what it takes to read this book, I'm going to challenge you— to shake your disbelief— to *force* you to think of things you've probably never even considered before. If you have what it takes to read this book, I'm going to rip those blinders off you and let in enough light to keep you blinking for the rest of your life.

You think you've heard it all before? No, my friend, you've never been more wrong. Nobody has heard it all. I haven't, you haven't, and neither have your parents or grandparents. The only one who's heard it all is God. And, as St. Catherine of Siena reputedly said, "There is a God, and we ain't Him."

I won't be able to tell you everything. But I'm going to tell you enough to make you think. If you have what it takes to open your mind and think beyond the blinders, then keep reading. Who knows? You just might end up being glad you did.

Chapter 2

THE IMPORTANCE OF TRUTH

How important to you is that thing called "the truth"?

Let's be honest. Everyone says they care about the truth. But when it comes to telling (or hearing) what's true, a hell of a lot of people don't like it. Not only that, but there are huge numbers of people who love to twist it, until it bears little resemblance to reality. Have you heard the word "revisionist"? It refers, of course, to writers, editors, producers, etc. (some of whom call themselves historians) who lie about history in order to promote their own views. I would include in this group those people who just tell half the story, leaving out the facts and details which they might find "embarrassing." As an example— after more than 120 years, you'd think everyone would be through fighting the Indian wars. But how can any good revisionist ignore an opportunity to crank out some great propaganda?

A few years ago my kids gave me a DVD of the movie *National Treasure,* the first one. Included with the disc was a paperback book titled *Don't Know Much About American History.* [Source No. 6] It looks to me as if someone— perhaps some nameless editor— was intending, not to teach people who were ignorant about American history, but to *keep* them ignorant.

Chapter 2 started off by telling about the Indians and the early English colonists. As it started describing the early conflicts, the book told about the first Indian war in New England in 1636-37, when the English settled the conflict by burning out the Pequot Indians in the Connecticut River Valley. The decisive battle took place on May 26, 1637. The Pequots had built up their forces, then made a stand in a tribal fort which contained about

800 people packed into 80 small huts. The colonists attacked the fort at dawn, and a firefight ensued. Finally, the English captain ordered the torching of the huts. Most of the Pequots died in the conflagration, with those escaping falling to English muskets. It must have been a scene reminiscent of the burning of the Branch Davidian compound in Waco, Texas, in 1993. (Of course, the English had no tanks to attack the fort with, as the ATF did in Texas.)

Nearly all the cornered Indians died within half an hour, and from that day on the Pequots ceased to be a tribal force. In later fighting, remaining Pequot warriors were ruthlessly put to the sword while their women and children were sold into slavery. One can see the cruel logic of all this. Other tribes were stunned, and quickly recognized the value of peaceful coexistence with the settlers. Still, the English colonists had indeed fought a war of extermination and shown precious little mercy to the enemy. Against the Pequots, it had assumed the nature of a genocidal war.

A lot of modern-day historians love to cite the Pequot War, because it tends to make all English colonists look like mass murderers. But in this book, the Pequot War was presented as if it were the *first Indian war ever fought* in colonial English America.

What the book completely ignored was the fact that an earlier (and far bigger) war had been fought in Virginia. It's known as the First Powhatan War, and it started in 1622 when the ruler of the Powhatan Confederation, a chieftain named Opechancanough, launched a sneak attack throughout the colony which *wiped out about a third of all the Virginia settlers*— women and children included. That war went on, being fought intermittently, for ten years. [15:17-18]

Now, the [2]First Powhatan War had started years before Connecticut even existed. It was ignited by a huge massacre of frontier families, perpetrated by the Powhatan Indians. The Pequot War in Connecticut was finished by settlers burning out

---

[2] Occasionally called the "Second Powhatan War," even though the earlier strife was not a war.

the Indians. (So obviously the colonists could be branded as mass murderers.)

What did these people do, to keep this "first clash" narrative about the settlers and Indians politically correct? They conveniently forgot that the First Powhatan War ever happened.

This isn't an isolated example. (As I said, revisionists *love* to cite the Pequot War.) In 2006 the famed History Channel put out a set of DVDs, titled "10 Days that Unexpectedly Changed America." The very first item on the menu was called "Massacre at Mystic." This was also about the Pequot War of 1636-37. On the back of the cover containing the first DVD, they described that battle as "the first time the English settlers engaged in the slaughter of Native Americans after years of relatively peaceful coexistence."

So this outfit calling itself the "History Channel" is telling us that either (a) the First Powhatan War never happened, or (b) it should be considered as "relatively peaceful coexistence." Apparently a war isn't a war (and a massacre isn't a massacre) unless the settlers can be tagged as the bad guys. If the Indians were the ones committing genocide, it simply doesn't count.

You can find examples of "revised" history all the time, if you have a passable knowledge of history yourself. There's plenty of such falsified history in movies made since the 1970s. I'll give just one example here. There was a movie made in 2005 called *The New World*. It was about the founding of Jamestown in 1607, and it starred Colin Farrell, Q'orianka Kilcher and Christian Bale. In the movie, Captain John Smith (Farrell) has a love affair with the princess Pocahontas (Kilcher). One scene— about 36 minutes into the movie— contains two tedious soliloquies by Farrell and Kilcher, where they both tortuously explain why the affair is so wonderful and good. (Apparently it was so "good" it had to be justified to the audience.)

It was all very tasteful— simply suggestive portrayals, with no sex scenes or any real nudity. But the implied affair between them was a central theme of the entire film.

In another scene from the same movie, when the Indians are visiting the English, a tribesman picks up a colonist's hatchet and steals it. The owner of the hatchet sees this, then takes a pistol and attempts to shoot the thief in the back. The movie doesn't actually show the Indian guy *dying,* but the intent of the Englishman is obviously to kill him.

What is wrong with this (motion) picture? Simply that one of the events depicted was wildly distorted, and the other never happened. When the English arrived in Virginia, the real Pocahontas was about 10 or 11 years old. There was *never* any affair between Captain Smith and the girl. In fact, Smith left the colony in October of 1609 and never came back. [33:113] The last time Pocahontas saw him was when she visited England with her husband John Rolfe in 1617, just before she died.

As for the incident with the tribesman stealing the hatchet, that really did occur in May of 1607, the very month the colony was founded. The visiting Indians were warriors of the nearby Paspahegh tribe, which was part of the Powhatan Confederation. But the English colonist never shot the thief. He simply yelled at the Indian and struck him on the arm, as he grabbed back his hatchet. Right after that, there nearly *was* a fight— at least one Indian raised his war club against the hatchet's owner, and then the colonists took to their muskets. But there was no shooting. The Paspaheghs stalked off in anger, then came back eight days later to launch a sneak attack on the fort. [33:50]

Now, this is a movie which is supposed to show how Jamestown was founded. But very selectively, those wonderfully "creative" Hollywood people mixed fiction with history— in one instance to make the movie sexier, and in the other to make the settlers look like murderers. How did they justify this? Simple. In the credits shown after the movie, they had a disclaimer, stating: "This film is based on actual historical events and public records. Dialogue, certain events and characterizations contained in the film were created for the purposes of dramatization."

So apparently it's just fine for Hollywood to *distort* history for the purposes of drama, and for the "History Channel" to *ignore* history for the purpose of political correctness. Where's the truth in all this? You tell me. It shouldn't be that hard to figure out.

It is said that truth is the first casualty in war. If so many people are willing to distort the historical record, it's no surprise that truth can be the first casualty in life as well.

WHY IS TRUTH IMPORTANT?

Truth is important, because it's like a yardstick. It can be used to measure all things. And in the final analysis, it's also a yardstick by which others will measure you. If you are not a man or woman who adheres to truth as a principle, others will soon see this. In other words, you'll be marked as a liar and a phony.

Truth can be a very potent weapon. Back in 1960, President Dwight D. Eisenhower (who was at that moment under a lot of pressure) denied that we were sending any spy planes over the Soviet Union. Then the Soviet premier, Nikita Khrushchev, brought out an American pilot named Francis Gary Powers, whom they'd just shot down over Russia. Not one to miss a golden opportunity, Mr. Khrushchev trotted Powers in front of the TV cameras. Eisenhower then became the first U.S. president ever to be caught in an official lie. It didn't help his credibility at all.

However, that kind of thing works both ways. In 1983, when the Soviet leadership denied that their air force had shot down a South Korean passenger jet, President Ronald Reagan released the audio tape of the Russian pilot being ordered by his superiors to shoot down the airliner. The Soviets had to confess to the atrocity, and their president, Yuri Andropov, died a few months later.

Everyone knows what happened in 1998 when Bill Clinton denied having any sexual relations with that White House intern, Monica Lewinski. He was caught in his lie, and then he paid the price with public humiliation and impeachment. (He wasn't removed from office, but he *was* impeached.)

Richard Nixon fared worse. When an audio tape was released in August 1974 proving that he'd authorized a cover-up of the

Watergate burglary, he found himself resigning from office a few days later. He had been lying his head off about his role in the cover-up, but it didn't do him any good. True, Nixon was never impeached. But the only reason he resigned is because he knew he *would* be, if he dared to stay in office. And even his most die-hard Republican friends were telling him so.

There's no doubt about it, the truth can be a powerful weapon. When people find out they've been taken in by a lie, most of them are not happy about it. They usually react harshly against the lie, and they turn against the liar who's made fools of them.

OTHER KINDS OF TRUTH

There are other kinds of truth, than simple factual truth. In the third Indiana Jones movie, *Indiana Jones and the Last Crusade,* Professor Jones (Harrison Ford) tells his class that archeology is a search for facts. He says that if they're searching for truth, then they'll have to take a course in philosophy. That was stated pretty simplistically in the movie, but there's a lot of wisdom in it. After all, what purpose does life have, if we never find truth and— ultimately— the real meaning of life?

Even an atheist *believes* in a higher truth. Even if his higher "truth" is the belief that there is no God, the atheist still has that to believe in. Then— once he's put his faith into the notion that there's no God, he can start sharing his "transcendent" idea with others.

As we've seen, in the twentieth century millions of people put their faith into belief systems called ideologies. In Italy they wore black shirts and marched to the drumbeat of Fascism. In Germany they wore brown shirts and added racism to the mix. What they got was an obscenity called Nazism, with their *Fuhrer* as their god. In eastern Europe an ideology took hold which would outlast the others, then threaten to engulf the entire world. That, of course, was Marxist communism.

These historical facts show just how extreme (and destructive) false religions in the guise of ideologies can be. And yet— the people who worshiped at those altars believed wholeheartedly that those ways were the truth. For doctrines, they had party lines. For deities, they had uniformed martinets in officers' boots or party leaders dressed in gray suits, who strutted around giving speeches and mugging for the cameras.

Seen in this perspective, it almost sounds ridiculous. But because so many millions of people put their faith in a lie, just look at the horrendous consequences! There were over *fifty million people* killed in World War II, including both combatants and civilians.

If any lesson can be learned from the history of the twentieth century, it's that no political leader can be truly a god on this Earth, and no human ideology can be trusted as the ultimate truth. Once people forget this reality, the results can be cataclysmic. And all we have to do is look at North Korea to see the same monstrous recipe cooking again on a smaller scale.

SEARCHING FOR A "TRUE" TRUTH

So then, what kind of truth are we to believe in? What kind of realities are *real* enough to put our faith in, and use as an anchor for our lives?

There are obviously plenty of contenders. We have a vast entertainment media touting the glories of sex as life's ultimate goal. And, of course, there are the four great preoccupations of power, riches, love and beauty. Let's face it, a lot of people think these things are what life is all about. And why not? We see this stuff on TV and in the movies every day. If we're living in a world that's like a darkened underground mine, then these things are the glitter and they definitely look like the gold. Why shouldn't they be the greatest goals in life?

But power, wealth and beauty are all objects of great competition, and there are never enough of these particular commodities to satisfy everyone. How could there be enough? In fact, the overwhelming majority of people come nowhere near achieving the level of goodies and glitter they see on TV and in the movies. Only genuine, lasting love can fill that part of the heart which was created for it. And that kind of love— while more abundant than the other things— can still be difficult to find.

The results can be seen in nearly every society. In the great world struggle, those who "lose" big often suffer the most. And many will do anything to escape the pain. Some people resort to addictive drugs; others stumble into an alcoholic swamp, clinging to a bottle as an escape hatch. A lot of people try to find refuge in endless television or other entertainment.

But let's be honest. Neither drugs, nor alcohol, nor videos, nor wild and frenzied sex are going to give our lives meaning. The emptiness we feel in fleeing from reality simply cannot be satisfied by things which temporarily numb the mind.

You can't keep doing illegal drugs without becoming an addict, either physically or psychologically. You can't keep drinking excessively without getting hangovers or worse. And you can't keep treating people like sex toys without eventually paying the price— either with child support, or AIDS, or any of the other countless risks involved. If one of these doesn't catch up with you, the odds are that someday a jealous spouse or boyfriend will. And if that doesn't happen, you'll wake up one day to find out that you're pushing fifty, and after wasting your best years on empty relationships there's damn little chance left of finding that happy ending you've always wanted.

Don't forget: All these "goals" in life are basically escape routes, used by those who want to *avoid* things like real truth, pain, and life's tougher realities. <u>But the realities are always still there.</u> One of the realities of life is that it will definitely end. There will be a time when you and I will no longer be walking on this Earth, breathing this air, or savoring this world's goodies.

Now, knowing this— and seeing how easy it is to get it wrong— doesn't it seem like a good idea to try to get it right? If there actually is a Creator up there, a God who formed us and watches over us and loves us, wouldn't it be a good idea to at least find out?

RECOGNIZING AN ULTIMATE TRUTH

Just look at it logically. Without some type of transcendent truth, life simply has no real meaning. And if God actually exists, then— obviously— **there can be no greater truth.**

Again, logically, when billions of the world's people believe in a personal God who takes an active part in the world, isn't there a very good chance that all these people may actually be— right?

And again, logically, if there is a real God up there, one who created the world and everyone in it, and who exerts vast power throughout all of creation, wouldn't it be a good idea to get as close to this God as possible, and even to see if we can get His help in life?

Now, one more logical proposition. Admitting that there is the *possibility* of such a God existing, how much harm can there be in finding out?

Really— by looking past the blinders of cynicism and smugness which are so easy to wear, just *what are we risking* by opening our minds and finding out if God actually exists? Should we worry that we'll have to give away our money? No way— there are plenty of people who worship God and enjoy their wealth at the same time. Being faithful doesn't mean you have to give away all your money, or even most of it.

Does it mean we'll have to give up sex and live like good monks and nuns? Not really. The Bible encourages married couples to have a healthy sex life. {1 Corinthians 7:3-5} Weakness of the flesh is simply part of the human condition. From any reading of the Bible, it's obvious that God knows our weaknesses and shows mercy to His people, to His adopted children. He's not going to send us to Hell the minute we make our first mistake. We've each been given enough good sense to learn from our mistakes, and to get it right.

However, like any good father, He's made rules for His children to follow. And as any loving father would have it, the rules are for our own good. All one has to do is look at the demolished lives of some of the people around us, to see that there *are consequences* for refusing to improve.

Is it wrong to seek power in this world? Nope. In both the Old and New Testaments of the Bible, it's clear that God Himself is the one who sets up rulers of nations. It's made pretty clear that even lesser officials, like governors, are in office at the discretion of His divine will.

So, what is there to lose? Your freedom? Does being faithful mean you'll have to spend most of your life in church? Most churches only ask for an hour of anyone's time in a typical week. How much freedom is lost with that?

As a former agnostic, I can tell you this with all honesty and certainty: The freedom and control you gain over your life and over your own weak impulses will vastly outweigh any diminished amount of free time. Nothing in this world is better than being set free from the things that drag us down.

Think about it. Is it better to be "free" to be a drug addict or an alcoholic, or to *be free* from those chemical dependencies? Is it better to seethe with hatred of your job, or resentment toward your boss, or to be free of the hate and let your better instincts steer you to success? Is it better to lurch from one empty fling to another, risking all sorts of STDs and dangerous "love triangles," or to find that one lasting relationship that brings genuine love and stability into your life?

Is it better to be known as an "easy" person with little self-control, or as an emotionally mature individual who doesn't jump into anything stupidly? Whether we like it or not, we all make our own reputations in this world. We're all going to be known to others in one way or another— some who're going to be cruelly judgmental. And the choice is all yours. God isn't going to force anyone to be decent or respectable.

So, what *is* going to be your choice of truth in life? And, speaking of that, what kind of actual life do you *want* to choose for yourself?

We can argue about it all we want. And sometimes it's impossible *not* to argue about it. Sometimes, life is just not easy to understand. After all, why would a God create us out of flesh and blood, give us all these primitive instincts, then tell us we should live in a way that *transcends* these things?

Why would a God put us in a world containing so much misery and suffering, filled with hostility and weapons and wars, and then encourage us to have inner peace? In a culture that depicts pride and arrogance as cardinal virtues, how can God want us to have humility? Why would God drop us into a society rife with political conflict, churning in an orgy of moral anarchy— a society which bombards us daily with endless confusion in the form of advertisements and commercials— then expect us to make sense out of it all? How can one even *find* God in all this chaos, much less believe in Him?

If we have the guts to think about it, there are answers to all these arguments. But the last question is the easiest. To find God, all you have to do is look for Him— "Seek and you shall find." I'm not the one who said those words. As just about everyone knows, Jesus is the one who said them.

Now, you may not be a Christian. (I wasn't.) You may even have a strong aversion to the word Christian, depending on where you are in your life. We do see countless anti-Christian messages in movies and other areas of our culture nowadays. In fact, it's just about the only form of bigotry left which appears to be socially acceptable.

But if you have a shred of logic (along with slightest bit of honesty) you'll recognize that this does make sense. If you look for God, you should be able to find out if He's there. And about the only way you're *not* going to find out, is if you *avoid* looking for Him.

IT'S REALLY NOT THAT COMPLICATED

The challenge here is fairly obvious. And, yes, it is being presented as a challenge.

When you seek God and find Him, the risks are very few and the rewards are obviously great— even beyond imagining. After all, what would you be risking? Would your super-cool friends be laughing at you? Is it even any of their *business,* if you check out a church once a week? Would you feel edgy by not dropping a dollar in the collection plate? Would that dollar even be important? Don't you think God will know if you can't afford it? Don't even worry about the damned dollar! I don't!

Do you think God won't accept you? Nonsense. Both the Old and New Testaments make it clear that there's not a single one of those Ten Commandments that He won't forgive you for breaking. {Psalms 32:5-6} also: {Mark 3:28} Of course, you eventually will have to make a serious effort to stop breaking them. (Darn!)

Have you killed, wearing your country's uniform? Maybe you were involved in a street gang at one time, and might even have killed someone to "prove" yourself? Did you put harmful drugs into your body? Did you fall into sexual quicksand, seducing (or being seduced by) others? How far did you find yourself sinking into your personal swamp before you realized your life was out of control? You don't have to tell me about it, or any of your friends. Your conscience— and your salvation— are strictly between you and God.

Ask yourself one thing. Do you think you'll be any better off punishing yourself for the rest of your life for your mistakes? Or do you think it might be better to approach a loving and forgiving God and bring your burdens to Him? The very fact that you feel remorse for your failings means that you're repentant for them. Don't you think God will know that, and have enough love to forgive you? Do you think He let those Roman soldiers nail His Son to a wooden cross just so you could sit there and damn yourself for the rest of your life?

There's one truth that we all have to deal with: Sooner or later we've got to reconcile our conscience with our beliefs. Some people will tell themselves there is no God, so there's no need for any conscience. But somehow, that doesn't make the conscience disappear. Lying to one's self very rarely works.

In a way, truth is one of those things that separates the people in this world into different groups. There are people who live their lives being true to themselves. They tell the truth. They care about what's true. When making decisions using their conscience, they take into consideration the truth. And they try to live by what they know is true.

There are people, also, who couldn't care less about the truth. They shun any notions of transcendent truth. Often, they express pride that they "live for the moment," and they encourage others to do the same. These people are rationalizing that— without any acknowledgment of a higher power such as God—there's no reason to look beyond the moment. This can be a very convenient philosophy.

As a former agnostic, I can remember what it was like to leave God out of my thinking. I can look back on that part of my life as a passage that I was going through. In my own way, I was trying to live by what I thought was true. And I think this is part of the answer for everyone. Even if you're at a point in life where it's difficult to believe in God, at least try to be a person of truth. Try to make truth important. Always speak the truth. If you can't answer a question truthfully, then just don't answer it. When you hear someone say something that's true, don't be afraid to acknowledge it. That won't mean that you're agreeing with everything else they're saying.

Perhaps most important, don't be afraid to look inside yourself. Are there truths there, that could help you to improve? We all have things inside of us that are not so pleasant. But is it better to ignore them, or to see them clearly?

Be a person of truth. At times, it may be more challenging than closing your eyes. Sometimes, it may even be a bit painful. But— trust me on this— in the long run, it will always be worth it.

AGAIN: WHY TRUTH IS IMPORTANT

Maybe this is the bottom line, on the "truth" thing. Jesus said that the truth will set us free. One doesn't have to be a Christian to appreciate how obvious that is. And one thing we need is to be free. Free from fear. Free from guilt. Free from the uncertainty that riddles our minds and our entire existence. And free from all the other things that drag us down.

God isn't just a word, or a myth, or a distant star with which there can be no contact. He's not an object of ³fear, but an inexhaustible source of hope. He's not a crutch, but a strengthener.

God is a reality— a truth— that each of us must reckon with. And truth is a curious thing. We can try to ignore it. We can try to avoid it. We can even try to deny it or laugh it off. But just like death and taxes, it's always going to be there. In the back of our minds and in the innermost recesses of our hearts, we'll always find it staring back at us. Nothing quite makes it go away.

How we deal with the truth pretty much defines each one of us— not just for others, but ultimately for ourselves. And this is the thing. We can turn away from others; we can shut out anything they want to say. We can close our minds, and shun things like churches and Bibles and religious speakers on the radio. For a time, we can even avoid our own conscience if we try hard enough.

But truth— real truth— is still there, and that tiny voice inside us will always keep reminding us of it. Whether we like it or not, the conscience which that loving Father gave us will always be a part of our inner self.

And the one person we *have* to live with is ourself.

---

[3] The term "God-fearing" harkens back to a time when the word "fear" had several meanings. The phrase actually means that someone has awe, or reverence, for God— not a feeling of terror.

Chapter 3

WHAT IS ATHEISM— REALLY?

Atheism is basically the idea that God does not exist. Atheists, simply stated, are people who believe there is no God, no supreme being at all. The word "atheist" is taken from the ancient Greek language, where *theos* is the word for "god," and another word, *a,* means "without."

Agnosticism isn't quite the same as atheism. An agnostic is someone who simply does not know if God exists. Or, an agnostic might say that he thinks there is a God, but that God is unknowable. The word "agnostic" is also derived from early Greek. Again, *a* means "without," while *gnosis* means "knowing," or "knowledge." (The word itself was coined by Thomas Henry Huxley, a 19th century English biologist who was an aggressive supporter of Charles Darwin's Evolution theory.) [9:Vol. 6:179]

These are simple concepts. But their impact on each one of us is enormous. Because the way we think about God, the way we perceive God, and the way we deal with our belief (or non-belief) in God, will affect every one of us— and our choices— throughout our entire lifetime.

I can give one example of this from personal experience. When I was still in my teens, I started thinking about the question of God's existence. I reasoned that since there's no real evidence or proof that God exists, it didn't make any sense to believe in Him. And I thought I was okay with that.

In all honesty, I can't fully blame myself. I was brought up in a family environment in which religious faith played no part. My parents didn't have any religion, so they never took me to any church. Neither did my paternal grandmother. My maternal grandmother's parents (my great-grandparents) were devout members of the Nazarene Church, and they brought me to church maybe three or four times during my childhood. I can remember only one of those visits, which must have been when I was about five. It was not a pleasant memory— I started missing my grandmother during the Sunday school class, so they took me back to her and my great-grandparents.

Years later, I was told that my parents had made a decision to not bring me into any specific church, so that later I could pick my own religion. Perhaps, in the long run, this was best for me. But to this day, I feel a certain amount of envy for people whose parents took them to church regularly. Because they were given a better start, and a firmer foundation to build their lives on, than I had.

Without any faith, or even any knowledge about God, the earlier years of my life were basically lived out in ignorance— one might describe it as spiritual darkness. Without any understanding of the teachings of religion, or of human nature, I was unable to even attempt to understand other people. And if we fail to understand others, we fail at life itself.

But paradoxically, when someone chooses to reject God, and even the concept of God, very often they think of this as a strength and an advantage.

To a typical atheist, those who believe in God are inferior. Compared to him, they are mental and spiritual weaklings. As far as he's concerned, religious faith is nothing but a crutch. He thinks himself stronger, because he can walk through life without it.

This is an atheist's "reward" in life. It's the towering strength of his own pride. He can do anything he sees fit without any pangs of conscience, because without God there are no Commandments and no such thing as sin. He is freed from all such "archaic" restraints.

It sounds pretty good in a way, doesn't it? By denying that God exists, anyone can (in a way) be their own god. They can construct their own belief system, make their own rules, and feed off their own pride. They *know* that they're vastly stronger than those who need the "crutch" of religion. I've read quotes from people who cling to atheism. One said that, "I don't believe in God, because I don't believe in the Easter bunny." Another I can remember went like this: "There just ain't no big sky-daddy up there." Apparently— for the atheist mentality— cynical one-liners are the types of things that pass for wisdom.

ATHEISM AS A FORM OF FAITH

The following statement isn't a new idea. Others have said it before me. But it's definitely worth stating again: When you think about it, atheists have every bit as much faith as any Christian. It's just that they put their faith in themselves— or anything else but God. Think about it. There are *countless* things that people put their faith in. One of the most popular is money. We've already looked at ideologies such as communism and Nazism. Throughout the twentieth century, we've seen religions based on everything from spiritualism to flying saucers. (Some people believe so strongly in space aliens influencing our world, it's actually like a modern-day cargo cult.[4])

But no matter what people put their faith in, they still can't get away from the reality that it is a form of faith. Of course, any good atheist will have trouble admitting this.

PERSONAL INSIGHT: THE GREAT FAILING OF THE ATHEIST MINDSET

Perhaps the greatest handicap of an atheistic belief system is the limitation it imposes on the person's ability to "step back" and look at himself objectively. A convinced atheist is hardened

---

[4] cargo cult — A religion once popular on some islands of the south Pacific, based on the hope that superior beings would return from the sky bringing gifts of cargo. [9:Vol. 2:866] also: [22:706] For flying saucer devotees, the "gifts" would be the wondrous alien technology.

into his beliefs. He's not interested in any conventional religious talk. It doesn't matter if you cite modern events, current news items or historical fact. An atheist usually won't even want to listen to it.

Now, the trouble with this is, having a closed mind is a distinct handicap. One is shutting out information which might be very beneficial. Of course, atheists have no monopoly on this. But in the case of an atheistic mindset, it can have disastrous consequences for someone locked into it.

There are numerous human weaknesses which we all share. (I'm well aware that I'm not made out of stainless steel.) But pride is a weakness which masquerades as a strength.

Someone who recognizes that there is a God, or even just some "higher power," can at least find comfort in the knowledge there's Someone in the universe who is in control. Also, it confers a certain amount of humility, knowing that God is in charge. But without that understanding, without that faith, there is no one in charge. And consequently, there's no need for humility. Each of us becomes the measure of all things— except himself.

Thank God, I've never had the experience of being in a prison. But there's probably no prison on Earth with walls stronger than the ones we can construct in our own minds. Those walls can be so thick that they can shut out any outside light— even if that light comes from a source that can help us achieve our own rebirth.

THE ESSENCE OF ATHEISM

As a former agnostic, I can understand what makes atheism (and to some extent, agnosticism) such a self-destructive force in those who embrace it. Someone who believes in God knows that such things as hope, salvation, and a rewarding afterlife are truly present in the scheme of things. No matter how difficult or heartbreaking life can be, there is more. And he knows that he can transcend this world's troubles, and even *prevail,* with God's help.

At the opposite end of the spectrum, atheism is a belief system which is almost totally negative. There is no God, no hope of any afterlife, and no such thing as salvation. There are no miracles except those provided by science and technology. Faith is not a strength but a weakness. Heaven is not a reality but a mirage. And death— at the end of the day— is exactly that: the end of everything.

With such a mentality, how can life have any meaning? What possible purpose can there be, except to satisfy one's personal appetites and cater to his (or her) own ego? In the modern world, can anyone find a philosophy *more negative* than atheism? I don't think so.

This is what makes atheism so destructive. It limits one's mind; it denies the existence of any real reason to "think outside the box." There are those who claim to get along just fine without any sort of religious faith. And— for a time— I'm sure it can appear possible to do so. But that's also an illusion. There will come a time in life when each of us goes through trials and tribulations that we never expected. Life is like that.

The men who built the *Titanic* thought they'd constructed a ship so great, they boasted that "not even God could sink it." All it took was a brush with an iceberg. A convinced atheist named Madalyn Murray O'Hair thought life was good. She had fame, popularity, and half a million dollars worth of gold. Then one day she and two relatives were murdered, and all the gold was gone.

These are both examples of human tragedies. Valid examples. The owners of the *Titanic* were inflated with pride. Madalyn Murray O'Hair was living a life that seemed like something out of a movie. Then came the unexpected.

It comes to all of us— trials and tribulations that we never thought would happen. Is it better to be guided and sustained through life by a reality that goes beyond personal pride? Or can we depend on a wall of our own making, that shuts out any annoying light during the journey?

One thing's for sure: Sooner or later, every one of us will find out.

Chapter 4

SEARCHING FOR GOD

As I said earlier, I had virtually no instruction in religion when I was a child. So I must confess a little envy for those who have had a religious upbringing. They've been trained in faith, and they've been brought up to know about God.

This doesn't mean that a religious upbringing is a panacea for life. Anyone can have a crisis of faith. But I can't help but think that it's an advantage to have some schooling in the basics of religion. Still, it's a fact that in our society huge numbers of people are brought up without it.

Countless people spend years asking the question, "Is there a God?" And it's a question that each of us must find an answer for. For some reason, our minds won't let us rest until we do. As mentioned in the second chapter, there is a way. Jesus said to "Seek, and you shall find." If we open our minds honestly and look for God, He *will* provide the answers.

BE PREPARED FOR SURPRISES

This is not a simple process. By realizing that God may exist, and by making a decision to find the answer, you are actually carrying out an act of tremendous courage. You'll be venturing into an area where many people are afraid to set foot. You will be approaching a reality which makes all the other realities of this world seem flimsy and insignificant. You will be daring to search for the supernatural— not the earthbound paranormal realm, but the supernatural which is above everything else.

In other words, you'll be approaching the genuine light which exists *outside* the dark, underground mine.

I remember my own experience. When I was seventeen, I decided there was no proof of any God, and so it "didn't make any sense" to believe in Him. When I was twenty-one I was in college, and going through some difficulties. Suddenly, spontaneously, I found myself praying for help.

I was amazed by what followed. God is not an exhibitionist. He won't force faith on anyone. He isn't going to have conversations with anybody, or send an angel with a flashing light show to tell you everything you want to know.[5]

There's a reason for this. It may seem a little puzzling at first, but it's not too difficult to understand. It's a basic theme which can be found in the Bible— both the Old and the New Testaments: One thing which God values very highly is faith. If He were to appear to anyone at the drop of a hat and perform miracles right in front of us, there would be no need for faith. We would *see* that He's there. We would *know* He's present. We would have no *choice* but to believe.

But God wants us to have faith. He wants us to believe in Him— strongly— even though we can't see Him. For some reason, this is a major part of what God wants of us.

But having faith isn't always easy— especially for those of us who live in this technological playpen of the Western world. Our society and culture don't teach us to have faith. On the contrary, we're taught to believe in science, in evidence, in material proof of everything. We're taught to be *not* believers, but skeptics. And there's something to be said for logic and rationality. After all, who wants to be a mindless fool? Who would want to be gullible enough to believe anything he's told?

Nobody's saying it's a choice between one extreme or the other. But— looking at it logically— in this violent, insane, lie-infested world, how can anyone get *through* it all without any faith? Is believing in God going to actually hurt us, or help us?

---

[5] I believe that angels do speak to people occasionally, but not with Hollywood-style special effects.

From my own experience, I can say with all certainty that it helps. And in this world, it can be key to survival.

Back when I was twenty-one, when I first opened my mind and started looking for answers, I was amazed by what followed. It just isn't possible to relate it all in words. But I'll record some of the things that happened, here and in Chapter 13.

To sum it up, I soon found out that God was there. Even more encouraging, I found that He cared about me, and that He was watching over me. This doesn't make me special. He watches over every one of us. It's just that I'd never known it before. For the first time in my life, I knew that I wasn't alone and helpless. I had finally found out that God is real.

In this chapter, I'll tell just one of the things that happened. At that time, when I was still in college, I enjoyed going to this local bar and having a few beers. It was a little like that situation in the TV show "Cheers." At the time you could buy a tap beer for as little as a quarter.

This one evening, I was feeling bored. I didn't have any cash on me— not a dime. But I felt adventurous. I'd already found out that God was there, watching over me. I had this sterling silver ring I'd bought several years before, and thought I'd sell it. I didn't have a car at the time, so I started out toward the bar on foot. It was an evening in December, so it was already dark.

As I started to cross a street, I suddenly felt that one of my shoelaces had come untied. I stopped right at that moment and reached down to tie my shoe. Now, just a few feet away from me was a street lamp. And when I looked down, right next to my foot was a quarter, with the light of the street lamp reflecting from it. I had just found my first drink. So I picked up the quarter, tied my shoe, and headed toward the saloon. I knew the bartender there, and he bought the ring. So I spent the evening sipping my drinks and enjoying the music.

Not a very spectacular sort of miracle. But it was definitely more than coincidence. My shoelace came untied just at that moment. When I bent down to tie it, the light from the street lamp was hitting the quarter at just the right angle— I couldn't miss it. My foot was right next to it. Anyone who calls all that a coincidence would call *anything* a coincidence.

I remember many more details. I can remember the exact date when I'd originally bought the ring, who bought it from me that evening, and so forth. But none of that's important. What's important is that God was there, watching over me. And He helped me out.

This was just one thing, out of maybe a thousand, which answered the "Big Question" for me. It wasn't the least important thing that happened, and it wasn't the most amazing thing, either. It's simply one example.

Don't forget, what we're looking for here is truth. We're looking for reality, not fantasy. We can get fantasy anywhere. It's available on cable TV, 24 hours a day. It's available on radio, in those rare moments between commercials when they're playing music. It can be found in any novel and in any board game. We're living in a culture that's *saturated* with fantasy. If you want to know that God is real, you won't find out from TV. There are a few religious shows and religious channels, but it's still coming out of a picture tube— which is usually a pre-recorded electronic illusion. And even when it's "live," the other 99 percent of TV is geared toward nothing but money.

I'm not a theologian and I don't have all the answers. To answer the Big Question for yourself, you'll have to search for it. But it's not that difficult. If you doubt this, there's a simple way of finding out. Just do two things. First, try to have the guts to see beyond the blinders. Use your mind as a sledgehammer, and bash a few cracks in those walls you've built for yourself. In other words, make a genuine effort to get your head around the idea that God is actually there. It's not going to kill you to be open-minded.

The second thing may be easier, or it may be harder. Once you've accepted that God may actually be there, try talking to Him. You don't have to call it praying. Just try talking to Him, and even try asking Him for something.

I'm not suggesting that you put God to the test. Jesus warned against that, and I'm not going to disagree. But Jesus also said, "Ask, and you shall receive." Just start talking to God once in a while, and don't be afraid to ask Him for something. Don't get greedy and demand to win the lottery. I don't think He'll be willing to cater to that one. (Very often, I think, too much money can do more real harm to our souls than not enough.)

But I just can't exaggerate the number of times I've said a quick prayer to God, and asked for some little thing— some small help in getting through the day, for instance. And I can't exaggerate the astounding number of times He says "yes." It must be something like nine times out of ten, or better.

Try asking Him for little things. Then— if your head's in the right place; if you're not actually *wanting* nothing to happen (to reinforce those precious blinders)— you'll find out what I meant by "a thousand little miracles."

Just try these two things. You'll be glad you did. Because when you're looking for the greatest truth in the universe, He's going to be worth finding. The thing to remember is, God is the one who created you. Sometimes, it's not really easy to comprehend this, but He really is a loving parent. He loves each one of us, He watches over us, and He cares about us *individually*. And He can be an amazing source of strength and courage.

He isn't going to force faith on anybody. But He's not going to be hiding in another solar system, either. Whoever honestly searches for God can find Him. It's as simple as that.

Chapter 5

WHAT MAKES GOD DIFFERENT FROM ANY OTHER GOD?

I can remember a conversation I had with my uncle when I was around eighteen. By that time I was an agnostic. I was saying that the God of Christianity and Judaism is basically no different than any ancient (pagan) religion. This was because I could see that, in Christian teachings, God wasn't alone. He was accompanied by countless angels. To my thinking, it was just like ancient polytheism. The angels were other supernatural beings, sort of like a company of gods in a pantheon.

My uncle replied that this was in favor of modern religion. By having this similarity to ancient paganism, it showed that even those ancient pagan religions were on the right track.

Both of us were wrong. I was putting down Christianity, when all I knew about it was from the few (usually negative) portrayals of it I'd seen on television. I had never studied Christianity, had never attended a church regularly, and basically didn't know what I was talking about.

My uncle was wrong, because he was trying to equate Christianity with ancient pagan religions, as if all religions had a common thread, linking them somehow. He was trying to guide me toward his own way of thinking, of course, by making my own statement sound closer to his own. But those pagan, polytheistic religions are so unlike Christianity as to rule out any real link between the two.

ANCIENT RELIGIONS

Can you remember the stuff they taught in high school about ancient civilizations? Like the Greeks, Romans and Egyptians? If you can recall anything you learned about ancient religions, you'll know that they all contained a multitude of gods and goddesses. Each of them had a chief god, whether he was called Zeus, Jupiter or Amun-Ra.

There's a popular theory that all ancient religions originally had a "mother goddess" as their main deity. But this has far more to do with feminist ideology than history. It's generally agreed that the most ancient inscriptions known are Sumerian. By around 2500 BC, the Sumerians began using cuneiform signs representing syllables, instead of whole words. [7:137-138] This meant that the language could finally be read as it was actually spoken. From these writings, we know that the Sumerian religion— just as the other ancient pagan religions— had a male deity as the head of its pantheon. Their chief god's name was Enlil, who was credited with creating civilization. Enlil, much like the top deities of other pantheons, was a male sky-god. [13:88] also: [19:83]

It's difficult for the modern mind to really comprehend what it was like to be immersed in an ancient pagan religion. It must have been like living in a mental universe of incredible confusion.

To the ancients, having many gods was considered a virtue, because it meant people were "more religious." As noted in Chapter One, the Hittites and Egyptians boasted of having a thousand gods— probably an exaggeration, but to them the boast was more important than the truth.

To some cultures (such as the Egyptians), the more obscure, complicated and contradictory their religion was, the holier it was. Confusion in the mind of man meant that their gods and the workings of their gods were too far above man's thinking for him to understand. That made their gods "greater."

Christianity takes pretty much the opposite view. When Jesus was speaking with a Samaritan woman at a local well, He criticized Samaritan customs, saying that her people worshiped what they didn't understand. {John 4:22} The Samaritans weren't pagans; they originated as an offshoot of Judaism. [9:Vol. 10:374] But Christ's criticism illuminates part of the essence of almost all ancient belief systems. Those pagan religions did not encourage worshipers to understand.

In pagan religions the priests were not servants, whose job was to bring man closer to his own salvation. In those religions, the role of the priest (or priestess) was to be a buffer standing before the deity and glorying in its presence, while the common herd could only gather at a spiritual distance, hoping that the gods would take pity on them. There was no true salvation, no assured forgiveness of sins, no loving and almighty Father God who would treat each person as His own.

True, there were a few semi-"personal" gods scattered among these religions during various periods in history, such as Amun-Ra, who in the New Kingdom era of Egypt was called the god who would listen to the poor man. There were also lesser deities, such as the Egyptian god Bes, or the *lares familiares* (household gods) of the Romans, which were popular with the citizenry and were considered more like personal gods. [17:180]

But by and large, the gods of ancient pantheons were distant deities, powerful and (except to the priests and priestesses) unapproachable. They could only be worshiped at a distance, and given sacrifices to appease them. Only priests and national leaders could claim to enter into their presence.

This was, of course, a very sweet deal for the priestly caste, as well as for the kings, emperors and pharaohs— who sometimes claimed to be deities themselves. Those chosen few who could speak directly to the gods were the same ones who enjoyed all the power and wealth of the world.

There was another aspect to the ancient gods, which differs greatly from the God we know today. And this can be described as the single greatest difference between the God of

Judeo-Christianity and all the distant deities worshiped in the ancient world.

THE ESSENCE OF THE ANCIENT RELIGIONS

To put it simply, the pagan gods of every age were invented by men. The chief deities of the pantheons were always the ones who controlled the most powerful aspects of nature, who reigned over the other deities, and who sometimes were the parents of them.

It wasn't often that the chief deity really "ruled" the others, because each god was typically the ruler over his (or her) own domain— such as Mars, the god of war, or Venus, whose fiefdom was sexual love. There were gods of writing for scribes to worship, gods of childbirth for expectant mothers, etc.

The gods and goddesses of these pagan religions were basically reflections of the human world, and their specialized functions in the pantheon often mirrored the role of earthly rulers. This, naturally, helped to legitimize the kings, emperors and governors who claimed the right to rule over others.

It was only rarely (if ever) that pagan gods personified any moral standards. We don't see too many of them representing what we would call self-discipline, or self-control. In the interaction between deities, they functioned much like human society, and they almost always shared the same weaknesses and flaws that all human beings have had since the beginning of time.

That's why we see such dubious deities as the Greek Dionysus (the Roman Bacchus) as the god of wine and drunkenness. The Egyptians worshiped a fertility god, Amun-Min, who was always depicted on temple walls as having an erection. In the New Kingdom period, he was another personification of their chief god, Amun.

In other words, the pagan religions had gods for every vice, but not for every virtue. Just about every human weakness had a god or goddess to sanction it and make it "holy." Again: Putting it simply, men in those times invented their gods, creating them in their own image. I'm certainly not the first to make this observation. It's a truth which has been well-known through the centuries. But it's a point worth repeating.

THE TREMENDOUS DIFFERENCE OF A TRUE GOD

The Judeo-Christian God has exactly the opposite origin of any pagan god. He revealed Himself to mankind. Again, I'm not the first to point this out. But the very simplicity— and the enormous meaning of this contrast— are worth some reflection.

I'm not pretending to be a theological expert here. I'm not an expert on the Bible, either. All I'm saying is that in my own life experience, through various ways, God has made it clear to me that He exists. As Jesus Christ had recommended in the New Testament, I looked for some answers and I found them. That doesn't make me special, or omniscient, or anything else. But I can speak about this from experience, and from the advantageous position of *knowing* that God does exist.

Many very wise and spiritual people throughout history have had things revealed to them as well— far greater things than I've ever seen or heard. Fortunately, some of these people recorded these events in a series of books which are found today in the Bible.

The Bible is a fascinating compilation, because the books it contains have formed the spiritual and historical foundations of Western civilization. These books were written over a span of more than a millennium, from the earliest parts of the Old Testament to the last book of the New Testament.

There used to be a certain amount of controversy over how well the ancient scribes maintained the accuracy of these writings. Then, in 1947, the Dead Sea Scrolls were discovered. They included nearly every book of the Old Testament, even though many were in fragmentary form. But some documents, like the Book of Isaiah, were virtually complete. Scholars were startled by what they found. The contents of the Old Testament books of the Bible were almost unchanged from what we already had. The latter manuscripts (the oldest ones available to scholars before 1947) were nearly identical. So we know that the scribes were very faithfully copying these books, from at least the second or first century BC. And there's no reason to think they weren't using the same care before that.

There's a good deal more. Thanks to the science of archaeology, a huge number of discoveries have been made which verify much of the information found in the Old and New Testaments. Archaeologists have found that pre-Exodus Semitic laborers in Egypt did in fact have a primitive pictographic alphabet— now called proto-Sinaitic. This is ironclad evidence that the Hebrews of Moses' time had writing. [29:151]

Archaeologists have found ancient inscriptions proving the existence of Israel in the late 13th century BC, and also the rule of the Roman governor Pontius Pilate in Judea in the first century AD. In modern Syria in the 1970s, an ancient city called Ebla was identified, and the thousands of cuneiform tablets discovered there proved that many personal names found in the Old Testament were in common use before 2000 BC. [4:249] also: [23:736] Ancient signet rings and clay seals have been unearthed which actually bear the names of a few individuals mentioned in the Old Testament— items which they possessed personally. Such discoveries are far too numerous to cover here. If you want to know more, there are plenty of books on biblical archaeology available.

What's the point of all this— to prove that everything in the Bible is true? No. Archaeology is never going to "prove" the existence of God. For some people, nothing could ever prove that. If God appeared personally in a burst of light and spoke to a hardened atheist, the latter would probably dismiss Him as a hallucination.

Obviously, the main themes of the Bible are messages of faith and ultimate truth. And only those who seek the truth with an open mind are going to find it. But what archaeology *has* proved, is that many of the incidental historical facts mentioned in the Bible are definitely true. Neither the Old Testament nor the New was formed from a tissue of lies and imagination. It's been shown beyond doubt that many of the details contained in these books were recorded by men who lived in those times, and who knew those cultures first-hand.

Some scholars think that a few of the accounts in the Old Testament (such as the description of the Flood, and the story of Joseph and his brothers) may be anachronistic— written down at a later time than the events they describe. But by and large, the historical information found in the ancient books of the Old Testament has proved to be very accurate in its details.

WHEN DID THE TRUE GOD REVEAL HIMSELF?

The Bible records three major events where God revealed Himself to men. The first was when He spoke to a man called Abram.

Abram is a pivotal figure in the Old Testament. It was to him that God first made Himself known as the true God. In this famous narrative found in the Book of Genesis, Abram was ordered to sacrifice his only son, Isaac, to prove his loyalty to God. At the last moment, Abram was told to spare his son. Abram's name was changed to Abraham, which is another form of the same phrase, meaning "the father is exalted." {Genesis 17:5} As God promised him, Abraham later became the ancestor of the Jewish people, and he has always been counted as one of the great Patriarchs of Judaism and Christianity.

From this seminal event originated the three great revealed religions we find today—Judaism, Christianity and Islam. So it's of some importance, to try to fix the date in history when this event took place. The modern science of archaeology has begun to shed some light on this.

The Bible records that Abraham had been born in a city named Ur. Scholars have most often taken this to be the Sumerian city of Ur, which was excavated by the great British archaeologist Sir Leonard Woolley in the 1920s and '30s. This city was the capital during last great era of Sumerian civilization, which flourished from about 2112 to 2004 BC. And so it was long assumed that Abraham lived around 2000 to 1900 BC.

More recent archaeological discoveries, however, have cast doubts on this particular city being Abraham's birthplace. Near the Dead Sea (modern Jordan), two archaeological sites have been discovered, named Bab edh-Dhra and Numeira. These buried cities are in the general area where ancient Sodom and Gomorrah stood. Those cities, of course, were the ones which God destroyed because of their extreme moral degeneracy. {Genesis, ch. 19}

The book of Genesis contains certain information dating back to very remote times. [29:85] It actually lists the cities of the region, naming some of their rulers. {Genesis, ch. 14} It's evident that these facts recorded in Genesis are from a far more ancient document, probably originating from tablets inscribed in cuneiform, which was still widely used in the Mideast when the Old Testament was being compiled.

Not only is Abraham linked with those cities listed in Genesis, but his nephew Lot was recorded as living in Sodom when that city and Gomorrah were destroyed. Lot, in fact, was the one warned by God to leave Sodom before its impending destruction. Therefore, the close association of Abraham with those cities— and Lot's residence in Sodom just before its end— should be reliable markers for helping to pinpoint the time when Abraham lived. And this is where the science of archaeology is prompting some re-thinking of Abraham's time (and even his place) of birth.

As mentioned, the buried cities at Bab edh-Dhra and Numeira are in the area where Sodom and Gomorrah once stood; therefore many scholars tend to identify these ruins with those two cities. Preliminary studies by archaeologists determined that both sites were destroyed by fire, just at the end of the Early Bronze Age III period— around 2350 BC. At the Bab edh-Dhra site a smaller population, apparently with different cultural remains, were inhabiting the ruins later, during the Early Bronze Age IV era (2350 – 2200 BC). However, it was found that both cities had actually been destroyed about 2350 BC. [37:36 & 160] More information on this can be found in the glossary.

That might seem to be in conflict with the Bible's account of Abraham's birth. For many years, the identification of his birthplace with Sumerian Ur has gripped the minds of biblical scholars; and it continues to do so. But if we follow the evidence, it may become necessary to break away from this mindset. In other words, Abraham may have lived earlier than once thought. If Bab edh-Dhra and Numeira are indeed the ruins of Sodom and Gomorrah, it's obvious that this was the time of their destruction— two cities in the right place, which abruptly ended some 400 years earlier than most biblical scholars expected. And this evidence doesn't stand alone.

As mentioned earlier, the archaeological dig at Ebla (a site called Tell Mardikh in modern Syria) has uncovered a civilization which shows uncanny parallels with the Old Testament world. A number of later Israelite personal names, such as Abram, Michael, Ishmael, and even Israel, have been found among the names recorded in its cuneiform archives. [4:249] also: [23:736] The name of one of Ebla's kings, Ebrium, was similar to that of an ancestor of Abraham listed in the Old Testament. {Genesis 10:21}

These discoveries have one feature in common: All these sites date back to the same era— around the 24th century BC. People with Israelite names were definitely living in Ebla at that time. Since the Old Testament describes Syria (then called Aram) as the homeland of the Patriarchs, this ancient tradition seems to place Abraham and his ancestors squarely in the region of Ebla; it's quite possible that Abraham was born in an Aramean city with the same name of Ur. [1:163 (footnote)] also: [23:736]

The preliminary destruction levels found at Bab edh-Dhra and Numeira, along with the thousands of inscribed tablets found at Ebla, seem to point to a date of c2350 BC as the time frame for Abraham. This is not ironclad proof that Abraham lived then; but it proves that he *could* have.

Whatever the details of his origins might be, Abraham was named as the first individual to whom God revealed Himself.

Of course, God had spoken long before to Noah and warned him of the impending Flood. But that was more of an account of man's survival from that primeval disaster, not the same as what Abraham later experienced. The encounter with Noah was basically a warning, rather than a revelation.

There is also, of course, the corresponding account of the Flood which has been found on very ancient cuneiform tablets, and which was incorporated into the greatest work of Mesopotamian literature, *The Epic of Gilgamesh*. [29:45-47] For some, those inscriptions have actually called into question the originality of the Flood story found in the Bible. All that can be said with certainty is that both Flood stories have strong parallels in their respective texts.

The Bible is not a like a secular history book. Although parts of it contain much historical information, it all centers on the common thread of what biblical scholars call Salvation History. Its purpose is not to record facts and details (like a daily newspaper), but to give a reliable account of mankind's relation to God— and to nourish faith in Him.

For religious denominations which have the doctrine requiring a distinctly literal meaning for every passage of the Bible, the details of Noah's story and the Flood are a matter of faith. For those who consider the archaeological record, the Flood account must also be seen in the light of faith. Although many biblical scholars have reached a consensus that various chapters of some Old Testament books— including Genesis— were composed at different times in history, this takes nothing away from the spiritual value of these books, or from the truths they contain.

THE SECOND GREAT REVELATION

God's next great appearance took place in the 13th century BC, to an outcast from Egypt named Moses. Moses is perhaps the most fascinating figure of the Old Testament. By the time he was born, his Hebrew people had been living in Egypt for several centuries, and ultimately working there as slave laborers. Although born to a Hebrew mother, in the Old Testament it's recorded that he was abandoned as a baby (to save his life), and subsequently found by an Egyptian princess. The princess took him as her own, and Moses was raised as an Egyptian in the surroundings of the royal palace. For anyone who has seen the classic 1956 movie *The Ten Commandments,* or who's read the Old Testament account in the book of Exodus, the story is familiar.

Ultimately Moses had a falling-out with the ruling pharaoh and he was banished from Egypt. Migrating to a country called Midian, he married there and settled down. Years later, he was called to the top of a nearby mountain, and found himself confronted by the presence of Almighty God. It was then and there— from a miraculous bush which burned without being consumed— that God revealed Himself to the man who would soon be the liberator of the Hebrew slaves in Egypt.

The following events are familiar to just about everybody. The pharaoh was adamantly opposed to freeing the Hebrews. God then punished Egypt with ten plagues, and the stricken monarch finally allowed them to go. A few days later, Pharaoh changed his mind and took off after the Hebrews with his army of chariots. Crossing a body of water called the Sea of Reeds, the Hebrews made it safely to the other side after the waters were miraculously divided to allow them to pass. When the Egyptian army pursued, the sea closed in on them. After escaping from Egyptian territory, Moses brought his people (numbering in the many thousands) to the holy mountain where God had spoken to him. It was there that God gave him the Ten Commandments, for the right conduct of His people.

God demonstrated His unlimited power time and again, with miracles which brought life, and a firm basis for His people's faith. His intercession at the Sea of Reeds— the manna and quail to relieve the people's hunger in the wilderness— these events were emblazoned on the minds and memories of the former Hebrew slaves.

Still, their hearts grew faint when they saw the dangers of entering the Promised Land of Canaan, along the eastern Mediterranean coast. God was disgusted by their cowardice and weak faith, and He decreed that they would wander in the wilderness for forty years (the traditional span of a generation), until all the adult members of that fearful group died and their children had succeeded them. Only two were exempted from this sentence, Joshua and Caleb, both of whom had favored an immediate invasion.

Before Moses died, he designated his chief lieutenant Joshua as his successor. After the people had completed their sentence in the desert, Joshua led the new generation into Canaan where they established settlements and waged war, capturing some cities. A new nation would appear called Israel— and it would have a tremendous impact on future world history.

THE SIGNIFICANCE OF THE SECOND REVELATION

In my view, the appearance of God to Moses and the Hebrews is essentially the greatest event in history before the birth of Christ. What can one say of other historical events in comparison to this? The world had known plenty of tyrants and conquerors, builders and destroyers. But how many of them had actually uplifted the mind and soul of man?

Everyone has heard of the Egyptian pharaoh, Ramses II ("the Great"). This so-called great pharaoh usurped many monuments that had been built by his predecessors, having their names chiseled off and his own carved over them. (Other pharaohs had done the same.) Apparently, from the propaganda he left inscribed on temple walls, he barely escaped with his life at the Battle of Kadesh. In typical pharaonic fashion, his inscriptions boast that he singlehandedly fought the Hittites to a draw, claiming a great victory.

To his credit, Ramses II later made a treaty with the Hittites which gave his people a generation of relative peace. He then spent the rest of his 67-year reign building temples and statues to glorify himself.

I can think of at least two Egyptian pharaohs who were greater than Ramses II— Mentuhotep II Nebhepetre of the 11th Dynasty, and Thutmose III of the 18th. Both of them were far more adept at conquering their enemies than Ramses. They spent most of their reigns building up Egyptian territory and unifying the country, instead of simply carving huge monuments for self-glorification.

Other great military leaders of other ages built empires— Sargon I of Akkad, Cyrus II of Persia, Alexander III ("the Great") of Macedon, Caesar and Octavian of Rome, the Mongol chieftain Genghis Khan— the list could hold maybe a hundred names.

But how many of those empires are around today? How many of those conquerors gave their people enlightenment instead of tyranny? How many of them freed the minds of their subjects from the false worship of stone and wood? How many of those rulers cared about anything more than their own personal power— and their own glorification in history?

When God revealed Himself to Abraham, it set the stage for far greater miracles, but still it had relatively little impact on the world. When He chose Moses to receive the Second Revelation, it was an event that not only changed history then, but which would have an incalculable influence on the world's future. This was the impact of the Second Revelation— one which has reverberated through the ages.

MOSES AND THE EXODUS: WHEN DID IT HAPPEN?

Since at least the 19th century, historians and other scholars have debated as to exactly when the events of the Exodus happened. The basic question was, did the Exodus take place in the reign of Thutmose III (in the 15th century BC), or was it during the reign of Ramses II (13th century)? [29:127-133] It's evident that this question has been answered by the science of archaeology.

In April of 1980, during the course of a [6]ground survey, Israeli archaeologist Adam Zertal discovered the ruins of a large stone structure. It was located on the slopes of Mt. Ebal, in the occupied West Bank territory administered by Israel. [16:139] After much excavation work, it was determined that the structure had been an altar of ancient Israelite design. [16:164-166] Along with the remains of burnt animal bones, artifacts found in and around the altar included ancient Egyptian scarab amulets and earrings, and sherds of very early Israelite pottery. The scarabs, as well as the sherds found in the fill of the altar, dated its construction to the 13th century BC.[16:121-122, 151]

The altar fits the description— and is in the exact location— given in the Bible for the altar built by Joshua during the settling of Canaan. {Joshua 8:30-31} The stones had not been worked with any iron tool. The burnt bones found there were from animals which would have been kosher under Jewish law, and acceptable for sacrifices. It's obvious that the date of the Exodus is now attested by physical proof.

Another artifact was discovered in 1896, which proves the Israelites were in Canaan at that time. A large stele (free-standing stone tablet) was found which dated to the reign of the pharaoh Merneptah, the son and successor of Ramses II. (It was carved on the back of a stele which had been originally used by the pharaoh Amenhotep III more than a century earlier.) The inscription, as with most Egyptian historical documents, is a boastful propaganda message claiming victories for the pharaoh over many enemies. One of those enemies named was the people of Israel— located, according to the context, in the land of Canaan. The inscription dates to the fifth year of Merneptah's reign, around 1207 BC.

The presence of the word "Israel" was a bombshell in the archaeological world. It was— and is to this day— the earliest intact and unmistakable mention of the nation of Israel yet found outside the Old Testament itself.

---

[6] ground survey — A process by which archaeologists survey a large area, scouring every square meter of ground for artifacts and recording the site of each find for later use. [16:78]

It's amazing, that even in the 21st century AD such discoveries can be the center of raging controversy. But whether we realize it or not, we are living in a world inherited from the ancients. There are many people (including some professional archaeologists) who refuse to accept that an altar mentioned in the Old Testament has actually been found.

Part of the problem is, such a structure would help to demonstrate modern Israel's right to exist in its ancient homeland in the Middle East. More embarrassingly, it proves that another of the historical facts mentioned in the Old Testament is authentic. Worst of all (for the cynics)— it stands as a concrete, visible witness to the reality of Moses and of the great revelation given to him by God.

This helps explain why the excavation of a rose-colored sarcophagus found in the tomb of King Herod of Judea in 2007, would be denounced as a "robbery" by Palestinian nationalists. [26:58]

This is why the archaeological site of Ebla, in Syria, would be subjected to a virtual news blackout in the late 1970s, after it was found to have Old Testament connections. (Modern Syria remains technically at war with Israel.) And this is why a so-called documentary would be touting the discovery of an Egyptian tomb as "proof" that the Bible was *wrong* about the death of the first-born son of Ramses II, during the biblical plagues of Egypt.

This last-mentioned documentary (titled *RAMESES — Wrath of God or Man?)* was produced in 2004. It was about a massive tomb being excavated in Egypt's Valley of the Kings, which had been built for the many sons of Ramses II. The entire thrust of the documentary was the idea that a particular skull— one of several found in the tomb— "proved" that Ramses' eldest son did not die as a child in the 10th biblical plague. [Source No. 34]

Interestingly, this documentary mentions no inscription identifying that skull as belonging to Ramses' eldest son. In fact, the Bible doesn't even say that every firstborn son was killed in the 10th plague— it simply states that every firstborn *offspring* died. {Exodus 11:5, 12:29} Ramses' first child could just have easily been a daughter. However, none of this was important in this so-called documentary. Its overall goal was to establish that this (unidentified) skull "proved" the Bible wrong. And the people behind it definitely weren't going to let any bothersome facts get in the way.

This is something that I see no reason to be objective about. On examination of the facts, it's obvious that some members of the scientific community (as well as the media) are conducting a persistent, not-so-clandestine campaign against the Bible, and even against people's faith in God.

When politicians, scientists, or media moguls deliberately distort the facts of history and archaeology, what other purpose can they have? When they use the power of the mass media to push such obvious propaganda, what cause are they serving? These are legitimate questions. **Once we see that we're witnessing a conflict between lies and the truth, those doing the lying should be held accountable for it.**

THE THIRD GREAT REVELATION OF GOD TO MAN

God had appeared to Moses and the Hebrew people with great miracles, liberating His people from their servitude in Egypt. The next great revelation would also be accompanied by miracles. But they would appear in a way that many hadn't expected.

The next great revelation came through a man called Yeshua. This was the name "Joshua," the way it was pronounced in the ancient country of Judea. In our own time, the man's name is usually known to the Western world by its Greek form— Jesus. The word Christ is also Greek. It means simply, "the Anointed One." This is another way of expressing the Hebrew term "Messiah." (In our own culture, it's sometimes used with the name Jesus as if it's a family name— which it isn't.)

I realize that everything in the last paragraph is pretty basic stuff. Many people are already fully knowledgeable of it. But I can recall that I knew nothing about *any* of this when I was a teenager. It hurts to admit it, but about the only time I heard the phrase "Jesus Christ" was when my uncle or stepfather was swearing. That's the reason for covering this basic territory here. I know what it's like not to know any of this. I'm mentioning it for those who are at the same starting point that I was.

WHAT IS THE MEANING OF "MESSIAH?"

The word Messiah is from the ancient Hebrew language. It has a number of connotations, meaning things like "savior," "deliverer," "liberator," etc. With apologies for those who aren't big on history, it is necessary to give a very brief sketch of the culture which produced this concept of a Messiah.

The Hebrews of ancient times were by our standards a primitive people. The word Hebrew itself has been found in numerous ancient sources, some dating as far back as c2000 BC. It appears variously as "Habiru," "Hapiru" and "Aperu." [29:66] In such non-biblical documents, the word always seems to have one common characteristic: It was used to describe various groups of people who were not highly thought of by those writing about them.

Some scholars think the word originally described a class of nomads, some of whom lived by robbing and pillaging others. It's really not easy to tell, because not much is said about them. However, because they appear in Middle Eastern inscriptions, it's obvious that they lived in that region. Some of these inscribed tablets are from the 14th century BC, during Egypt's 18th Dynasty. [29:128]

The ancient Israelites may have been simply one particular group of these shadowy Hebrews. When they migrated into Egypt, around the 17th century BC, they were allowed to settle in certain areas. Later they were pressed by the Egyptians into forced labor— perhaps as state-owned slaves. {Exodus 1:11-14} This was their situation when the Exodus took place in the 13th century BC.

After the Hebrews (now called Israelites) entered Canaan, they began to establish settlements there, and some Canaanite cities they captured by military operations. It was there, in ancient Israel, that the books of the Old Testament began to be written and preserved.

It's not easy for us nowadays to visualize the world those people lived in. The Israelites were a small nation who worshiped one God, surrounded by other nations (some of them more powerful) who worshiped many gods. They never seemed to "fit in" with their ancient counterparts. This is why the worship of idols is expressly forbidden in the Ten Commandments. But occasionally in their history, many Israelites fell back into idol worship. Surrounded by other peoples who worshiped numerous gods, it was a constant temptation for them.

Eventually God punished the Israelites by allowing them to be conquered. First— after the reign of their King Solomon— the country split into two, which made them easier prey for their enemies. The northern kingdom (called Israel) was destroyed by the Assyrians in 722 BC. The Babylonians conquered the southern state, Judah, in 586 BC. For about fifty years, many of the Israelite people were forced to live in the Babylonian Empire. This period of the "Babylonian captivity" produced some of the truly great literature of the Old Testament.

And a theme began to emerge. It was prophesied that— even though they were a conquered people— there would ultimately be a Messiah who would deliver the Israelites from their quagmire of degradation and misery. This theme is found time and again, sounding throughout many books of the Old Testament. By the first century AD, the people were ready for that prophecy to be fulfilled.

But it wasn't that simple. There were two basic, but very different, ideas of what kind of Messiah they were to expect. In one view, the Promised One would be a liberator, a great military leader who would establish the permanent kingdom of God's people on this Earth. In the other view, the Messiah was thought to be the one who would free God's people from their sins— bringing them a different, less worldly kind of liberation. He was seen as more of a savior than a conqueror.

FULFILLMENT OF PROPHECY

Jesus was born about 6 to 4 BC, in the last years of King Herod "the Great" of Judea. The reason Jesus' actual birth year isn't correctly designated as 1 AD is because Dionysius Exiguus, the 6th century Catholic monk who calculated the start of the Christian era, was off by a few years. [9:Vol. 4:109]

To understand the full significance of Jesus' birth, we must try to view the entire Jewish culture in the context of that age. In Jerusalem, the center of the Jewish faith was the Temple, which had been built by that same King Herod. (All that's left of it now is the Western Wall, which contains some of the stone foundation blocks which originally supported the Temple Mount.) [26:41]

But at the time of Jesus' birth, it was the most magnificent structure in the Jewish world. It was considered to literally be God's house— the place where His presence came to rest. Unlike the earlier Temple of Solomon, Herod's Temple did not contain the lost Ark of the Covenant. But the sacred status of the new Temple was just as important to the people who worshiped there.

In those times, the Jewish faith in Jerusalem was led by priests who stressed the absolute authority of the ancient Mosaic law, and the importance of the traditional sacrifices. These laws had been observed for centuries, and were considered to all have divine authority, since they were in the sacred Scriptures of what we now call the Old Testament— the modern Jewish Bible.

The largest religious group in Judea were known as Pharisees. [18:133] They were the most extreme interpreters of the law. They may have been sincere, faithful Jews; but they had an unpleasant tendency to label as sinners anyone who didn't observe all the laws as strictly as they did.

We might think of them as religious police, who believed in upholding every letter of the law. We can compare their attitude on biblical laws to our enforcement of modern ordinances.

Nowadays, we would all agree that a murderer should be locked up. If the Pharisees had had their way, jaywalkers, smokers and sidewalk-spitters would be in prison right along with him.

Another powerful group were the Scribes. They also interpreted the Jewish laws and applied them to the details of everyday life. One might compare them to modern lawyers.

There were other denominations of Jews at this time, such as the Sadducees and the Essenes. Another force were the Zealots— Jewish nationalists who wanted political independence from the Romans. The Zealots were what we would call the extremists of their day, essentially revolutionaries.

The legions of the Roman Republic had taken over Judea in 63 BC. The Romans were often despised by the native Jews, but they kept order and (as a rule) didn't interfere with local religious practices. At first they ruled Judea through client kings such as Herod. But in 6 AD the first emperor, Augustus, dispensed with such niceties and appointed a Roman governor to rule directly.

This was the environment into which Jesus of Nazareth was born. It was a religious milieu where numerous groups claimed the mantle of the Law, with each of them vying for influence. It was a political climate where a foreign empire (and a pagan one) operated the levers of power. It was a curious blend of political stability and religious ferment— a culture where the true God was acknowledged and worshiped, yet still remained distant to those who worshiped Him.

THE GREAT LIGHT BROUGHT BY JESUS

The beginning of the Gospel of John describes Jesus of Nazareth as the real light, or the true light. {John 1:9} As you may have noticed, I don't do an extreme amount of actual quoting from the Bible in this book. I'm not an expert on the Bible, and I don't pretend to be an authority on biblical teachings. I'm only one man, speaking from my personal background and experience, and from my limited knowledge of history and theology. Usually,

I feel it's more fitting to refer readers to the biblical quotations, so that they can check the actual source.

But this simple statement from the Gospel of John sums up the meaning of Jesus and the Third Revelation better than anything else I know of. Jesus brought hope to a people who had been conquered time and again. He brought new— and full— meaning to the ancient Scriptures of the Old Testament. And [7]He brought the kind of light that can destroy any darkness, in any individual's mind.

The four Gospels of the New Testament are the only reliable eyewitness reports we have of Jesus during His mission in the world. It's tantalizing, considering how much more there could be. At the end of the Gospel of John, it's said that this world probably couldn't hold all the books which would be needed, if all Jesus' works were described in detail. But— limited though they may be— these brief accounts provide an amazing picture of the events which took place.

Jesus spoke with such love and simplicity, that countless people accepted Him immediately as the promised Messiah. His words were so powerful that they are best described in the Gospel of John, where Jesus asks His apostles if they want to desert Him. The chief apostle, Peter, replies simply, "Lord, to whom shall we go? You have the words of eternal life." {John 6:68}

But Christ's mission consisted not just of words, but of deeds. He started out with an unplanned miracle at the request of His mother; at a wedding feast He easily transformed water into wine. It was only the beginning of His public mission. In a mind-boggling torrent of miracles, Jesus traveled throughout Judea healing the sick, restoring sight to the blind and mobility to the lame. Perhaps two of His miracles overwhelmed His followers more than any others: Christ demonstrated His awesome divine

---

[7] The reader must bear with me here. I may not be a professional scholar or a biblical expert, but I believe my priorities are in order. So I will explain one thing. As a convinced Christian, being a confirmed Catholic, from this point on I will be using capital letters for personal pronouns such as "He," "His" and "Him," in relation to Jesus. My reason for this is simple: As the only begotten Son of God, Jesus is God as well as man. I believe that God deserves capital letters. As a former agnostic, I will totally understand if this statement is met with skepticism. I am asking only for the reader to understand my thoughts on this subject— not to unquestioningly agree. If such a sign of respect is unpalatable to anyone, then let me be blamed for poor punctuation.

power over nature— not only by walking on the surface of the Sea of Galilee— but also by resurrecting a man who had been dead and buried in a tomb for days.

A good many people may have been following Him in hopes of receiving cures. In the 21st century, we take "miraculous" medical results almost for granted. But in those days, going to a regular doctor was often a gamble between what would kill you first— the physician or the ailment.

Regardless of the "medical benefits" to His followers, the main draw was what Jesus had to say. Living today in a modern civilization which has gone through the Renaissance and the age of the Enlightenment, it's almost impossible to fully understand how the people of those times thought. Perhaps we could compare their basic mindset to that of people living now in countries like Saudi Arabia.

The majority of people in Judea were taught the Hebrew Scriptures since childhood, and precious little else. Most classes of society were kept in educational and political ignorance. Their lives were governed by religion, custom, and a powerful political authority. They were not only conditioned to accept rule by monarchs, but their ruler was a foreign emperor, represented by the Roman governor.

In other words, Judeans were taught from birth to obey (but to loathe) the Romans, to accept the customs of the day, and above all to follow the scriptural Hebrew Law. Women were expected to marry young and devote themselves to family life. Many (if not most) men in their culture earned their living in the same line of work as their fathers. About the only big choice they had in life was to decide which sect of Judaism they would follow— the Scribal legal tradition, the Pharisee interpretation of the Law, the Essene separatist doctrines, or the extreme revolutionary path of the Zealots. Their entire society was dominated by Jewish law and Roman soldiers, while the anti-Roman agitators (especially the Zealots) were trying to foment as much rebellion as possible— all in the name of God. This was the sea of confusion and contradictions in which Jews were living at that time.

And then this *nobody* named Jesus shows up, preaching in the streets and hills, gathering together a band of disciples, healing the sick and the handicapped with astounding miracles, and on one occasion making His own whip and driving the money changers out of the Temple! People either loved Him or they hated Him. And (not surprisingly) the ones who sided against Him included almost all of the local power structure— such as the priests, the Pharisees and ultimately the Roman authorities. Just about the only authority figures who didn't resent Jesus were the tax collectors. He treated them like human beings, while most of the rest of the Jewish populace hated their guts.

Nowadays, you pay to get into an auditorium to see celebrities. Major seminar organizers will sell you their wisdom on being a "success." Or, you can pay even bigger bucks to sit at the feet of rock stars while they belt out their songs about life, love, philosophy— and, of course, the glories of casual sex.

Commercial promotion isn't an American invention. In the 5th century BC, teachers in Greece were charging people big bucks to listen to them too. They were called Sophists, and they taught that truth was always relative. (Perhaps they could be described as the Einsteins of their day, except that their "relativity" theory was rooted in cynicism rather than nuclear physics.)

This Judean upstart named Jesus just didn't fit the mold. He seemed to stir people up and cause controversy wherever He went. In that respect He resembled the earlier Socrates of Athens, except that not even Socrates could heal the sick or resurrect the dead. Like Socrates, this Jesus wasn't charging people to listen. Instead, He would *give* to people— with frequent and public miracles. He would heal their broken bodies and occasionally feed them by the thousands.

In the title song of the '70s musical, *Jesus Christ Superstar* (sung by the actor playing Judas), the singer asks why Jesus appeared at "such a backward time and such a strange land?" And this much is true: There were no news media at that time.

There were no reporters, no evening news, and no videocams (in fact, no cameras of any kind).

But there are very good answers to that question. First, if Christ had initially appeared in our modern society, He might have gone almost unnoticed. His voice and His message could have been drowned out by the glitz of MTV and Ticketmaster. His example of giving and self-sacrifice would have been ignored by all political parties— except maybe by efforts to co-opt His presence for their own benefit. The media "opinion makers" would probably have treated Him like a joke.

Or (secondly), they might have put Him on the same shelf as all the false messiahs we've seen. Or (thirdly), Jesus may have been been treated as an object of fascination, a source of entertainment— at least until the public became bored, at which time He would be ignored, just like all the celebrities who had their moment in the spotlight until they were dismissed and forgotten.

How would Jesus have been seen by most people in our Western culture? As a curiosity, a media-painted malcontent, or a head case? What kind of amusement would He have provided, for a society hooked on amusement?

When God the Father chose the ancient Roman world as the "fullness of time" for His Son's birth, He knew exactly what He was doing. The entire Mediterranean region was in a state of relative peace. And the peace imposed by the caesars— even in a military dictatorship— provided fertile ground for the growth of a new way of life.

THE GREATEST REVELATION IN HISTORY

The miracles Jesus performed were electrifying. The crowds He drew must have been the biggest in living memory. The words He spoke were miracles themselves; they lifted people up and poured out spiritual life to everyone listening. But greatest of all was the message Jesus delivered— the great revelation He gave us about the God of Heaven.

At least two thousand years earlier, God had revealed Himself to Abraham as a God of power and absolute authority. He had demanded that His people reject the orgiastic ways of the surrounding nations, whose dissolute religions included such things as ritual prostitution and child sacrifice. He had shown the strength of His moral laws by destroying the degenerate cities of Sodom and Gomorrah.

Then— twelve centuries before Jesus— God had shown Himself to be a liberator. He had taken Moses, a man raised as an Egyptian prince, and called him to lead the Hebrew people out of their servitude in Egypt. The ruling pharaoh, Ramses II, was powerless to prevent it.

After the Exodus, God had taken His people and forged them into a nation, settling them in Canaan where they supplanted the Canaanites and outlasted the Philistines. Not simply a moral beacon and a liberator, God had revealed Himself to be a nation-builder as well. Not only that, but He had sent prophets to the Israelites. After their country suffered conquest by the Babylonians, it was promised that a new Israel would arise in a future age. {Ezekiel, chapters 36 & 37}

Now, after these great revelations from God Himself— after all these tremendous events— after all those prophets had spoken and all those kings had perished— after the Romans had exploded out of Italy like an eruption of Vesuvius and conquered the Mediterranean world— after their ancient country of Judea had become a mere province in a vast empire— after all those centuries of faith and all their hopes for a promised Messiah— the one Man was suddenly there, who would bring the greatest revelation of God the world would ever know.

And what Jesus taught people was as simple as it was astounding. God— that same God who had brought their ancestors out of Sodom and out of Egypt— was not just the harsh moralist of Abraham and Lot. He wasn't limited to being the stern and dynamic commander of Moses, nor even the severe punishing master who had brought upon His people the Assyrians, Babylonians and Romans.

Through all these various guises, through all these faces seen over the centuries, God— at His heart— was finally shown to be a powerfully loving Father, who views every last man and woman as His own child; a Father who is willing to adopt every single one of us who wants to be His. This was a revelation and a liberation like nothing ever known. Jesus, God's only begotten Son, was sharing His Father's love with all the lost and alienated children who'd never had a clue.

This was something that [8]few of the prophets had foretold, or even glimpsed. Who could have known that a God powerful enough to destroy cities and liberate nations, would ever bother to love individual people? Who would have guessed that He wants *each one* of us for His own? It was a type of divine love and even intimacy that men were not prepared for. Yet this was what Christ, the Messiah, revealed— that God, that same creator and ruler of the universe, is the Father of each of us, who wants us to be close to Him.

That's why this Third Revelation has to be the ultimate one. What could be more central to human existence, than knowing that God Himself is our own loving Father? What could have more meaning than that? What could possibly bring greater enlightenment, or surer salvation?

Christ did more than reveal the reality of God's fatherhood. Jesus created a Church, to bring His followers into a community and keep their minds focused on true worship. He promised that whatever His Church allowed on Earth would be allowed in Heaven; and whatever it held bound on Earth would be held bound in Heaven. {Matthew 16:18-19} Some churches in the world today trace their origins back to that original group of Apostles. The Catholic Church still is governed from Rome, where St. Peter served as bishop.

Christ also gave His people warnings. He foretold that terrible tribulations would come. He warned of future persecutions, and a number of Roman emperors did just that— from Nero to Diocletian. Jesus also warned about false prophets and false

---

[8] One of the few was the great prophet Isaiah, in one of the most beautiful and sublime passages of the Old Testament. {Isaiah 63:16 – 64:8}

messiahs— that many would come in the future claiming to be Him. In recent decades we've seen them in plenty, people such as Jim Jones and his "cult of death" in Guyana in 1978. Then there was Vernon Howell, who changed his name to David Koresh and brought his followers to a terrible end in Texas in 1993.

Christ also predicted the destruction of the Temple in Jerusalem, which took place in 70 AD. But through all the miracles of Jesus— beyond all the prophecies, and even transcending the Church He founded— is the great revelation of God's role as a loving Father.

Christ, for the first time, made God *reachable* for every one of us. He made salvation attainable, and set the Church in place as His foundation for our pathway to redemption.

PUTTING THE THIRD REVELATION INTO PERSPECTIVE

Throughout fifty centuries of history conquerors have subdued nations, and many kings have posed as gods themselves. Tyrants have butchered thousands and even millions. Some (such as Ramses II) built vast stone temples, while others (like Josef Stalin) leveled countless churches. Powerful ideologies such as communism and Nazism have marched across continents, destroying nations and threatening civilization itself. Vast numbers of innocent human beings, including Jews, Slavs and unborn children have been deemed "sub-human" in order to justify their mass slaughter.

Even today, mass murderers call themselves "holy men" as they try to justify the deliberate bombing of civilians. And in our own country, there are those who claim that every mother carrying an unborn child has a license to kill. Right now in the 21st century, in what some smugly call the era of "New Age" wonders, there are atavistic forces trying to impose a new *dark age*— a darkness where human life itself has no value.

But through all the centuries of wars and conquest, eclipsing all the conquerors and tyrants and mass murderers, shines the revelation of love given to the world by Jesus. No wonder His message has survived millennia of wars and persecutions. No wonder the tiny Church He founded in a small province of the Roman Empire has grown to inhabit nearly every corner of the globe. And now the light of Christianity shines from many churches, illuminating the souls of countless millions.

Only those countries which impose the greatest tyranny are so fearful of Christianity that they try to blot it out. But tyranny and darkness can't win. Not in the long haul. Regardless of every obstacle and persecution, the revelation of God as a loving Father continues to shine through it all. No wonder so many regimes opposed to it have ended up on the ash heap of history. Who can doubt that this will always be the same?

This is the God who revealed Himself to Abraham and Moses. No product of a darkened human mind, He chose the times and places to show mankind the blessings of true worship of a true God.

But we still have the great gift of free will. People can still choose other roads to follow. They can put their faith in money, magic crystals, ideologies, mother goddesses, false messiahs— anything they want. It appears so incredibly easy, for some to turn their backs on a God who chose to reveal Himself. To my thinking, it's nothing less than amazing— how some people can so readily put their faith in something *less* than God, but find it so difficult to believe in *Him*.

But this only sharpens the contrast between false gods and the real one. Only the true God revealed Himself to the world. Only the true God put His indelible stamp on history by liberating His people from Egyptian slavery. Only the true God sent His Son to redeem very man and woman, through His great sacrifice on the Cross.

And there's more. For any devotee of those man-made religions— for any dedicated, hardened atheist— there's a great deal more that *has to be ignored,* than just the eyewitness accounts found in the Bible. Fortunately for mankind, this loving God gave us not only miracles in ancient times, but also many proofs of His existence in later ages. In the next chapter, we'll see examples of God's power that anyone can recognize— if only they have the courage to look past those comfortable blinders.

Chapter 6

AN AMAZING GOD, WHO GOVERNS AND GUIDES THE WORLD

We live in an age of healthy skepticism. We live in an age that demands proof, or at least convincing evidence. We live in an age of logic and reason. And these are generally good standards. After all, we no longer force accused criminals to suffer "trial by ordeal" to establish their innocence. We no longer bleed people in order to restore their health. The age of the Enlightenment— and the growth of science— *have* brought some definite benefits to mankind.

But at the same time, we've lost something. Even though they were ignorant of science, the people who lived a thousand years ago were secure in their knowledge that God is in charge. They *knew* that He exists. They *knew* that He set down certain rules for people to live by. And they *knew* that God is the ultimate arbiter of life, death and justice.

People in past times suffered from widespread illiteracy, primitive medicine and a host of other handicaps. But they had a strength of faith that many of us today never experience. They had a certain peace of mind that only real faith can bring. Their very societies and culture taught them from birth that God is there, and Heaven and the angels with Him. Those people were secure in that knowledge, no matter how tough life was in this world.

While science and scientific inquiry have brought countless material benefits to mankind, society's fabric of faith has been frayed at every edge. In the world we are now born into, skepticism and doubt reign supreme. And nearly every precept of Judeo-Christian teaching has been attacked from all directions.

But— when we think about it— God Himself *gave* us these rational minds which have embraced science. We can see everywhere the day-to-day benefits; we live longer, healthier lives due to medical advances. We've even set foot on the Moon, and envisioned the colonization of Mars. Science, after all, is a result of our God-given minds. How can we condemn it out of hand?

But still, this raises a valid question: Have all these scientific wonders actually disproved the existence of God?

Only in the minds of those who refuse to see everything.

The God who created us, who revealed Himself to us, who loves us as a patient and caring Father, still lives. He still governs the world with the same awesome and limitless power that He has exercised from the beginning. And we can see Him working in the world, if we just open our eyes honestly and look at the proof.

I don't get messages from God. I'm not some special individual who somehow just "knows" all this stuff, or who has some sort of unique ability to expound on such matters. I'm simply stating this from the perspective of one who was once an agnostic, but who has been brought through the jungle of doubt and confusion. I'm just one more individual (out of countless millions) who has struggled through that jungle in search of sunlight. It doesn't take an Einstein to point out that the sunlight is real.

It isn't that difficult, really. As the Son of God promised long ago, "Seek and you will find." The answers are there, under our noses. All we have to do is open our eyes and recognize the truth when we see it. All we have to do is use these marvelous minds He gave us— and use them honestly.

THE FALLACY OF DEISM

Deism is a word we've all heard before, back in our high school history classes if nowhere else. It describes a type of religious thinking that was especially popular in the 17th and 18th centuries, and which emanated from the age of "the Enlightenment."

There were various shades of deistic thought and theology. But it basically taught that all religious truth is inherent in the human psyche, and can be accessed by human reason; this meant that (for most deists) any *revealed* truths were unimportant at best, fraudulent at worst. Deists believed that the most prominent organized religions were artificial and unduly wealthy, and that their priesthoods had concocted all the rituals of their faith in order to enhance their personal power, just so they could lord it over their flocks.

Most classic deists accepted the idea of a God— but it was *their* idea of God. For the most part, they conceived of God as an organizer of nature, a natural God, who (lacking a true personality) sits in benign neglect of the world, presiding over it merely as a distant observer. Deism teaches that a God had indeed created the world, but then left it to be governed by the laws of nature. Essentially, its hazy doctrine says that God had set the world in motion, and then let man do the rest. (Even some Christian believers today seem to have a deistic view, rejecting the idea that God continues to shape events.)

To deists, God was a loving, distant and harmless deity. He played little or no part in worldly affairs, but He emanated love and stood mainly for benevolence, sweetness and niceness. Their God was a god of convenience, who never got angry and who never would think of favoring one set of religious beliefs over another. (Although the most organized and traditional Christian churches were held in suspicion.) Some deists leaned toward pantheism, which teaches that God is in everything— from rocks and trees right up to stars and galaxies. To pantheists, these things are not mere creations of God, but are all part of their god.

It has been asserted that the first three presidents of the United States subscribed to deistic thinking. [9:Vol. 3:965] And it's well known that the third president, Thomas Jefferson, definitely leaned toward [9]deism and had strong suspicions against organized religion— especially those with priesthoods and traditional rites. Although Jefferson was a renaissance man and a great thinker, he was also a product of his 18th century culture. (Perhaps this made him the perfect instrument whom God would use to advance the idea of religious freedom in the modern world.)

So, in deistic thinking, we find a remote god who created the universe and then retired from any active role in it. However, in Judaism and Christianity, we are shown a God who is always present, who is definitely pro-active in this world, and who actually sent His own Son to redeem mankind.

We've got to face up to this: These two types of deities cannot be reconciled. It has to be either one or the other. The universe— the real universe— simply isn't big enough for the both of them.

The deistic god, in many ways, seems attractive. He is certainly convenient. After all, with a god like that, we can basically ignore him and live our lives any way we want. But he's nothing like the God who revealed Himself to man. Could it be that the deistic god is just one more deity which (like so many others) *sprang from the minds of men?*

Today, we live in a society which in many ways is a direct descendant of the culture of skepticism that shaped Thomas Jefferson. With the rise of science, we've seen a technological explosion and amazing advances in medical knowledge. Our children are growing up in a world where interplanetary probes have become ho-hum events and manned Moon landings are old news. Computers, linked by the World-Wide Web, seem to offer every possible answer to every possible question. Heart, kidney, and even lung transplants are everyday stuff.

In short, many people look at the world around us, and think that man produces all the miracles. They just don't see any need for faith in a God whom our culture basically ignores, or— more to the point— makes "obsolete." Looking back, I can see that this

---

[9] Although deistic in his thinking, Jefferson described himself as a "REAL CHRISTIAN," and "a disciple of the doctrines of Jesus." [40:278] He actually took the New Testament and clipped out those passages he disagreed with— perhaps in an effort to blend deism with Christianity.

is what made me an agnostic as a teenager. God simply seemed to be absent from our society. Way back in the '60s, some journalist had even come up with the notion that "God is dead." (Sort of like that fellow who announced that we had reached the "end of history" right after the Cold War ended.)

There I was, never taken to church regularly, never taught any religion, and watching a rectangular tube every day that showed me images of a world without any real reference to God. There were plenty of "miracles" and marvels to see, but they were all man-made. I didn't have the eyes to see beyond that. A culture heavily steeped in a secular mentality had got me thinking that God was— at the very most— unprovable.

But there's definitely another side to this coin called proof. After all, we do live in an age of science. So the next question is quite legitimate: If God is real, and if He is indeed an active God who cares deeply about us and takes a strong interest in human events, there must actually be evidence of this. If He's real, then there *must* be some type of objective lens that we can use to find Him. **And there is. All we have to do is have the honesty to see.**

THE LORD OF HISTORY

The ancient Hebrews, to whom God first revealed Himself, had many titles for Him. As is well known, they wrote His name with the Hebrew letters for YHWH, which omitted the vowels and lost for us the original pronunciation. The two most common English transliterations are "Jehovah" and "Yahweh."

When He appeared to the prophet Moses in the 13th century BC, God gave Moses a new name to know Him by— "I AM." (Believers in modern existentialist philosophies no doubt love that, because the core of existentialist belief is Descartes' famous phrase, "I think, therefore I am.")

But God gave the Hebrews more than just words. He ordered Moses to go back to Egypt and free His people. Then He performed amazing miracles to secure their freedom— from the famous ten plagues of the Egyptians to the crossing of the Sea of Reeds on dry land. This was no distant, apathetic god, such as the deists describe.

It's obvious that the God of Moses took an active interest in His people's lives. When He found His faithful ones living as slaves, He brought about their liberation. When He found them homeless, He gave them the land of Canaan. In other words, God stretched out His arm and changed the course of history. This is one of God's attributes which has been known from very early times. He is the Lord of History— a God who decides the outcomes of great issues, whether by using nations as His instruments in war or by exercising His decisive power of life and death. He sets up rulers and removes them as He sees fit.

And we find in the New Testament that this hasn't changed. When the Roman prefect Pontius Pilate warned Jesus that that he, as governor, had the power to set Him free or to crucify Him, Christ responded by reminding Pilate that all his political power had been given to him from above. {John 19:11} In the New Testament, God's power over life and death is undiminished. Jesus demonstrated this when He resurrected His friend Lazarus from a tomb in front of witnesses, four days after the man's death. And after the Crucifixion, Jesus Himself rose from death.

Those who scoff at Christianity love to dismiss such events as "myth." Even though there were plenty of eyewitnesses still living when the four Gospels were written, cynics love to laugh at the idea that anyone in this modern age could take such things seriously. And the scoffers seem to have an advantage on this point. After all, no one has been resurrected for a long time— unless you care to consider the thousands of "near death" experiences recorded in recent years.

But the active participation of God in history is another matter entirely. There are quite a few instances in history— and not just ancient history— where sudden, unexpected, and clearly miraculous events have changed the direction of history itself. These are far more numerous than I can recount here. But there's room in this chapter for a few good examples.

THE VISION THAT TRANSFORMED AN EMPIRE

In 312 AD, the Roman Empire still covered most of Europe. But it was no longer the stable, peaceful empire established by Augustus three hundred years earlier. For generations it had been a battleground between opposing generals fighting for power. At the same time, barbarian tribes constantly lurked at the borders, waiting for an opportunity to invade. To the once-proud Roman citizenry, freedom was a distant memory. Their great empire was now nothing but a military dictatorship. Most emperors were petty tyrants who managed to rule for a few years until they were killed by rival generals, or their own troops.

There were exceptions. One recent emperor had been both capable and far-sighted. His name was Diocletian, and he had managed to stay in power for twenty years. Diocletian somewhat stabilized the Empire, but he took draconian measures to do so. In an effort to halt inflation, he issued a decree (301 AD) fixing maximum prices on all items sold throughout the Empire. It didn't work. Instead of selling at a loss, merchants simply removed their goods from the shelves. (Apparently the laws of economics are in some ways immutable. A similar effort to freeze prices by President Richard Nixon in 1971 also failed.) Diocletian's decree was ultimately repealed. [9:Vol. 4:106]

Another of his measures had a more permanent effect—though not with the result that he expected. Diocletian appointed three colleagues to help govern the Empire. He and another served as joint emperors, while the other two were supposedly subordinate to them. The Roman Empire was theoretically still one political unit, but in actuality it was now divided. This was a radical measure, intended to make the task of guarding the borders easier.

As part of his economic program, Diocletian made an effort to put the Roman coinage system on a firm footing. He also imposed new rules for taxes, making it possible to collect them more regularly. And in a move which set a precedent for feudalism, he decreed that the Empire's people must remain in the jobs they had— and even continue the work their parents had done— *on a hereditary basis*. He wanted to stabilize the Empire, and individual freedom was not one of his priorities.

Diocletian was a firm believer in state control, and he didn't think much of any organized religion that was independent of the government. So he renewed the persecution of the Christians with a vengeance, closing churches and confiscating all the Christian writings he could. He was one of the few emperors to attempt the total suppression of Christianity. Despite this, from a strictly political perspective, Diocletian was one of the more capable Roman rulers. His reforms did help preserve the Empire. Ultimately, he did something unheard of: In 305 he voluntarily abdicated, leaving the Empire in the care of his hand-picked successors.

The peace did not last. Inevitably, the new rulers began waging civil war to determine who would be top dog. And this is where the course of Western history would be changed forever.

After more than a year of fighting, the forces of two of these rival generals— Constantine and Maxentius— were squared off for a major battle at the Milvian Bridge, a structure located on the Tiber River near Rome. [10:Vol. 16:687] It was October 27 of the year 312. [14:85] On the eve of the battle, Constantine had a religious experience which was variously recorded as a vision or a dream. In this vision, the general saw the monogram for the word Christ, which was a combination of two Greek letters resembling an "X" and a "P." (This is now known as the chi-rho symbol, from the Greek letters.) Along with this monogram he was shown the Latin words which said, "In this sign you shall conquer."

Being a practical man, Constantine took the advice to heart. He ordered his soldiers to inscribe the chi-rho symbol on their shields. When the Battle of the Milvian Bridge was fought, his enemy Maxentius drowned in the waters of the Tiber along with thousands of his troops. [36:226] Constantine went on to rule the Empire with his ally Licinius, who became co-emperor.

This single event brought tremendous consequences. Constantine immediately devoted his loyalty to the God who had given him victory in this decisive battle. It wasn't just the conversion of one man which made this important. The history of the *entire Western world* was now set on a new trajectory.

The next year, 313, Constantine and Licinius issued a decree which is now called the Edict of Milan. It was declared that Christians would be free to worship without any harassment, and that all the properties which had been seized from them must be restored. Although paganism continued in strength for some time, the Christian religion was now legally protected by the Roman state. Nearly two hundred fifty years of official hostility and persecutions had come to an end.

The two men who now ruled jointly were not simply politicians, or bureaucrats accustomed to blissful harmony and compromise. They were first and foremost soldiers. Eventually— perhaps inevitably— Constantine and Licinius fought it out for control of the Empire. Again, victory was given to Constantine. From the year 324 he was sole emperor and would remain so until his death.

Every victory of Constantine turned out to be a victory for Christianity. In May of 330 he founded the city of Constantinople, which would become the alternate— and later the sole— capital of the Roman world. Unlike the pagan origins of Rome, it was established as a Christian city.

Christianity was allowed to grow and flourish— not hidden underground in catacombs, but building great churches where anyone could worship freely. Only one more emperor, Julian, would attempt to role back the tide of Christianity. He perished in an ill-conceived border war against the Persians in 363, after just two years in power.

Formerly organized in secret communities to evade the swords of Roman troops, the Christian faith now became like a blazing sun, relegating the old pagan gods to the shadows. In 380 another emperor, Theodosius I, declared Christianity the official religion of the Empire. Eleven years later he banned every form of pagan worship. [36:272-273]

WHAT ABOUT FREEDOM OF RELIGION IN THE ROMAN EMPIRE?

This can be seen from two perspectives. Constantine's Edict of Milan declared that Christians and pagans alike would be free to worship as they please; it was much like the First Amendment to the U.S. Constitution in that respect. Three generations later, when Theodosius made Christianity the official religion of the Empire and then banned pagan worship, it was another great victory for Christians— but a giant step backward for religious freedom.

As an American, this makes me ambivalent toward Theodosius' actions. Yes, here was a ruler who advanced the cause of God and Christ— but at the same time he suppressed other religions. He was simply another tyrant, but one who happened to be on the right side.

Let me say right here, that I fully support freedom of religion. What a Roman emperor did sixteen centuries ago was simply standard procedure for those times. We have to remember that— after the fall of the Roman Republic— the concept of freedom (as we know it) was pretty much a thing of the past. But the *Pax Romana* which followed brought a renewed stability which had been lost during the civil wars that destroyed the Republic.

This can all be seen in historical perspective. The Roman Empire— which was chosen by God as the birthing place for His Son— served its purpose. It preserved Western civilization, gave Europe two centuries of relative peace, and provided a fertile field for the growth of Christianity. The very persecutions which the Empire inflicted on Christians forced them to build an organized and resilient Church. How can anyone without blinders doubt that this was all part of God's great plan?

We have to remember that God is the Lord of History. He guides history in His direction. As stated in the Old Testament, even Egyptian pharaohs and Babylonian kings were used as instruments of His will. And it is in the record of man's history that God's handiwork can be clearly seen— provided we have the honesty to recognize it when we see it.

CONSTANTINOPLE PROTECTS THE WESTERN WORLD

When Constantine chose the Greek town of Byzantium as the place for his new capital, he was thinking like a soldier. The site was situated strategically so that it could defend the strait of the Bosporus, a gateway from Asia to Europe. It was an ideal location to withstand just about any assault from the East. And this was exactly what it did. (The Eastern Roman Empire is often referred to as the "Byzantine" Empire, from the original Greek name of Byzantium.)

For over 800 years Constantinople remained unconquered. It withstood every enemy, even the assaults of the Muslim Saracens, who tried repeatedly to take it. Finally, in 1204, an army of treacherous crusaders from the West managed to overthrow Constantinople and sack it. Although the city was retaken by Byzantine forces in 1261, the Eastern Roman Empire was never as strong as before. Constantinople was conquered by the Ottoman Turks in 1453 and became part of the Muslim territories. (Now, of course, it's known as Istanbul.)

But for 1100 years after its founding, Constantinople had served as a Christian fortress, a bulwark against Eastern invaders. By the time it fell to the Turks, Europe was strong enough to defend itself. The last of the Muslim invaders were being driven from Spain, and the so-called Holy Roman Empire (a loose coalition of European states) could raise armies to defend western Christendom.

A single, momentary vision given to a Roman general before a battle had changed the course of history. Instead of persecuting the Christian faith, the world's strongest empire would protect, nurture, and finally embrace the Christian faith. The city founded by that same general would be a fortress to defend the Christian faith. And the Church which had looked like an endangered flame, flickering in the dark world of paganism, grew into a beacon of light which would penetrate every corner of the globe. Such are the workings of God in history— visible in a way which annihilates the possibility of coincidence, and transcends any attempt at denial.

THE INTERVENTION THAT SAVED WESTERN CIVILIZATION

There is one event in Western history which has been vastly under-reported. And that is the devastating invasion of Europe which took place in the 13th century. There was one immense army of warriors who simply went *around* the Byzantine Empire, through Russia. In fact, they had *conquered* Russia, cut through eastern Europe, and then virtually stood at the threshold of Vienna— ready to absolutely *drop the hammer on European civilization itself.*

This time the invader wasn't an army of Germanic tribes or conquering Muslims. It was an enemy much more dangerous than either of those. The barbarous German tribes at least tried to assimilate with the civilized peoples whom they conquered. And the Muslims had a reputation for allowing their subjects to continue in their own religions if they paid a special tax.

The enemy facing western Europe in the year 1241 was far more destructive, far more ruthless, and far more deadly than any of the others. They were the Mongols.

The founder of the Mongol Empire was, of course, Genghis Khan. By 1206 he had united all Mongol tribes under his rule. Then he began to conquer elsewhere. Within a generation, his realm was the greatest expanse under one ruler that the world had ever known. With the arguable exception of the recent British Empire, the regime established by Genghis Khan retains that distinction to the present day.

The name (or title) Genghis Khan still conjures up images of conquest and imperial glory. But in reality, it was similar to the "glory" which Josef Stalin earned as he strengthened communist rule in the Soviet Union. It was identical to the "glory" earned by Adolf Hitler as he rounded up helpless civilians for the death camps. It was a "glory" built on the most savage kind of destruction and mass murder.

Genghis Khan had a hobby. He would send his armies to conquer a neighboring state, then he would kill off the ruling families and anyone else who might be a potential rival. In addition to this, if he thought it would bring the slightest advantage, he would order the rest of the population slaughtered. Any city which dared to hold out would pay with the lives of every last inhabitant. If a city surrendered without resistance, the population (if they were lucky) would only be enslaved.

For all his expertise in warfare, Genghis Khan was at heart a nomadic horseman. His view of an idyllic world was pasture land for vast herds of horses, to sustain his people in their tents. After conquering the northern Chinese city of Peking (Beijing) in 1215, he looked forward to razing every building and killing every inhabitant in the region, so that the Chinese grasslands could be entirely dedicated as pasturage for his people's horses. (Very fortunately for millions of Chinese, an adviser explained to him that live subjects provide more tax revenues than mountains of corpses.) [10:Vol. 19:748]

Aside from the terror (and frequent submission) inspired by his sheer savagery, the main reason for his military success was simple: The Mongol armies were the finest in the world. Mongol warriors were renowned for being able to "live in the saddle." Not only this, but their fighting capabilities were far ahead of their time. With a communication system using colored pennants, their ability to wage war was not only enhanced by lightning speed, but also a unique battlefield flexibility which gave them a huge tactical edge over every enemy. [44:100]

After Genghis Khan's death in 1227 his third son, Ogadai, was chosen by the Mongol chieftains to rule the Empire. Ogadai completed his father's conquest of northern China, taking the Chin Dynasty capital of K'ai-feng in [10]1234. [9:Vol. 8:886] Like his father, Ogadai contemplated the massacre of the entire population. This time a Chinese adviser convinced him to spare the inhabitants of the country, in order to exploit China's productive wealth as well as its military technology.

Then, unlike his father, Ogadai turned his attention to the West. In 1237 he sent his armies into Russia. City after city was besieged and leveled. In 1240 Kiev was destroyed, and Russian resistance collapsed; for the next two centuries Russia was a tributary state of the Mongol Golden Horde. The interior peoples of Siberia paid tribute for nearly 400 years. [9:Vol. 8:886] also: [10:Vol. 24:349]

After the fall of Kiev, the other medieval states of Europe realized they were next— and they were right. Back in Mongolia, while the great Khan Ogadai held court at his new capital of Karakorum, his army cut through eastern Europe like a knife through a porterhouse steak. Their leader, Batu Khan, along with his chief general Sabotai, easily overcame the armies of knights and infantry which the Christian Europeans sent against them. At the Battle of Liegnitz on April 9, 1241, a great coalition of Germans, Poles, Teutonic Knights and Templars marched from Liegnitz (modern Legnica) to confront the Mongol horde, which they more than matched in numbers. The Christian army was virtually annihilated.

The following day an army led by King Béla IV of Hungary attacked the Mongol host at the Sajo River. At sunrise the next morning, April 11, the Mongols counterattacked, smashing the Hungarian forces and slaughtering nearly all of them. Only King Béla and a few of his followers escaped, fleeing the field and making a humiliating run back to the capital at Buda. Béla himself didn't slow down until he got to an island in the Adriatic Sea. [44:96]

As was their custom, the Mongols spent the rest of the spring and following summer resting their horses, grazing them on the European grasslands and preparing for the next season's

---

[10] Another source [25:10] gives the year as 1233.

campaign. Eastern Europe having fallen before them, the Asiatic horde was marching ever westward.

Late in the year 1241, the Mongol armies were encamped on the plains of Hungary. Every city they'd attacked had been destroyed. Every army thrown against them had ceased to exist. In the north, Mongol forces had advanced to the Elbe River of Germany. Modern-day Poland and Hungary laid prostrate in their path. And now it was the turn of Vienna. Raiding parties were already conducting sorties into Austria, preparing the way for conquest. The helpless Viennese could do nothing but watch, wait and pray. They knew the outcome was inevitable— barring a miracle.

One morning in January of 1242, they looked over the city walls and saw that the Mongol raiders had vanished. Then came word that their army had vanished as well.

Ogadai, great Khan of the Mongol Empire, conqueror of northern China, Russia and much of the Middle East— ruler of all Mongol forces in Europe— was dead. Well known as a heavy drinker, the emperor had expired suddenly during a drinking bout with his friends in Karakorum late in 1241. Weeks later, Batu had learned of the death by messenger. Dutifully following the ancient Mongol nomadic custom, he and his army packed up their equipment and went home, anticipating the shift of power that was taking place.

But there was no election of a new khan. Ogadai's widow, Torogene, ruled as regent for her eldest son for the next four years. [9:Vol. 8:886] In the future the Mongols would turn their attention again to the East, never returning to Europe.

No one will ever know how different history would have been, if Ogadai's armies had continued westward. Vienna would certainly have suffered the same fate as Kiev. Also certain is this: No power on Earth could have stopped the Mongol army on its path of conquest, wherever it chose to go— only a Power greater than that on Earth.

The Old Testament records an attempted conquest of Jerusalem by the Assyrian king Sennacherib, in a campaign which took place in 701 BC. The Assyrian monarch had taken numerous other cities, and then decided to add Jerusalem to the list. His army surrounded the city. However, on waking one morning and exiting his tent, Sennacherib found all his troops dead— evidently struck down by bubonic plague. {2 Kings 19:35}

Modern skeptics might try to dismiss that narrative as myth. But Assyrian cuneiform records from the same period (while ignoring the ignominious destruction of his army) do state that Sennacherib besieged Jerusalem. They also tacitly acknowledge that he failed to capture the city. [29:237] It's the closest thing to an admission of defeat that anyone is likely to find in the records of ancient Assyria.

Just as the death of an army in 701 BC prevented the conquest of the ancient Israelite kingdom of Judah, the death of an emperor in 1241 AD prevented the destruction of European civilization. The latter event was a more subtle— but nonetheless obvious— occasion where the Lord of History took matters into His own hands.

A HUMBLE PEASANT GIRL LEADS AN ARMY TO VICTORY

The Mongol invasion of Europe has been almost ignored by modern Western historians. But there probably isn't anyone in America who hasn't heard about Joan of Arc. The word "saint" is often used loosely now. In secular Western history, there are only a few people whose entire lives can be called a miracle. The simple peasant girl who became known as the Maid of Orléans was one of them.

This girl, whose name was Jeanne, or Jehanne, in French, was born in a small village called Domrémy in what is now northeastern France, around the year 1412. She was just another girl from a family of tenant farmers, unremarkable in her childhood.

At that time France was embroiled in a conflict known as the Hundred Years' War. (Actually, it was an "on-again, off-again" war which lasted 116 years.) The country was a battleground between the French monarch and the English, while many French nobles had allied themselves with the latter. The English, of course, claimed much of France as the legacy of William the Conqueror, who had ruled the Duchy of Normandy.

To make matters worse for the French, by the late 1420s the heir to the throne, the Dauphin— five years after his father's death— had still not been officially crowned King. The city of Rheims, where coronations traditionally took place, was under the control of one of his political enemies. Without the coronation ceremony, the Dauphin's claim to the throne was shaky at best.

It was in May of 1428 that this peasant girl first showed up at Vaucouleurs, which was the closest stronghold to her village maintaining its loyalty to the Dauphin. Explaining her mission, she asked the officer in charge of the French garrison to be taken to the Dauphin. The captain, Robert de Baudricourt, didn't take her seriously and sent her back to her village. [10:Vol. 22:377]

She showed up again the following January. By this time de Baudricourt's attitude had changed. The girl spoke with firmness and clarity. He could see that she wasn't insane or feeble-minded. It's doubtful that in this present age she would be seen in any other way. The 16-year-old peasant girl gave an astonishing account of how she had been commissioned by St. Michael the Archangel, and also Saints Margaret and Catherine, to rescue the Dauphin and save France. The voices of these saints, she said, had sent her on her mission.

Anyone nowadays who talks seriously about hearing voices soon gets "measured for a straitjacket" by friends and relatives. Psychiatrists today must make a fortune off the percentage of their clients who hear voices. But in 15th century Europe, people didn't always scoff at such things. Those people were raised in a culture of faith. They knew that God rules events on Earth as well as Heaven, and that the saints and archangels are just as real. The French commander listened to her.

Captain de Baudricourt's reaction was— for his time— pretty level-headed. At first he'd dismissed the peasant girl with the unusual story. Then he took a second look at her and listened.

He told her to dress in men's clothes (probably for her own protection from attack), then ordered a squad of six soldiers to take her to the Dauphin's court at Chinon. The journey, which involved crossing enemy territory, took eleven days.

Then she arrived at the royal court. After two days of listening to conflicting advice, the Dauphin (the future King Charles VII) granted Joan an audience. He had decided to test the peasant girl. Putting a friend on his throne when she arrived, Charles was himself standing among the crowd. But the maiden from Domrémy went straight towards him, recognizing him as the heir to the throne. She passed the test. There followed several weeks where Joan was interrogated by churchmen. After all, they had to consider the possibility of heresy. They were satisfied by her answers. Then the Dauphin did something unparalleled in history. He commissioned Joan as an officer in his army with her own squire, gave her armor, weapons and a horse, then assigned her a squad of soldiers.

Incredibly, this teenage girl— with no education or military training— led the French forces from victory to victory. Her very presence inspired the army. Within a matter of months her troops had captured numerous English strongholds; finally the royal city of Rheims threw open its gates to the French army. There, on July 17, 1429, Charles VII was officially crowned King of France.

However, France was still embroiled in its war with the English. Joan continued to lead the army for Charles. Most of her battles ended with victory. But in May of 1430 she was forced into a tactical withdrawal and— as she held back to cover the retreat— was captured by troops of the Duke of Burgundy. (Burgundy was at that time an independent state, allied with the English.)

What followed was a travesty of injustice and political cynicism. She was handed over to the Bishop of Beauvais, one Pierre Cauchon, who was also an ally of the English. The bishop brought together a group of churchmen who prosecuted Joan on no less than 70 trumped-up charges. [10:Vol.22:379] She attempted to escape, but unsuccessfully. She was confined and shackled, guarded round the clock, threatened with torture and subjected to numerous interrogations. When she asked to appeal her case to the Pope, her request was ignored.

Although Joan weakened and agreed at one point to sign a statement admitting guilt and to wear women's clothing, a few days later she put on men's clothes again. When questioned about this, she said that the voices of St. Margaret and St. Catherine had reprimanded her for giving in. The churchmen handed her over to secular officials, who condemned her to death by burning at the stake.

On May 30, 1431, Joan of Arc was executed. To the very moment of death she maintained her faith. Although she'd been "convicted" of heresy, she was given permission to make a last confession and take Communion. Even as she died at the stake, a Dominican priest held up a crucifix so that she could see it, as she had requested.

Although Joan died for her cause, her cause did not die with her. The French continued fighting the invaders. By 1453, only the port city of Calais remained in English hands. Charles VII was still king, and the Hundred Years' War was over.

The Maid of Orléans wasn't forgotten. In 1455 Pope Callistus III ordered an inquiry into her trial, and as a result her conviction was officially reversed. [32:246] Joan of Arc remained a national heroine of France. And— in one of those delicious ironies of history— in 1920, nearly 500 years after her struggle, she was canonized as a saint by the Catholic Church. Her betrayer, the corrupt Bishop of Beauvais, was forever disgraced. Of course, some people couldn't care less what the Catholic Church has to say about anything. But this chapter isn't about the Catholic Church— it's about God's role in history.

The mission of Joan of Arc can be seen in various ways. To historians, it was a pivotal event in the development of the modern nation state; from a loose patchwork of duchies and principalities, Europe was evolving into a continent of modern countries. To patriotic Frenchmen, it can demonstrate that

France stands out among nations. To fervid feminists, it can be taken as proof that women make the best generals.

But one overriding fact is clear: In 15th century Europe, a teenage girl from the countryside— unschooled in courtly manners and untrained in war— led an army to victory and inspired a nation. To almost anyone, one aspect of this is obvious: Some events in history can only be described as miracles. And genuine miracles are not man-made. Nor are they woman-made.

THE TIMING THAT DOOMED AN EMPIRE

As Europe was transforming in the 15th century, so was the scope of world events. The voyages of Columbus turned Europe's attention to an entirely New World.

Everyone knows about the Aztec Empire of Mexico, and how it was conquered by Hernan Cortés. We've all been told about the brutality of the conquest, about the Spaniards' ruthlessness and their greed for gold. And it's true, those conquistadors were a very rough crowd.

But that's not the whole picture. To see this clearly, we've got to just forget the whole "noble savage" idea, and all the propaganda we've heard about the "evil Europeans." For the sake of honesty, it's going to be necessary to set aside any such preconceived notions. Regarding the Aztec Empire of Mexico, one thing is abundantly clear: Whatever faults the Spanish conquistadors may have had, the Aztec rulers were far worse— in just about every category.

The Aztecs weren't nearly so desirous of gold; that much is true. But the Spaniards had no monopoly on greed. The Aztec rulers taxed their conquered subjects to the hilt. They demanded vast quantities of jade, and also rare tropical bird feathers which were highly prized for rich clothing. They also took tribute in the form of hard labor, for constructing temples and other public buildings. [5:287] Cacao beans were used as a form of money throughout the Aztec Empire. But the substance they produced— chocolate— was reserved for rulers and nobility alone. Commoners were not allowed.

However, the worst feature of the Aztec world was not mere greed, or elitism, or even the incredible level of tyranny— it was the sheer brutality. There were other civilizations we know of which regularly practiced human sacrifice; ancient Carthage, for example. But nowhere in the history of man is any other society known where *countless thousands* of people were slaughtered as a regular feature of their religion. Although earlier Mexican cultures had developed the custom, the Aztecs brought it to its greatest depths.

The most common method of Aztec sacrifice is well known. The victims were led to the top of the temple pyramid, held down and stretched over the sacrificial stone. Then they had their chests ripped open by a priest wielding a stone knife, and their living hearts torn out. While each extracted heart was still beating, their convulsing bodies were thrown down the temple steps as if they were last week's garbage.

Not only the mode of killing, but the sheer scale of the slaughter staggers the mind. As one example, it was recorded in Aztec documents that when their Great Temple was dedicated in Tenochtitlan, from ten thousand to eighty thousand victims had their hearts torn out. [24:727] (Since the slaughter went on for four days, the higher number is probably more accurate.) [31:14] This took place in 1487 under their eighth emperor, Ahuitzotl. [5:81] It was noted that the Emperor himself, being quite an enthusiast, performed many of the killings personally, until he finally grew tired and handed the job over to others. [2:68]

The Great Temple was, in fact, the epicenter of the Empire. It was a huge, pyramidal stone pantheon devoted to the two highest Aztec deities. One of these, Huitzilopochtli, was a war god as well as a sun god. In Nahuatl, the Aztec language, his name meant "Hummingbird Wizard."[11] The other idol housed in the Temple was called Tezcatlipoca. This latter deity, known as the tempter of men, was considered to be "in charge of the

---

[11] The name of this deity has also been translated as "Left-Handed Hummingbird." [2:62] Tezcatlipoca has been translated as "Smoking Mirror."

souls" of the Aztecs; one of the Spanish soldiers present simply described him as "the god of Hell." [31:31] These were the types of obscenities people worshiped in that culture. These were the things for which countless thousands were led to their deaths like cattle.

Of course, it was important to maintain trophies of the sacrifices. For this purpose a huge structure stood in Tenochtitlan, which served as a multi-sided rack for the skulls of the victims. At any given time, passers-by could view thousands of human heads in every stage of decomposition. The Aztec capital was praised in all Spanish accounts for its magnificent beauty and the splendor of its buildings; it also boasted many open-air markets and plazas. It was a good thing there was so much outdoor space in that city, because without it the stench of rotting flesh might have asphyxiated every inhabitant who remained alive.

The slaughter was not restricted to Tenochtitlan. Surrounding cities— many of them subject to the Aztec Empire— carried out similar sacrifices. When the Aztec army fought with enemy tribes, it was called a "war of flowers." The clash was usually not for the purpose of killing the enemy or winning the war. The objective was to *capture* enemy soldiers for use as human sacrifices. This was a mutual understanding between Aztecs and their adversaries. Human sacrifice was what they lived for. Those people were taught from birth that their gods could have nothing less.

In addition to their monopoly on chocolate, the Aztec priests and nobles had other culinary privileges. They were entitled to take part in cannibal feasts on the bodies of sacrificial victims. It must have been quite a spectacle to see great pots boiling in the vast dining rooms, as the gorgeously dressed nobles gathered to dine on the corpses of the peasantry whom they so cheerfully disposed of. Warriors who captured enemy soldiers for sacrifice were also alloted certain portions of the remains. [5:228]

There were other quaint customs held dear by this great civilization. To honor the ancient god of spring, Xipe Totec, this deity's priests would don special attire. They would actually clothe themselves with the freshly flayed skins of sacrificial victims, who had the honor of being sacrificed and skinned for the occasion. [2:67] also: [24:738-739] By some accounts, the devotees would wear this unique garb until it began rotting to pieces.

Is it even possible for us to imagine living in such a society? What it would be like, to be taught from birth that slaughter is a way of life? That it was simply your fate— and a glorious one— if you happened to find yourself in line for the sacrificial knife? This was the kind of "civilization" which greeted Hernan Cortés when he landed at Yucatan on April 22, 1519. He knew nothing of the shocks which awaited him, or the ordeals which lay ahead. The Aztecs who had heard of his coming knew a good deal more; or at least they thought they did.

In the 52-year cyclical calendar of the Aztec Empire, it was the year *Ce Acatl*— One Reed. [39:11] And in the Aztec religion, One Reed was a year steeped in symbolism. Another of their more important gods was Quetzalcoatl, a deity inherited centuries earlier from the Toltec culture. Quetzalcoatl was a sort of demigod— a mythical hero-turned-god— and their legends said that he had been exiled by the ancient Toltec priests for opposing the practice of human sacrifice.

The thing was, Quetzalcoatl had supposedly been born in a One Reed year, and then had been sent into exile 52 years later, in another One Reed year. Therefore, many Aztecs believed that Quetzalcoatl was destined to return in a One Reed year.

The appearance of this host of armor-clad warriors, riding monsters which looked to them like huge deer, jolted the Aztec officials to their core. Could this be Quetzalcoatl, returned from that ancient exile to restore his kingship? With this in mind regarding Cortés, they definitely didn't want to offend him.

Other events had unsettled the Aztec rulers in recent years. Tenochtitlan and its people had been visited by ominous portents. Strange lights had been seen in the sky. Inexplicably, raging fires had ignited in some of the temples. And in the night, a woman's voice could be heard crying through the streets, "O my beloved sons, now we are about to go." [2:139]

These omens, and others, had deeply troubled Emperor Montezuma II. He was known to be unusually superstitious (even for an Aztec), and generally of a gloomy and negative nature. [2:139] All these factors— the legends, the strange portents, the year One Reed, even the mind of Montezuma himself— tended to work in the Spaniards' favor.

The story of the following events is well known. Cortés was plied by an Aztec official with gifts, which included objects of gold. Battles had to be fought with local tribes along the journey. Nothing, however, could deter the Spaniard from his course. Finally, after reaching Tenochtitlan on November 8th, 1519, he was ushered into the presence of the Emperor Montezuma. A week later, Cortés made him his captive and his puppet. [31:51] The days of the Aztec Empire were now numbered.

If the Aztecs had acted decisively, overwhelming the Spanish troops on the beach at Yucatan, the name of Hernan Cortés might be nothing but a wispy footnote in history. But the year One Reed, the apparent return of the demigod Quetzalcoatl— even the very religion of the Aztecs— all paved the way for the greatest overthrow of any empire in the Americas.

If Cortés had arrived a year earlier, or perhaps a year later, what might have happened then? But the one true God who controls history had set the board, with all the chess pieces in place. He had timed the start of the match. And this particular contest began in the Aztec year One Reed.

THE SHOWDOWN

With Montezuma serving as a Spanish marionette in Tenochtitlan, things went well for about half a year. Shortly after arriving in the capital, Cortés had demanded that the human sacrifices be stopped. The Aztecs balked, although the numbers of victims were reduced. At the Spaniards' insistence, a Christian altar with a cross was set up in a room within the Great Temple.

Then came the showdown. Cortés himself, seized by a spirit of religious zeal, destroyed one of the idols of their blood-soaked gods. A few days later he had their priests remove it— along with the other idols— from the Temple. The sacrifices were ended, and the Cross of Christ surmounted the former pantheon of death. [31:54-55]

By these actions, Cortés had put his own faith above safety and personal gain. It was no longer a mere clash of civilizations, but a war for men's souls. Although most of the Aztec people resented this new regime and grew sullen, with Montezuma's cooperation Tenochtitlan remained quiescent. But soon a rush of events took place which would transform the city into a seething cauldron of death.

The following April, Cortés was obliged to return to the coast with some of his men to deal with an opposing force sent by the Spanish governor of Cuba— who was no friend of Cortés. While away from the Aztec capital he left his most trusted officer, Pedro de Alvarado, in command of the garrison.

In Tenochtitlan at this time, a major festival called *Toxcatl* was approaching. During the festival many of the Aztec nobility would be gathered to dance, lightly armed with their obsidian-edged weapons. It was reported that the customary human sacrifices would be carried out, regardless of the ban imposed by the Spanish. Then two Aztec officials came to Alvarado with a warning which was a thinly disguised ultimatum: There was a plot afoot to massacre every Spaniard in the city, unless the Christian symbols were removed from the Great Temple and the idols restored. [31:59]

Pedro de Alvarado was a soldier who had no scruples about ruthless preemptive action. He ordered the courtyard (where the dance would take place) to be sealed with all exits blocked. When the appointed hour came and the Aztec nobles commenced their festival dance, on his orders the Spanish troops moved in and put them all to the sword. The slaughter was murderous, gruesome and complete. Six hundred or more of the ruling elite were massacred within the space of a few hours. [2:144]

The Spanish had been the first to throw off the mask of false friendship. Along with it went the peaceful submission of the people. Every Aztec man in the city rose up to attack the Spaniards. Their emperor, the pliable and helpless Montezuma, was killed— allegedly by an object thrown by his own people as he tried to calm them with a speech. (The Aztec accusation that he was murdered by his captors seems unlikely, as the emperor was said to have lingered several days before dying.) [9:Vol. 8:288]

Cortés' expedition to the coast went well, and he returned not only with his own men in his force, but also most of the Cuban governor's. But he returned to a city that was up in arms. In the midst of overwhelming numbers of the enemy, the Spaniards were forced to attempt an escape.

It was the night of June 30, 1520. As the Spaniards were crossing a hastily repaired bridge over the lake, the Aztecs discovered the sneak-out attempt. Then all hell broke loose. Under the relentless attack, two-thirds of the Spanish soldiers were killed, drowned, or captured and sacrificed. Cortés himself was taken prisoner at one point, before being rescued by one of his men. The surviving troops fought their way out of Tenochtitlan and gained the shore. Forever afterward, that horrific evening has been known as *la Noche Triste*— the Night of Sorrow.

THE MIRACLE VICTORY THAT SEALED THE EMPIRE'S FATE

What was left of the Spanish force had got out of the city; now the march to find refuge began. The "army" which was left consisted of some 440 men (along with some Tlaxcalan allies) and 23 "debilitated" horses. [5:191] A dozen men still carried crossbows. Apparently they had none of the harquebuses, the primitive matchlock guns, with which they had arrived. These took so long to reload that they were of little use in pitched battle anyway. Of course, there'd been no chance of escaping Tenochtitlan with any of their artillery pieces. The best weapons they had left were their fine swords of Spanish steel, along with their daggers and a few lances.

Lightly armed, sparsely mounted, physically strained to the limits, the Spanish soldiers were now in a forced retreat, trying to get to a place of refuge where they could regroup. But there were no roads, no humvees, no air transports and no trucks to carry them. In the real world of 1520 they were on foot, moving slow, cutting their way through the jungle.

After a week's march, they arrived at a place called the Plain of Otumba. It was [12]July 7, 1520. A sight greeted them there which might be sufficient to kill a man.

In front of them was a fully armed Aztec army, consisting of countless warriors. Spanish veterans of Otumba reckoned the number of Indians at around 200,000. [39:65] Some recent chroniclers, oozing with the comfortable skepticism of modern-day historians, have asserted that it must have been more like 40,000. As if either number would really make any difference. At best, the Spaniards were outnumbered by about 100 to one.

For the small force of surviving conquistadors, there was no choice. They had to fight their way through the enemy host before them— or die in the attempt. There could be no turning back. Every Spaniard immediately knew it. Can anyone imagine being faced with such an ordeal today?

Characteristically, Cortés ordered his men forward. The Spanish troops threw themselves into the sea of Aztec warriors. As the enemy whittled their numbers with arrows and obsidian-studded clubs, the Spaniards pushed ahead.

This, then, was the stunning picture of that day: a few hundred lightly armed Spanish soldiers, trying to cut their way through the countless thousands of enemy warriors surrounding them. The Spaniards fought with the desperation of doomed men, who nevertheless refused to give their lives away. They fought throughout the morning and into the late afternoon. They fought for hours, slashing, killing and dying under the merciless tropical sun.

---

[12] Many years later, one of the Spanish soldiers present, Bernal Diaz, recorded the date as July 14.

Then something happened. The Spanish commander, Cortés himself, saw in the distance the great feathered crest of the *cihuacoatl*— the Aztec leader directing the battle. [5:186] With a sudden surge of fury, the Spaniard ordered his troops to cover his sides while he drove his horse forward. Thrusting and slashing, the Spanish vanguard made their way toward the enemy chieftain's position.

Finally they were close enough. [13]One of the men at Cortés' side, Juan de Salamanca, spurred his horse up to the Aztec general, ran his lance through the man's chest and then hurled his body to the ground. [31:66] By some accounts, one of the Spaniards took the necklace from the dead chieftain's throat (his symbol of leadership) and held it aloft for the Indians to see.

What happened next was astounding. The host of Aztec warriors fled the field. With all their weapons, with all the magnificence of their feathered costumes, those remaining tens (or hundreds) of thousands ran from the Plain of Otumba as if they had seen their own ghosts.

That moment witnessed the death knell of the Aztec Empire.

The astonished Spanish survivors had become the victors. They continued their march and made their way to the refuge of Tlaxcala, an independent Indian state opposed to the Aztecs.

There was a second event which spelled doom for the empire of human sacrifice. It was reported that the force of Spaniards sent earlier by the governor of Cuba (to oppose Cortés) had brought with them a man infected with smallpox. [39:67] In any case, within two months after *la Noche Triste* a sudden plague of smallpox struck the land. The Indian people suffered horribly, and the Aztec fighting strength (along with the regional population) was greatly reduced.

By this time the Spanish troops had taken refuge with the Tlaxcalans. They proceeded to build a fleet of boats, then returned with their Indian allies to overthrow Tenochtitlan. On the 13th of the following May, the invading force laid siege to the city, and the inhabitants suffered countless agonies. [31:73-76]

---

[13] By another account, Cortés himself dispatched the Aztec general. [39:65]

The Aztec capital fell on August 13, 1521, and with it fell the most monstrous and blood-soaked empire which the world would see until the rise of Nazi Germany.

AN "UNCOMFORTABLE" HISTORICAL FACT

The Battle of Otumba is one of those events which make some historians uncomfortable. How can one explain a force of hundreds seizing victory from a host of tens (or hundreds) of thousands? Was it all due to the excellence of Spanish steel? Did a few hundred swords clear the field of Aztecs?

Was it mere chance, that Cortés found the enemy general through a sea of warriors? Was it simple luck, that enabled him to slash his way through the Indian hordes to see their leader impaled on his comrade's lance? Was it just the "law of averages" that prevented an Aztec arrow or spear from stopping him cold?

None of these factors seem sufficient. There was obviously something more to it— something which some historians would rather not speak of. In fact, many modern historical accounts simply skip over the Battle of Otumba without mentioning it at all.

If the Spaniards had been overwhelmed at Otumba— as all factors (except the miraculous) indicate they should have been— the entire Spanish conquest would have been stopped, or at the very least delayed for some years. The Aztecs would have had time to regroup and reorganize their empire. Even after the devastating smallpox plague, they could have rebuilt their remaining forces into a formidable army. They might even have "sacrificed" the practice of mass sacrifice, to avoid depleting their numbers further. Or, more likely, they would have offered mostly women and children to their stone gods. In any case, the Aztec Empire would undoubtedly have survived for some time— perhaps to rise in strength again, able to resist any new assault.

But Otumba sealed their fate. The historical fact is, a few hundred surviving Spanish troops emerged victorious, made their way successfully to the refuge of Tlaxcala, then returned months later to finalize the conquest of the Empire.

It wasn't luck, or chance, or Aztec superstition that decided that battle. It was the Lord of History who had it all planned out. The same God who saved Europe in 1241, and who commissioned a teenage peasant girl to lead an army in France; that same God had arranged for a force of hundreds to destroy an empire of blood. This is what the Battle of Otumba shows. And this same God is seen to intervene repeatedly throughout history, for anyone with enough honesty to see past their own self-deceiving blinders of skepticism.

THE ARRIVAL THAT SAVED JAMESTOWN

We can all remember from school, how the first English colony was planted at Jamestown, Virginia in 1607. The story of Captain John Smith and the Indian princess Pocahontas— and the fictional romance between them— has become the stuff of legend and countless movies.

What isn't so well-known, is the fact that the colony at Jamestown was abandoned. At one point in time, all the remaining English colonists actually packed up their goods and left. They were headed back to England.

Captain John Smith, of course, had pretty much held the colony together. But in the autumn of 1609 he suffered some serious burns from a gunpowder explosion. On the first of October, he took a ship back to England to seek better medical attention. [33:113] His departure was a disaster for the English. Smith— more than anyone else— had been able to deal effectively with the tribes of the Powhatan Confederation which surrounded the colony. Upon learning he had left, the Indians intensified their harassment of the settlers. But that was just the beginning of their new agonies. The winter of 1609/10— in its impact— was the worst in American history. In fact, it very nearly put an end to the colony of Virginia. To give us an idea of what this means, at the time Smith left there were 490 settlers at Jamestown.

When the following spring came, sixty were left. From then on, that winter would simply be known as the Starving Time.

On May 23, 1610, two English ships dropped anchor off Jamestown. Their main passenger was Sir Thomas Gates, the new deputy governor of the colony. [33:120] Gates had left England nearly a year earlier, on June 1, 1609. His ship, the *Sea Venture,* had been hit by a hurricane and run aground on the shores of Bermuda. (It's been said that this event was William Shakespeare's inspiration for his play, "The Tempest.") After using the wreckage of the ship to build two new pinnaces (the smaller ships which arrived at Jamestown), Gates and the surviving party of new colonists had finally landed.

When Gates went among the survivors and saw what was left of Jamestown, he was stunned. It was like a town of living ghosts. Some of the remaining settlers were in the final stages of starvation, others shuffling with vacant expressions through what was left of the buildings. Most of the dwellings within the fort had been dismantled after the deaths of their owners— the planks used for firewood, so that the survivors wouldn't have to venture into the forest for fuel. To do so was to court death from Indian snipers, who were often lurking outside with bows and arrows. [33:58]

After all the ordeals of the voyage, the man who was slated to be the new leader of the colony saw what remained— and he decided that it was best to pack up and leave. After conferring with the two ships' captains and evaluating the situation from a military standpoint, the decision was made. The colony would be abandoned. Over the previous three years, some 900 settlers had come to Jamestown to build new lives. On June 7, 1610, the sixty survivors of that colony— along with the surviving emigrants from the *Sea Venture—* loaded the remaining supplies aboard the two pinnaces. Then both ships weighed anchor and headed down the James River toward the sea. At sunset they anchored at Mulberry Island, nearly halfway down the river. The next day they would exit the James and begin their transit of the Atlantic.

But in the first morning light, they were greeted by a sight which no one had dreamed of. Before they'd even weighed anchor an English longboat appeared, heading towards them from the direction of Point Comfort. [Source No. 20] The men in the longboat brought amazing news. The colonists learned that a small flotilla of relief ships was near. The ships had just arrived from their Atlantic voyage.

The three ships were bringing Thomas West, who was also known as the 12th Baron De La Warr. He is often referred to simply as Lord De La Warr, or Delaware. (Both the state and river are named for him.) Lord De La Warr had been appointed governor and captain general of Virginia that year by the Virginia Company, and he was coming to assess the conditions of the colony personally. [9:Vol. 3: 933] His name is given prominence here because, along with Capt. John Smith and Pocahontas herself, he saved the colony of Virginia— setting firmly the first jewel of the English-speaking world into the crown of North America.

De La Warr returned the colonists to the fort and replenished their supplies from his ships. After presenting his commission and being received as governor, he remained there to personally govern the colony until the next year. He rebuilt Jamestown, ordered two new fortifications constructed at the mouth of the James, and "in general brought order out of chaos." [9:Vol. 3: 933]

This was the miracle which preserved God's plan for the future of America. The only English colony in North America had been stripped of supplies, vacated and abandoned. The ship had been loaded and set sail. If De La Warr had arrived three hours later, he would have found no more than what was found twenty years before at Roanoke— a deserted ruin. [9:Vol. 12: 627]

A skeptic could just as easily say, "If he had arrived two days earlier, everything would have been hunky dory." But the fact is, the settlers *had abandoned* the colony. And after a voyage of some two months across the Atlantic, the rescue ship arrived— literally— in the nick of time. Hollywood itself couldn't invent a plot better than that. Only rarely will the titans of Hollywood glorify God rather than fictional love affairs. But the glory can be found somewhere better than the great fantasy factory. It's recorded in actual history. And all we have to do is look at it with open eyes, to see the reality of God's workings with man.

THE INTERVENTIONS THAT SAVED A CAUSE

What would modern history be like, if the British colonies in North America had remained just colonies? Would the Appalachian boundary line for western settlement (fixed by royal proclamation in 1763) have halted westward expansion? Would half of North America still belong to Spain? If the American Revolution had failed, what example would there have been to inspire independence movements within the Spanish Empire? All that can be said with certainty, is that world history would be very different. Perhaps that's reason enough to attach a certain importance to the events which took place at the birth of the United States. Looking closely at those events, it's quite evident that the Lord of History deemed it a matter of some importance.

It's been often said that during the American Revolutionary War, both sides made so many mistakes that the outcome was very much in doubt. In other words, the American colonies could easily have ended up staying in the British Empire. Nowhere is this more obvious, than in several occasions where the outcome of a military engagement was decided by sudden changes of the weather.

Ten months after the start of the War of Independence, General George Washington and his army were outside Boston, which was occupied by the British Army. But the British had failed to take possession of an area just south of Boston, called Dorchester Heights. Washington recognized this as an opportunity. First, he would bring in artillery pieces which had recently been captured at Fort Ticonderoga. After this, he would seize Dorchester Heights and place the cannon there, in a position to shell the town. Then he'd send in some 4,000 troops to overwhelm the British forces and take Boston. It was a grandly conceived scheme, which actually opened up the possibility of winning the war then and there.

The plan seemed to go well. Dorchester Heights were seized, and the cannon brought in as planned. On the night of March 4, 1776, the artillery was set in place over the frozen ground, using prefabricated materials. The soldiers worked feverishly throughout the night. One eyewitness commented that, "The night was remarkably mild, a finer for working could not have been taken out of the whole 365. It was hazy below so that our people could not be seen, tho' it was a bright moon light night above on the hills." [38:178]

The next morning, the British were astonished by what they saw. From out of nothingness, it seemed, there were now countless Patriot cannon up on Dorchester Heights— all aimed at their positions. The British general, Sir William Howe, "was seen to scratch his head and heard to say... that [Washington's troops]... had done more work in one night than his whole army could have done in six months." [38:178]

Both Washington and Howe decided to go on the offensive. Both readied their forces for an attack. However, at sunset on March 5, a freak storm suddenly arose. One of Washington's junior officers, in an oft-quoted notation, called it a "hurrycane." The sudden gale brought shrieking winds, throwing rain and hail on both armies. The downpour continued into the following morning, bringing everything to a standstill. Since the firearms of the time were often rendered useless by rain or snow, both generals called off the engagement. Afterward, the British promised to refrain from burning the town, if they would be allowed to evacuate without being fired upon. They left on March 17. General Washington had taken Boston without a fight.

But he may have been surprised most by what he found afterward. When he saw the British fortifications, he admitted that they were "almost impregnable." [44:163] This is what Washington had not known before. If his battle plan had gone forward and he had led his forces to attack Boston, the Continental Army (including himself) might well have been shot to pieces at the ramparts. The war might have indeed been decided right there— in favor of the British.

Or another scenario might have been played out, with equal disaster for the Americans. If both armies had marched forward and gone at each other (as both generals had been preparing), the well-seasoned, better-trained British regulars might well have carried the day. In either eventuality, the small Continental Army could likely have been destroyed— along with its commanding general.

But the God of Battles decided that there would be no battle. And General Washington, along with his small army, had not only won Boston but lived to fight another day.

AN ARMY SAVED AGAIN

1776, of course, was to be the pivotal year in American history; but militarily it would be a year of mixed results. In an abortive southern campaign, the British fleet was repulsed in an attack on Charleston on June 28. [42:45] This stalled British efforts in the southern states for more than two years.

The northern campaign was a different story. After a terrific storm on the night of August 21, British invasion forces landed on Long Island. The British and their allied Hessian soldiers were in almost a holiday mood— and they had every right to be— as the initial landing was unopposed. Their troops poured into Long Island, plucking bright red apples from orchards as they moved forward. [38:430] The conquest of New York City had begun.

On August 27, when their forces reached the entrenched American left flank at the Jamaica-Bedford road, the inexperienced Continental troops "fled in terror before the British and Hessian bayonets, falling back to the fortifications on Brooklyn Heights." [42:48]

Well over a thousand Americans had been killed or captured; the remainder were hunkered down on Brooklyn Heights. Almost by accident, British forces were now in a position to destroy Washington's army. Then came the unexpected. A sudden storm blew up, bringing strong winds from the northeast and heavy rains. There would be no military assault in the midst of the downpour. [Source No. 45] The commanding British general, once again Sir William Howe, decided to attack Washington's forces by using "regular approaches," or siege warfare. His troops began digging trenches. For the second time in six months, it looked as if the main Continental Army was on the verge of destruction.

Washington knew that the situation was desperate. Numerically, the odds against him were overwhelming. He also realized that the storm would stall any enemy troop movements. But he might have no more than a few hours of grace. He decided on a risky stratagem: a forced withdrawal. The General sent men out, to quietly procure every possible boat on either side of the East River.

After sunset on August 29, Washington commenced the withdrawal. [42:101] Incredibly, after the rains had subsided, a thick fog covered the area of his encampment. Visibility from the enemy side was down to zero. At the same time, the continuing wind over the East River blew into the bows of the British fleet, effectively preventing them from sailing eastward. Washington's retreat across the river continued, unopposed on the water and unnoticed on land. By morning's first light, his troops had completed the crossing without loss of life. The main Continental Army had once again been saved. And once again, a sudden and almost freakish sequence of weather anomalies had saved the cause of Liberty.

THE TEMPEST THAT DECIDED THE WAR

We all know about the surrender of the British Army by General Cornwallis at Yorktown, Virginia, in 1781. It was the decisive moment when the United States— along with our French allies— actually delivered the knockout punch of the war. But what is *less* well known, is that Cornwallis almost got away.

In May of 1781, Lieutenant General Lord Charles Cornwallis had marched his main force from North Carolina back to

Virginia. [42:77] Cornwallis wanted to win battles in that state. But his commander in North America, Lieutenant General Sir Henry Clinton, had other plans. Clinton sent him a direct order to establish a base on the coast of Virginia, to prepare for a joint operation farther north. The two men did not get along.

So, on August 1st Cornwallis occupied Yorktown, which at that time was a "small tobacco port." [42:77] Now, General George Washington may not have been another William the Conqueror, but he was nevertheless a great soldier and an extremely astute strategist— who knew an opportunity when he saw one. And what he and his French allies saw now was a major British army holed up in a one-horse town with its back to the sea. Washington quickly sent word to French Rear Admiral Count Francois de Grasse, who set sail for Yorktown, arriving on August 30th. [12:292]

The Allied forces were not operating in a vacuum. British intelligence was well aware of this maneuvering, and Rear Admiral Baron Thomas Graves sailed down to the Chesapeake Peninsula, in a bid to scatter or destroy the French fleet. De Grasse fought a running sea battle with Graves from September 5th to the 9th, and drove the Englishman back to New York. While this was going on, General Cornwallis dutifully maintained his post, hunkered down at Yorktown. When Washington and the Continental Army arrived on September 26th, "the French fleet was in firm control of the bay, blocking Cornwallis' sea route of escape." [42:80] The stage was now set for the Siege of Yorktown.

Some 6,000 French Army troops arrived, bringing the total Allied land forces to about fifteen thousand. Lord Cornwallis was now even more firmly in place at Yorktown. He couldn't break through the Allied entrenchments, even if he wanted to.

While the siege works were being constantly extended under the direction of French engineers, the steadily-growing cannonade was taking its toll in British casualties. Cornwallis began considering desperate measures. He must have recalled how— just five years earlier— the Rebel army had once stealthily retreated from Brooklyn Heights on Long Island, preserving their main force. Why shouldn't it work for King George's troops?

It almost did. On the night of October 16th, Cornwallis' men assembled sixteen boats, and it was calculated that it would take three crossings of the York River to bring his entire force to safety at Gloucester, on the opposite shore. The first crossing was completed by midnight, and many of those troops were unloaded at Gloucester.

Then, in the words of Cornwallis himself, "...at this critical moment the weather, from being moderate and calm, changed to a most violent storm of wind and rain, and drove all the boats, some of which had troops [still] on board, down the river. It was soon evident that the intended passage was impracticable..." [38:1238] In that letter, written to General Clinton the following day, Cornwallis went on to explain how his boats had been scattered, leaving insufficient time to complete the evacuation. The operation had been carried out "with the utmost secrecy". [38:1238] The first contingent of troops had been partly landed. Then— once again— a sudden storm intervened to change the outcome.

The storm was a fact. So too, was Cornwallis' surrender three days later, to those same Rebels whom the British aristocracy of that era so deeply despised.

It wasn't just another surrender. It was the event which decided the outcome of the entire Revolutionary War. When Lord Frederick North, the prime minister, received the news on November 25th, one of the men who delivered the message said he took it "As he would have taken a ball in his breast." The stunned nobleman shouted out, "Oh God! It is all over!" According to this eyewitness account, he waved his arms wildly, repeating that phrase several times. [38:1243-1244] (To his credit, King George was said to have taken the news quite calmly.) [38:1245]

Lord North knew what he was talking about. The remainder of the war was essentially a few minor battles and skirmishes, fought while American emissaries negotiated the Treaty of Paris with their British counterparts. But the end result was determined on that fateful night at Yorktown. Once again, the course of history had been decided by something far more than coincidence.

A GOD WHO INTERVENES— WHAT CAN WE MAKE OF THIS?

No doubt there are many other occasions where a decisive event has turned on similar— or even more obvious— divine interventions. These are just some of the more glaring examples that I know of. But they all happen to be well-documented facts of history.

There's something to be gleaned from this. It's not possible, of course, to put God in a box and fully comprehend Him. After all, how can any creation take the measure of its Creator? I certainly don't pretend to do so. But looking clearly at some of His more obvious interventions in history, we can try to catch a glimpse of His great plan for mankind.

Was the United States meant to play a role similar to the Eastern Roman Empire centered at Constantinople? Was this country destined to be a bastion against the forces of modern barbarism, as we saw in the two World Wars of the twentieth century? Could there be a wider purpose— can America be seen as a sort of great midwife to the world, assisting in the birth of individual freedom around the globe?

It would be quite delusional to think that God— the Creator and Father of everyone— has set the United States above all other countries. Some authors of the Old Testament books, writing under divine inspiration, made it clear that God can use *any* nation as an instrument for His will. This has included pagan nations such as ancient Assyria and Persia. {*e.g.*, Isaiah 10:5-8 also: 45:1-5} But what does history teach us of His will? What kind of vast plan does He have for the world? *This is what's worth learning from it all.*

There are other examples in history, not just the American Revolution, where sudden storms changed the outcome of great battles. In the first attempt of the Spanish Armada to attack

England (May 1588), gales forced the Armada to return to the port of La Coruna (northern Spain) to be refitted. That gave the English more time to prepare. When the Armada attacked again in July, unfavorable winds again thwarted Spanish sails. The English ships then devastated their enemies. [9:Vol. 1:562]

Three centuries earlier, in 1274 and again in 1281, sudden typhoons destroyed Mongol invasion fleets which were attacking Japan. The Japanese hailed these storms as "divine winds," or *kamikaze,* a word which they applied to their suicide bombers in the Second World War. (Fortunately, the modern suicide planes were sent by men, not God, and they were much less successful.)

Following Joan of Arc's campaign, the English were almost totally expelled from France by 1453. This marked the end of the so-called Hundred Years' War. It was also a decisive event in Western history, because the victory of French forces signaled a great change in Europe. The old era of petty principalities was drawing to a close. Modern states were rising from the ashes of the medieval age.

France, England and Japan survived and grew to nationhood, partly because of miraculous interventions. There must be many other, lesser-known examples as well. From this series of events, it looks as if God wants nations to be free and self-governing. Throughout history, few of the world's great multi-national empires have outlasted the conquerors who founded them. In the twentieth century, the First World War eliminated most of those still remaining.[14]

But nations appear to survive. Egypt and China are perhaps the two most enduring examples. And in Europe, the nations tied together by true ethnic and language bonds seem to have the best survivability.

A second conclusion can be drawn from all this. When God gave the English victory over the Spanish Armada, it showed that He plays no favorites. In a religious war waged by a Spanish Catholic king against an English Protestant queen, the English

---

[14] The Russian Empire, the German Empire, the Austro-Hungarian Empire and the Ottoman Empire were all extinguished as a result of the war. Of course, after the war the victorious Bolsheviks succeeded in retaking nearly all of the former czarist realm, forging it into a communist empire.

were awarded victory. Loyalty to the Church founded by Christ was no trump card for Spain. Nearly two centuries later, when He saved the struggling American forces from destruction, He brought about the defeat of the most powerful army (and navy) in the world— that of Great Britain. What did these two conflicts have in common? What's the common denominator, the deciding factor, which God found pleasing in His eyes?

Apparently it's freedom— freedom of thought for every individual. The Protestant English were fighting not only for England, but for the freedom to worship God in their own way. Also, the English nation had spelled out the principle of individual rights in the Magna Carta more than three centuries later. True, that document had applied basically to the liberties of knights and nobles. But like a contagion, the idea of individual rights spread into the general population.

In 1775, when the American colonies took up arms against the mother country, they did so to uphold their rights as Englishmen. That type of thinking can be a dangerous thing for kings and tyrants of every sort. When independence was declared in 1776, the Continental Congress spat on the monarchist ideas of nobles and commoners, by declaring that "all men are created equal…"

The British armed forces had numerical superiority throughout the war. There were times— such as at Brandywine and Long Island— when they nearly destroyed Washington's army. At the end of the war, George Washington himself said that credit for the American victory must be given to "divine providence." His conclusion is difficult to avoid. It looks as if God wants not only nations, but individuals to be free. The English nation represented freedom of thought in their war with Spain. The American colonies represented the concept of rights and liberties in their war with Britain. Both conflicts witnessed God's direct intervention in critical battles. Both victories advanced the idea of individual freedom— the right of every human being to have his mind and spirit unshackled.

There's one more conclusion that can be reached. From all these examples, **it's clear that God does not want to**

micromanage things. He seems to intervene directly only when it's necessary.

At the Battle of Brandywine (September 11, 1777), General Washington was outflanked and his army shattered. His troops fled into the woods and regrouped. There was no sudden storm, no direct intervention. But none was needed. The men simply escaped by running. They fled, then lived to fight another day.

But a year earlier, at Long Island, it was a different story. If the British had noticed Washington's troops withdrawing, it (the entire war) might have been all over for the Americans; the ocean was at their backs. But the storm, the favorable winds and thick fog all worked to conceal the retreat. On that occasion intervention was obviously necessary.

We see this again in the Mongol invasion of Europe. The Asian horde had swept over Russia like a tsunami and beaten every force the West could bring against it. They had crushed the Russians, then a multinational army of European knights and then a Hungarian army. Finally the Mongols were threatening the gates of Vienna, poised to destroy the very civilization which was the seedbed of our most cherished ideals. In other words, *they were ready to bring on a dark age that would make the fall of the Roman Empire look like a three-minute eclipse.* That was when God removed the great Khan, Ogadai, from the picture, forcing the Mongol hordes to return to their homeland. Only after the best efforts of man had failed, did the hand of God intervene.

Those who think like deists are fond of making God into a clockmaker. He created the universe and the world— He built the clock— then He set it into motion and took the rest of the year off. So basically, now it's all in man's hands, and God is pretty much "irrelevant." But when we look at the facts with open eyes, we see a far different picture. It's a picture that a lot of historians prefer to ignore, or at least gloss over. To many minds, it simply isn't fashionable, or "cool," to see God in history. It might be too controversial to dwell on. It might draw too many jeers and sneers. It might not sell as many books.

But should we be more concerned with being cool, or with the truth? Is it better to ignore facts, to shut one's mouth with a polite smile, to turn away when someone mentions the word "God?"

We all go through life seeing the world through the prism of our mind. And there is a danger to this. It can become a distorted view, especially if we allow our preconceived notions to block out the parts of the spectrum we'd rather not see. But just because we can't see the ultraviolet band with the naked eye, does that mean it doesn't exist? How much truth are we willing to shut out, to keep those blinders on? How many facts must we ignore, in order to maintain that precious air of sophistication?

There's another question worth asking. If there is a God— and if we can find proof in history as well as religion— is this really a smart thing to ignore? Or, once we realize there's really a God, wouldn't it be a tremendous advantage for us to know Him better?

Chapter 7

HOW THE EXISTENCE OF GOD CHANGES EVERYTHING

Once we've let down the blinders we find not only that God is real, but that He's a personal, all-powerful God who takes a direct interest in the world we live in. There is another aspect of God we can easily see: He puts a great value on faith— much greater than on any amount of knowledge.

In the Old Testament, God is sometimes seen criticizing not only His people Israel, but such great men as Moses, for occasional displays of weakness in their faith. {Numbers 20:12} Anyone scanning through the New Testament will find also that Christ put the emphasis on faith. Often after Jesus had healed someone, He would tell them that their faith had made them well.

That may puzzle many of us living in the modern world. It's said that we live in the "Information Age." Vast stores of knowledge are available on the Internet. Education is greatly valued in today's world— and should be. Compared to knowledge, our culture pushes the quality of faith into a distant back seat.

Why does God prize it so highly?

I don't pretend to understand the mind of God. But going by simple human reasoning, perhaps faith is something like love. Each of us is an individual creation— an individual child of the Creator. God loves each of us greatly, and He wants us to love Him. I know this, because Christ taught that.

But it's evident that God doesn't *force* His love on anyone. And He doesn't force anyone to love Him. We each still have that gift of free will, along with our rational minds. We retain our natural instincts for survival; but unlike dogs, cats and duck-billed platypuses, we can also think. Few animals have any real thinking capacity at all, and of those few (such as higher apes), none of them come close to human abilities.

Actually, when we think about it, knowledge is the easy thing. We can *see* the Moon overhead at night, so we *know* it exists. In ancient times people used to worship the Moon, along with other celestial bodies. It was easy to worship things like the Moon and planets and stars, because everyone could see that they existed.

Going by all this, one can conclude that God wants us to *choose* Him. He very rarely performs public miracles as He did in Portugal in 1917. (This event will be discussed in Chapters 12 and 19.) He very rarely gives us obvious, glaring proof of His existence. He wants us to look for Him, and to find Him. He wants us to grow in faith, to know inwardly that He really is there for us.

Perhaps it goes deeper than the mere word "faith" can express. Perhaps God wants to be part of us, to be so saturated into our hearts and souls that we can bind with Him, in a sort of spiritual unity of love, trust and inner peace.

I don't think this is easy to achieve. I know that everyday life tends to smother my own sense of spirituality. All the cares of the world seem to work together, trying to snuff it out. I hope that it's easy for some people. I know it isn't for myself. Too often, I don't feel very spiritual at all.

This emphasis on faith would explain why God directly intervenes only when necessary in human history. What would be the sense in striking every bad guy with lightning, or sending a storm to decide every battle, if you want people to have faith? Why would anyone even *need* to have faith, if God made Himself so obvious?

We can see that God not only is active, but that He shapes history in a distinct pattern. It other words, it's evident that He is acting according to a plan. And looking at the moments in history where He's chosen to intervene, we can even get a clear glimpse of that plan. And knowing this *changes everything*. It puts everything we know— including our own lives— into an entirely different perspective.

WHAT THIS MEANS FOR OUR LIVES

Just think about it for a second. There is a God. He is a personal God. He's active in the world's workings; He cares about what happens in the world; and He even cares about us *individually*.

And there's more. Not only is God a real presence, but He's infinitely powerful. He can literally work miracles, and occasionally He does. Also— perhaps most unsettling of all— as a living, genuine person, He actually has a will of His own. He has His own plan, and He has all the power in the universe to carry it out.

What does this mean each of us— for the great "me"? The reality of God means that each of us is no longer his (or her) own world, with the rest of the universe revolving around it. The very fact of His existence tells us that **He** is the center of the universe. (Now we know how those 17th century churchmen must have felt after Copernicus and Galileo had shown that the solar system revolves around the sun, instead of our world.)

When someone finds out that God exists, it means essentially that there's a new person in their life. And He's a very important person. How do we get to know this person better? How can we improve our relationship with Him? How can we please Him? (Since this is God the Almighty we're talking about, that just might be important.)

My own journey toward faith was a relatively slow one, which ran in fits and starts. When I was seventeen I concluded that the existence of God can't be proved. So I became an agnostic. When I was twenty-one I had a crisis in my life, and I spontaneously began praying again. More than that, I opened my eyes and tried to see if God was actually there. What was that thing Jesus said— seek, and you will find? It actually worked. For myself, the great question had been answered. He is there for us.

But the knowledge alone wasn't enough. The real challenge was to build a relationship with God, to stay centered on Him to some extent. The real challenge was to not let the cares and headaches of this world snuff out my spirit and faith. I realized that trying to maintain my faith alone, as if I were marooned on my own spiritual island, wasn't enough. I realized that I needed some churching.

It's interesting, that when Jesus carried out His mission on Earth, He never bothered writing His teachings down. Jesus was undoubtedly literate. {John 8:6 & 8} But He wrote no books Himself, and it may have been decades before any of His followers did. However, He did do one major thing to establish His teachings and— in a sense— to make them official. He founded a Church. This was recorded by one of Jesus' followers, Matthew, in the New Testament gospel by that name. {Matthew 16:18} Also in the New Testament, the Book of Acts records the growth of the early Church during the following decades. Additional, unrelated comments by contemporary historians such as Tacitus also show that the Church was growing around the Mediterranean at that time. [3:365 (Tacitus: Book 14)]

It made sense to me— and it still makes sense— that the Son of God knew what He was doing. He knew that people need a sense of community and brotherhood. Looking ahead (with a view to the future that only the Son of God could have), He could see that it would take a strong organization to withstand the vicious assaults of a pagan world. What He did was establish a Church, an organized community for believers.

For the first time in my life, in my mid-20s, I started going regularly to church.

That didn't change my life overnight, or make everything easy. I had been through a difficult childhood. I couldn't relate to other people very well. Just about all my friends were other college students, and our friendships were not that solid. Most of the time I didn't communicate very well with girls, even though

I went "steady" with one for a while. I just wasn't much of a people person. (I'm sure there are some who would say that I haven't improved much.) While in school, most of my social life was centered on parties, where I could at least feel like one of the crowd. And the more beer I drank at those parties, the better I felt. Unfortunately, that did not help much in communicating with others.

In other words, even after taking the decisive step of going to church, I was still the same person. But I realized that improvement doesn't come instantly. I was in it for the long haul. I knew there was no other way.

Of course, it seemed strange to me at first— sitting among a crowd of strangers, and trying to follow along as everyone participated in the Mass. Reading the booklet provided for the services helped. But I had just never been in the habit of going to church. It was an entirely new environment for me, and of course I felt out of place. But it wasn't a matter of comfort, or convenience, or social improvement for me. It was a choice. It was a path I had taken for a certain goal. More than that, it was a revolution in my life. Neither fear, nor unfamiliarity, nor any sense of self-doubt was going to stop me.

As I said, there were no instant changes in my life. And for the first months, I would miss going on the occasional Sunday. My old mentality kept telling me that it wasn't that important. I think I must have missed once in a while after going to parties on Saturdays. However, there was one thing which was new. It was still a challenge to keep up with the booklet and follow the services. It still seemed new and different, being there in Church. I still hadn't been baptized or confirmed. But I did notice one change. While sitting in Mass— and for some time afterward— I experienced the overwhelming feeling that *everything was going to be all right.*

It was something I'd never sensed before. It was a feeling of calm, and inner peace. I didn't understand it, but I didn't question it either. I just wanted it to stay. I'm going to say right now, that seeking that feeling of inner peace is still a challenge for me. Not only internal tensions, but the external pressures of life are always forces working against it.

And each of us, I'm sure, finds that the world is— in a great sense— a challenging place. Many forces in our society tend to wear us down. And as we go through life, those same forces try to tear us down. This world just isn't a very friendly place when it comes to things like inner peace.

GOD IS THE ADVANTAGE

When you think about it, God is the best thing we have going for us in this world. On the "down" side of life, there are countless disadvantages. For one thing, we're born into a condition of weakness and helplessness. If we have good parents, that makes a huge difference. We can start out being loved, nurtured, taught the things we need to know— there is just no real equivalent to having a mother and father who care for you.

But the world is still there. From your earliest days in front of the TV, you're hearing that toys and "fun" are the things that bring happiness. The cartoon characters weave a fantasy world where everything turns out right and the good guys always win. At the same time, the commercials are trying to sell you all the toys and gadgets that you *desperately need* in order to be happy.

Some aspects of this are wholesome. After all, there's nothing wrong in being taught that good should triumph over evil. But when you see cartoon "heroes" that look like inhuman monsters and robots, then obviously the lines between good and evil are getting blurred.

Kids are vulnerable. They start out totally trusting, which in ideal circumstances works to their advantage, with their trust invested in their mother and father. Also, kids have a strong sense of their own smallness and weakness, as compared to the size and strength of "grown-ups." To a certain extent, for many of us, this sense of weakness persists into adult life. The world can be a scary place— and that's no illusion.

Being in school is a sort of cocoon for kids. But school can't last forever. Sooner or later we're thrown into the world— the great testing-ground of life. Soon enough, there are credit cards, taxes, collection agencies, and an ocean of laws and regulations to deal with. And that's not even considering the things we should be avoiding, like illegal drugs, sexual predators and unscrupulous auto repair places.

Let's face it, there are a lot of things out there which are geared toward wearing us down and grinding us up. And for those who get ground up, there's a vast network of jails and prisons (supported by public taxes) which is just waiting to add them to the millions of Americans already behind bars. This is the world each of us has to deal with.

But this entire wicked world, and every evil thing in it, is trumped by the power of God.

God is the wild card. Don't forget, He was the one who created this world to begin with. (That was long before man began screwing it up.) We're talking here about the God who set in place the laws of nature, and who can suspend them whenever He chooses— a God who can intervene directly in human events. When that happens, it's called a miracle. As we've seen, history itself is a witness to many miracles.

We're talking here about the God who created not only the world itself, but every one of us who lives in it— that same God who cares about each of us individually. This is a God who will listen when you talk to Him. This is a God who will help you when you're in trouble. In fact, the Bible promises us that **everyone who calls on the name of the Lord will be saved.** {Romans 10:12-13} Can you just sit back for a moment, and try to savor the *magnitude* of that?

THE "LOGIC" OF ATHEISM

Atheists love to say that the Bible was simply written by men. They'll laugh at the idea that God actually inspired anyone to write those books. But then, cynics will laugh at anything.

Their laughter and cynicism are their answer to everything. It's an "answer" that constitutes a form of despair. When an atheist— or any cynic— tries to put down the Bible, he's basically trying to put down the idea that the biblical God even exists. Because: to simply acknowledge the *existence* of such a God, is to acknowledge *everything*.

First of all, by admitting God exists, an atheist is admitting to himself that he is not his own god. Then he has to admit that the Bible may actually contain divine wisdom— and *that* idea threatens everything atheists claim to stand for. An atheist likes to think he's on the side of logic, reason and rationality. But once we've established through logic and reason that God exists, it demolishes the "logic" of the atheist. To his constricted thinking, there can be no God— and no moral authority— above himself. He is the center of his own universe, a universe *which has no meaning except whatever his own tunnel vision might allow*. This is a central tenet of the atheist mindset, just part of that precious pride which is one of the "rewards" of atheism.

A hardened atheist can't even consider the reality of God, because doing so would threaten his self-ordained world view. Even worse, it would be close to admitting that all those simpleton believers might just be as intelligent as he is.

Just think about it. Knowing that God exists puts the *entire universe* in a totally different perspective. Instead of each of us being a random microbe stumbling around on a speck of rock at the outer rim of the Milky Way Galaxy, we are now an individual creation of a loving Father— who not only watches over us, but actively answers our prayers when we need His help.

We now have Someone who can empower us to stand up against the world. We now have Someone who can help us to win the struggles of life. We now have Someone who can lift us up from any defeat. Of course, there will still be some defeats in life. The way that we deal with them shows our true character. But with God, even the setbacks work toward the ultimate victory. He can give us strength to wade through the adversities of life.

He *will* give us the ultimate victory. All we have to do is cultivate our faith, and learn from our setbacks.

So far, I've referred only to how God can help us to win in this life. But we have to remember that there's more. Much more.

This life itself is nothing compared to the eternity that follows. I'm not going to go into a long, speculative spiel about the glories of Heaven. I haven't been there yet, and so I'm not qualified to describe it. But Jesus Himself made clear to us that the Father's house (in one translation) "has many mansions." {John 14:2} One can only guess at the astounding vastness and beauty that will be there. But knowing the reality of God is enough. That means that His house and His Heaven are also real.

There's not only victory in this world, but an eternity of rewards to make us glad that God is real. And nothing in our human thinking can be greater than eternity itself. What could this world possibly give, in comparison to that?

Chapter 8

THE CHALLENGE OF BEING AN AMERICAN

I don't like the title of this chapter. I love this country, and I always have. But I have to admit one thing regarding America: Living in this society does not make it easy to have faith in God. Let's face it— most aspects of our culture are geared toward getting our minds on other things. From the day we're old enough to sit in front of a TV set, we're bombarded with commercials telling us we've got to have material things to make us happy. Whether it's breakfast cereal, dolls or toy trucks, kids are taught to think they've got to have them. And when we grow up, the commercials are simply selling us bigger toys.

How did things get to be this way?

It's interesting to realize, that in the first century of settlement, most Americans were just trying to survive. In the next century (the 18th), the foundations were set in place for a modern, workable republic— one built on the concept of individual freedom. In the 19th century we saw the great westward movement, and the U.S. became a continental power. After the Civil War had resolved the issue of slavery, the country forged ahead with a dynamism unmatched in previous generations. The three-month conflict with Spain in 1898 made the U.S. a global power.

Then, in the 20th century, things changed. The western frontier had vanished and many Americans found themselves living in cities. All of a sudden we were beset with crisis after crisis— two World Wars, a Great Depression, then a long, torturous Cold War fought against world communism. The Vietnam War and its aftermath nearly tore this country apart.

In the 1960s a strong counterculture emerged; at first it was comprised largely of hippies and hippie wannabes. Psychedelic lunacy and moral chaos were the core of their philosophy. A drug subculture was suddenly flourishing in this country, and a "sexual revolution" exploded onto the scene. Like a cancer growing on the soul of America, radical movements[15] sprang out of the '60s and '70s. A number of them remain powerful well into the 21st century.

One overriding fact must be understood: This resultant counterculture is essentially hostile to Judeo-Christianity. Some of these radical groups view Christianity itself as nothing more than an obstacle— a thing to be attacked and swept aside. (Atheism, in other words, is not the only anti-Christian force operating in our society today.)

AMERICA IN THE HERE AND NOW

At this point in history, we have a cultural landscape which is a battlefield of ideas. On the one hand, we're taught that our heritage of freedom, and our society built on the bedrock of family values, are what make America great. At the same time, we still have radical forces attacking every moral standard this country has ever had. And here we are at the very core of the conflict which grips our nation. It is a conflict encompassing more than Christianity. **What we're seeing is nothing less than a titanic war between faith and anti-faith.**

This is the central dynamic of the culture war in America. *This is what impels the people of the counterculture to become the people of the lie.* Because— once they had rejected Judeo-Christian moral standards, it became necessary to invent an entirely new type of "morality"— one contrived not only to make themselves look righteous, but also to undermine those who

---

[15] To illustrate just how bad things got in the '70s, there was an organization which called itself the "North American Man-Boy Love Association" (NAMBLA). One of its most highly publicized spokesmen was a renegade Catholic priest. Brazenly advocating pederasty, this was just one of the radical movements originating at that time.

build their foundation on authentic standards which comply with God's moral laws. {1 Corinthians 6:9-11}

Their strategy is simple to understand. The basic counterculture "moral" tenets are (a) sexual gratification without moral restraints; (b) the assumption that traditional moral precepts are obsolete; (c) the denial of virtually all inherent differences between men and women, in an attempt to confuse the natural male/female roles; and (d) the view that the United States has (throughout most of its history) been a force for evil in the world.

Since traditional morals are out the window, Christianity itself— except for those churches which renounce biblical moral standards— must be seen as outmoded at best, an enemy of progress at worst. And for those counterculture heroes who love to call themselves "progressives," the definition of progress includes just about anything that draws this country further away from God.

For them, history is not useful as an actual record of events, but as a tool to further their own aims. At the same time, it's used as a bludgeon to pound a sense of guilt into anyone who doesn't think the same. Decent, family-oriented pioneers in American history are painted as villainous murderers; the bombings of Hiroshima and Nagasaki are condemned as war crimes— and we should all feel very *guilty* about that. Curiously, (as we've seen in Chapter 2) whenever those pioneer settlers were *victims* of massacres, that doesn't seem to be worth mentioning. The half-million or so lives that were saved by not invading Japan never seem to get mentioned, either. (This would include, of course, both American and Japanese lives.) These are just a couple of examples of how revisionist "history" works.

There's no doubt that the counterculture has had an impact. Great numbers of people have been taken in by such propaganda, and this has definitely had a corrosive effect on this country. Not only moral standards have been degraded; with the spread of legal "euthanasia"— along with virtually unrestricted abortion— human life has become dirt cheap.

And there's more. We now have a country where children are torn between conflicting forces. We have garbage television which starts out by teaching them materialism, then goes on to saturate their minds with sexual images. We have a national Press that vigorously supports homosexual "marriage," and then crucifies the [16]Catholic Church for not cracking down fast enough on a tiny number of pederast priests. We have a powerful entertainment industry cranking out movies filled with blood and gore, and video games showing people as nothing but targets. (Then we wonder why we have a violent society.) Is it any surprise that fewer people attend church regularly? How can anyone catch a glimpse of God, when the devil controls so much of the media?

ANOTHER DISTURBING TREND IN OUR SOCIETY

There's another aspect of our society, that makes life more difficult for many people. As much as I love this country (and I love it more than my life), I'll be the first to admit that it's not perfect. When the founders of our Republic established the machinery of government back in the 1780s, they were very idealistic. At that time, they never really foresaw the forming of political parties. George Washington, the first president, tried to remain aloof from such notions. He didn't approve of "factionalism" and he wanted no part of it. And at first, there actually *weren't* any organized parties.

But in those early years, there were two powerful ideas in the air regarding America's future. Thomas Jefferson was Washington's first secretary of state. As a lifelong planter, Jefferson's vision for America was one of farmers tilling their lands. In his view, farmers would be the backbone of a society of fairly static character, with its economy based mostly on agriculture. Alexander Hamilton (also serving in Washington's

---

[16] Not just the Catholic Church has been targeted by the "news" industry. Recalling the media lynchings of Jim Bakker and Jimmy Swaggart, it's clear that any Christian leader caught in sin will be hung out to dry by the Press. The only exceptions seem to be pastors or priestesses in some churches who openly boast of a homosexual relationship. (These become media heroes.)

cabinet as treasury secretary) had a different vision. Having been a merchant in his youth, he believed in what we would call a "money economy," with banks and credit and all that goes with it.

As we know, political parties became a standard feature of American politics. Jefferson's followers formed into one of the first political movements in the United States. They were at first called Republicans. Later, a major faction of Jefferson's party evolved into the modern Democratic Party. [9:Vol. 9:1035] Hamilton and his followers formed another group called the Federalists, who stood for a strong central government, as opposed to the sovereignty of individual states.

Ultimately, the policies of Alexander Hamilton prevailed. As a result, we now have an economy where banks, credit, and industries are accompanied by great stock markets, along with every type of commercial enterprise imaginable. Hamilton's "money economy" has become the engine that drives this country. And I would say that this in itself is not a bad thing. But along with that money economy, we've developed a brand of capitalism which raises large corporations— "big business"— to the highest level. At the same time, in many cases the individual working American is reduced to a level approaching insignificance.

CORPORATE AMERICA— MAKING THE INDIVIDUAL NEGLIGIBLE?

We live in a society where money doesn't just talk— it rules. Corporate giants employ full-time lobbyists to influence members of Congress to vote their way. Countless loopholes are written into laws, exempting many companies from paying various taxes. At the same time, the votes of individual citizens seem to count for less and less. How many congressmen, senators, or state legislators are going to care about what their constituents think, while some of their re-election money (or their political friends' re-election money) comes from their corporate backers?

To me, it looks as if we've evolved an economy that has reduced the individual citizen to a place of insignificance. Corporate power whittles away individual rights. Many companies will do a credit check on anyone before hiring them— and it's perfectly legal to *discriminate* against someone because of poor credit. (These "lawmakers" just don't seem to pass any laws against that.) Of course, without an income, one's credit will continue to get worse. No credit, no job. No job, no life.

And then there's the insidious use of credit. Credit companies do their best to get us into debt, by tempting us to borrow money. That way, whenever we get a paycheck, so do they. Ordinary Americans are like a crop, and the corporations are doing as much harvesting as they can. Your money becomes their money. That's how the economic system works in this country.

No wonder so many people feel alienated and helpless. No wonder there's so much petty crime, and so many Americans in prison. Even the prison systems make money off of them— federal and state dollars for every inmate. To a terrible extent, our prisons have actually become an industry, feeding off people's wrecked lives.

DESPAIR IS NOT AN OPTION

This is the challenge of being an American. This is why it's so difficult to pull aside the curtain of darkness that surrounds us, and make our way towards the light. That curtain is simply so widespread, and has so many layers, that it takes a real effort to see past it. Some people would try to tell us that it's hopeless. For some, despair is the answer to every challenge. Surrender is their only real solution.

But with God, surrender is never an answer. Because defeat is impossible. We have to remember—*the final victory will be His*. And for those of us who are with Him, it will be ours too.

Again: We must remember that God is the Lord of History, and He *will bring* the victory. No matter how powerful His enemies might seem, they are always the ultimate losers.

That's why the fall of the Roman Empire wasn't the end— but a new beginning— for civilization. That's how the Mongols were stopped in their drive toward western Europe. God was in charge, and He always is.

There are signs of stabilization. The AIDS epidemic put the brakes on the "sexual revolution." Many scars from the Vietnam War era have healed. But America is still very much a battleground. The chaos that exploded out of the 1960s continues to rend the fabric of our society.

I don't pretend to know what God has planned for the United States. If someone's destined to appear out of nowhere to solve America's problems, I'm sure not the guy. Maybe no one but God can solve them. But that's no reason to give up. Eventually America's problems *will* be solved. And God's side will be the winning side. That's all we really have to know.

So, the real challenge of being an American is not to ignore what's happening in the country, but to get on the winning side. It isn't necessary to throw up our hands in despair. All we have to do is look to the God who created us, pray to Him, and remember that *He is in charge.* We can help where we can. There are plenty of people fighting to bring this country back from the darkness. Just by staying on His side and raising our children well in His sight, we're making a huge contribution to that victory.

The challenge of being an American is not the challenge of winning the victory single-handedly. The challenge is in seeing past the darkness and becoming part of the light. It's not that difficult. Remember— when we want to reach God, our prayers go directly to His ears. The same great God who made us can hear us at anytime. He's never far away.

The challenge can be met. No curtains of darkness can be dense enough separate us from God. No matter how many people are putting out propaganda against Him, they can never defeat Him. And once we know that, they can never defeat us either. Knowing that He is with us, each of us— in our individual lives— will savor the victory.

Chapter 9

SINCE THERE IS A GOD, WHICH GOD?

Once we understand that God is real, we've found the answer to the biggest question. But— as happens so often in life— that very answer can raise new questions. The first thing we might ask is, "Who is God?" In today's world, there are three major divisions of people who worship that one God: Christianity, Judaism and Islam. Each of these faiths has a starkly different view of God and His nature. Each of them has a history of being a "revealed" religion— one which is not derived from human invention.

In the case of Judaism, God appeared to Abraham. Christianity recognizes Jesus Christ as the Jewish Messiah and Son of God. In this light, we can see His entire mission as a direct revelation to man. Muslims base their faith on scriptures which Muhammad said he received from the archangel Gabriel, who was acting as God's messenger. (The word "angel" itself is simply from an ancient Greek word meaning "messenger.")

As a former agnostic, I can fully appreciate the negative reactions that such a jumble of teachings can produce. The very lack of agreement on the nature of God makes it more difficult for a nonbeliever to build faith. I know this from experience. But the challenge remains. Once we realize that there is a God, it is a matter of the greatest importance that we understand Him more fully. After all, what can be of greater benefit to us, than having the best possible connection with the God who created the universe?

It just makes tremendous sense that it would be better to have Him as a friend than shun Him as a stranger. Of course, if one chooses, he can go through life trying to live without God, ignoring Him, or even hating Him. But that's like trying to cross the Atlantic ocean on a one-man raft, when just for the asking you can have a steamship ticket. Why choose to be self-destructive?

HOW TO DISCERN THE TRUTH?

Just tearing off the blinders— allowing ourselves to find out there's a God— was the courageous part. Figuring out who He is takes not just courage, but the use of our intelligence as well. This may take some effort. We may have to spend a little of our TV time doing something else (like reading). We may have to get into the habit of talking to God (praying) once in a while. But no one's saying we have to go into the desert and live like hermits. All it takes is common sense, perseverance, a little humility and honesty, and the faith we have in *knowing that God is there.*

I think that one of the best ways to get a better view of these three great religious movements, is to take a look at the historical record. As we've seen in Chapter 6, this is also a sure way to get a glimpse of God's plan. I realize that a lot of people don't find history interesting. So I'll try to keep this part of the chapter as brief (and hopefully readable) as possible. What we're looking for here is a basic outline of God's purpose in the world— not the mere achievements of men and women.

THE ORIGINS OF JUDAISM, THE FIRST GREAT REVEALED FAITH

We've seen in Chapter 5 how God revealed Himself to Abram (Abraham), and gave mankind the first real understanding of Himself. The ancient Hebrews were originally a nomadic people. Eventually they migrated to Egypt and settled there. Ultimately, one of the pharaohs decided to draft them into forced labor. After some four hundred years in Egypt, God sent the prophet Moses to liberate the Hebrews from their slavery. Following the Exodus from Egypt and a generation of wandering in the desert, the Hebrews settled in the Promised Land of Canaan (modern Israel).

Ancient Israel went from being a land of isolated settlements to a united country, then divided into two independent states— Israel and Judah. The division weakened both kingdoms. The Assyrians extinguished the northern kingdom of Israel in 722 BC. Judah was eventually conquered by the Babylonians. Centuries later, the Jews (as they were now called) were able to re-establish a state of their own in the Promised Land. After setting up a last independent monarchy (the Hasmonean Dynasty), their country was finally taken over by the Romans in 63 BC. The Romans were stern occupiers, but they allowed the Jews to practice their religion. The great Temple built by Herod was the center of the Jewish faith; and for a time there was stability in the Holy Land, even if it was under Roman rule.

THE BIRTH OF CHRIST AND CHRISTIANITY

When Jesus of Nazareth began His ministry (about 30 AD), great numbers of Jews in Judea (as the land was now called) acknowledged Him as the Messiah— the Savior promised in the Scriptures. With frequent healing of the sick and many other miracles, Christ continued to preach until the Roman authorities were persuaded to have Him arrested and executed in the spring of [17]33. But Jesus reappeared to His followers two days later, and His resurrection became the cornerstone of Christianity.

In spite of numerous persecutions, the Church founded by Jesus grew steadily within the expanse of the Roman Empire. From Mesopotamia to Britain, Christian communities appeared and took root. Finally, in 313 AD, the co-emperors Constantine and Licinius issued the Edict of Milan, guaranteeing religious toleration to all peoples, Christian and pagan. With the exception of one brief episode which took place in the 360s, the persecutions had ended. Christianity continued to grow. In

---

[17] A reconstruction of the ancient Jewish calendar and other research has determined that the Crucifixion of Christ took place on Friday, April 3rd, 33 AD. [Source No. 27]

380 it became the official religion of the Roman Empire. But the Empire was in trouble. A century later Rome itself was conquered by Germanic tribes and only the Eastern Empire continued to function, with Constantinople as its capital. Still, Christianity continued to thrive in Europe.

THE APPEARANCE OF ISLAM

One more major religion appeared on the world stage. Around 570 AD, there was born in the Arabian city of Mecca a boy named Abu al-Qasim Muhammad ibn 'Abd Allah ibn 'Abd al-Muttalib ibn Hashim. He is known today simply as Muhammad. [10:Vol. 22:1] About the year 610, Muhammad reported the appearance of a "majestic being" who identified himself as the Archangel Gabriel. This being gave many messages to Muhammad, which were said to come directly from the true God, or (in Arabic) Allah.

Before long, Muhammad had found many converts in people he knew personally. They acknowledged him as a prophet and took the messages which he described to them, accepting them as having a divine origin. Eventually those messages were written down, and they now constitute the Muslim holy book, the Koran. Perhaps the essence of Islam is the idea of submission to God's will. The very word "Islam" has been translated as "submission."

Unlike Jesus of Nazareth, Muhammad was well-connected in society. His grandfather had been head of an important tribe, the Hashem clan, and was prominent in the Meccan political scene. Muhammad's first wife, Khadijah, was a wealthy woman of the Asad clan.

As Muhammad's new religion grew among the population of Mecca, opposition arose. Tensions developed between the followers of Islam (as the new religion was called) and those who opposed it. Eventually Muhammad left Mecca to live in Medina. This migration, or flight, on his part is known today as the *hijrah,* and is considered a milestone in Islamic history. The Muslim calendar begins in that year (622 AD), just as the Christian calendar begins with Christ's birth.

Within a couple of years Muhammad began leading raids on pagan caravans. After a number of unsuccessful raids, he and his followers began to win battles. This was taken as a sign of favor from Allah. It was at this time that Islam grew into a military force. Raids became a standard part of Muhammad's program. In 630 he marched on Mecca itself with some ten thousand men, and the city surrendered with little resistance. By the time of his death in 632, most of Arabia was united under Muslim rule.

ISLAM'S EXPLOSION ONTO THE WORLD SCENE

While Christianity grew gradually, like a mustard seed requiring the fullness of time to bloom, Islam expanded in a more explosive way— rapidly and violently changing the world surrounding its birthplace. Muhammad's stunning victories among the Arab city-states had set the seal on Islam's future. In those victories, the zealous firebrands of the new faith believed they had found its mission and its destiny. Apparently Islam was going to be a religion of conquest. During the following century, the faith established by Muhammad exploded onto the world scene. Syria was wrested from the Byzantine (Eastern Roman) Empire. Persia (modern Iran) was conquered. Egypt was taken, and the triumphant armies of Islam pushed westward. By the year 656 they had established an empire which stretched from western Asia to the north African coast. Eventually the new Islamic realm surpassed the empire of Alexander the Great, in both its expanse and viability. [10:Vol. 22:109]

THE REAL FIRST CRUSADE[18]

Contrary to the complaints expressed by some modern Muslims, the first major clash between Islam and western

---
[18] Although the word "crusade" is from the Latin word for cross and implies a Christian expedition, it's being used here in the generic sense, to describe any religious military campaign.

Christendom took place when Muslim forces invaded Europe—
not when Europeans invaded the Holy Land centuries later.

In the year 710, an Islamic army comprised of Arabs and
north African Berbers invaded the Iberian Peninsula (modern
Spain and Portugal) under the leadership of Tariq ibn Ziyad.
They defeated the local monarch, King Roderick, in 711. [10:Vol. 22:111]
Then they proceeded to sweep northward until nearly the whole
of the peninsula was conquered. Muslim forces continued
on, seeking further victories. Eventually, in 732, an Islamic
expedition was defeated at the Battle of Tours (or Poitiers) by the
Frankish leader Charles Martel. That battle would represent the
high water mark of Islam in western Europe. There, the Islamic
crusaders had reached their limit of conquest.

AFTER THE INITIAL EXPLOSION

This early string of electrifying victories established an
Islamic empire which encompassed modern Spain, the whole
of North Africa, Egypt, the Levant, Syria and much else in the
Middle East. Muslim forces had formed a permanent presence
in the region, a presence which was destined to menace (and
ultimately destroy) the Eastern Roman Empire of the Byzantines.
It was this initial explosion of Islam onto the world scene which,
to its followers, seemed to show the direction in which God was
pointing. But these newly-established bastions of Islamic culture
broke up into feuding factions, and various petty monarchs
ended up ruling the subject states conquered by Islam.

A few overriding doctrines emerged from this early period.
Muhammad was declared to have been the last prophet of God—
Moses, other Hebrew prophets, and even Jesus were defined
as his predecessors in that capacity. The divinity of Christ was
denied (as it had to be— because if God's Son were acknowledged,
Muhammad and all other prophets would automatically assume
secondary importance).

Clashes between Islam and Christendom would be an
inevitable part of future history. The European Crusades from

the 11th to 13th centuries put their stamp on Western civilization. In Spain, a sustained effort over several centuries rolled back the original Muslim crusade and forced the invaders from the peninsula. This was finally achieved in January of 1492, the same year as Columbus' discovery of the New World.

The Muslim conquest of Constantinople in 1453 put Islam at eastern Europe's doorstep. Several minor European Islamic enclaves were established, some of which survive to this day in places like Albania and Kosovo. The most decisive clash was at sea, with the Battle of Lepanto in October 1571. Although there would be further fighting in Europe, the Muslim tide was then checked. The Ottoman Empire eventually lost its stranglehold on Greece, and the Empire itself disintegrated after its defeat in World War I.

Islam remains the unchallenged culture of the Mideast and North Africa, although split by its own divisions, such as Sunni and Shiite. Yet through it all, there remains in the minds of some Muslims a lingering resentment over the idea that the clashes between Islam and Christendom were never quite resolved. At least not to their satisfaction. It's almost as if, at the beginning, the finger of God pointed toward glory and world domination— and then suddenly stopped writing. And this causes a problem. To this day, there are some Muslims who cannot reconcile themselves to anything less than the vision of a world ruled by Islam.

WHAT CAN BE LEARNED FROM THESE EVENTS?

Now that we've reviewed the briefest possible background of these three great revealed religions, we can try to get an overview— to see how they actually relate to each other. Again, history is our window. Outside the inspired books of the Bible, through history we can get our clearest, most objective view of God's workings among men.

Judaism started out as a religion virtually unnoticed on the world scene. After God revealed Himself to Abraham, the nomadic Hebrews kept their faith largely among themselves, evidently doing little to bring it to other nations. It was as if God allowed His early faith to be contained in a womb. It was only after centuries of servitude in Egypt that Judaism set its stamp on history. Once Moses led the Hebrews out of Egypt and they had settled in Canaan, Israel then became a player on the world stage— entering "the full blaze of recorded history." Even so, ancient Israel was a relative backwater power, flourishing while the rest of the Mideast was in decline. Her golden age of David and Solomon went almost unnoticed by surrounding nations, as far as contemporary records have shown.

Judaism survived every catastrophe— even conquest by the Assyrians and Babylonians. When the Romans became dominant in the Mediterranean world, these new conquerors recognized the antiquity of Judaism and respected its customs, so long as the Jewish people were peaceful subjects. Through it all, the religion of the Jews remained the most ancient— and only successful— form of monotheism to appear in history. They were the very first to worship the one true, self-revealed God we know today.

The fact that most Jews of his day did not recognize Jesus as the Messiah troubled St. Paul a great deal. {Romans 9:2-5} He had been a Pharisee, one of the most fervent of the Jews, before Christ called him to be an apostle. {Philippians 3:5-6} And yet, most of the Jews of that era failed to see salvation in Jesus.

Perhaps this can be better understood in the context of God's plan. In the Old Testament Book of Ezekiel, it was prophesied that the nation of Israel would one day be restored. {Ezekiel, ch. 36-37} At the time that book was written (6th century BC), much of the Israelite population was being held captive in Babylon. Undoubtedly, the prophet Ezekiel was writing for his own generation. But, like St. John writing the Book of Revelation nearly 700 years later, Ezekiel was writing an inspired book destined to reach far beyond his own time. He was also speaking to countless Jews of future generations.

The two Jewish revolts against Rome were disastrous for followers of Judaism. In the first, the Temple at Jerusalem was destroyed by a Roman legion (70 AD). After the Second Revolt (132-135 AD), the emperor Hadrian actually re-named the city. The Jewish people were banished from Jerusalem and scattered among the nations. It was only in the 20th century that the state of Israel was reestablished. The long centuries of the Diaspora (the great dispersal of the Jews) had finally come to an end. In this event, we can see a clearer view of God's plan, as well as His astonishing power revealed again in history.

The 20th century rebirth of the nation of Israel answers certain questions. Obviously, the Jewish people had to continue— in their own original identity, not as Christians— in order to fulfill the ancient prophecy of Israel's resurrection. It staggers the mind, to realize that God has the power to fulfill a prophecy delivered more than 2500 years earlier. It brings into full focus the meaning of a certain phrase in the New Testament— that in the eyes of God, a thousand years is like one day, and one day is like a thousand years. {2 Peter 3:8} Nowhere in human history is the truth of that statement better illustrated.

It's evident that more history— more of God's plan— will be played out in this world, before the final answer is revealed regarding the Jewish faith. Until that event, Judaism will retain its own identity, still searching for the Messiah, still striving to fulfill its part of God's design.

CHRISTIANITY'S ROLE ON THE WORLD SCENE

Following God's revelation to Abraham Judaism had grown slowly, in relative obscurity. Christianity had an almost immediate impact on history. However, the early Christian faith didn't take root by rioting or conquest. On the contrary, its apostles preached compliance with the ruling authorities. The earliest Christians wanted nothing more than to follow their faith peacefully. But a society ruled by gods of war, sex and drunkenness, by gods steeped in lies and chaos, saw the new religion as a mortal threat to the established order. And Christianity was exactly that. Because of the very essence of Christianity— a spiritual strength which was *unwilling to compromise* with the chaos of paganism— it was inevitable that the political powers would react against it. It was as if a world saturated with evil could not stand a growing "vacuum" where evil did not rule.

It may be the greatest paradox in history, that a religion which was repeatedly subject to severe persecution actually grew stronger as a result. It may be the greatest irony in history, that a faith started by a humble Jewish carpenter in a backwater of the Roman Empire, ultimately *transformed* the empire which had repeatedly tried to destroy it. The Christian religion— thriving in an underground Church that was far better organized than any of the pagan priesthoods—survived and grew despite every effort to stamp it out.

The history of Christianity isn't hidden from view, as were the first 1,000 years of Judaism. It's there for anyone to see. An inscription with the name of Pontius Pilate, the Roman governor who ordered Jesus' crucifixion, was found in 1961 at Caesarea in Israel. Excavations in Rome have uncovered the hidden catacombs where early Christians survived during times of persecution.

Some anti-Christian historians love to write about nothing except the later alliances between Church and state. They revel in tales of corrupt popes and heretics being burnt at the stake. But they aren't so interested in discussing the barbarian tribes that overthrew the western Roman Empire, and the churchmen who went out (at great risk to their own lives) to convert those same barbarians to Christianity.

These "historians" will paint the medieval Church as a hotbed of politicians, bribe-takers and libertines. But they won't say much about the saints, such as Francis of Assisi, who emerged to guide the Church in ways of spirituality. They'll gleefully (and falsely) paint a modern pope like Pius XII as a Nazi collaborator, but they won't mention courageous churchmen like Bishop

Konrad von Preysing of Berlin, Cardinal Michael von Faulhaber of Munich, or Archbishop Clemens August von Galen of Munster, who openly denounced Nazi crimes from their German pulpits. Those men risked their lives to oppose the Nazi regime— *even after the war began.*

Some modern writers love to grind out anti-Christian propaganda. But the world owes much to Christianity. Classical Western literature is just one of those debts. Except for the inscriptions we've found in stone and clay, and the few papyri preserved in the dry sands of Egypt, nearly everything we have today was transcribed and handed down by Christian copyists working in monasteries centuries ago.

Some years ago I read a quote in a *Reader's Digest* magazine, which I will paraphrase here: Civilization still has its conflicts in spite of Christianity. But stretching our minds to the fullest, can we imagine what kind of jungle the world would be *without* it?

Like Judaism, Christianity started with one event, one revelation. Both religions grew at their own pace— Judaism at first hidden in the womb, then born into world history with the Exodus. Christianity appeared as a peaceful and spiritual faith; the pagan world reacted with violence. Despite numerous persecutions, Christianity grew into a world religion found today in every corner of the globe.

It is important not to forget the eternal link between Judaism and Christianity. Both are on the same continuum of faith. Christ is the Jewish Messiah. He was— and is— the fulfillment of every Jewish messianic prophecy. That part of God's plan will eventually be as obvious as the rebirth of Israel. If it might take another thousand years, we can understand that God sometimes works in such ways. But there are, of course, other claims to divine revelation.

THE MEANING OF ISLAM'S ORIGINS

If Christianity appeared suddenly compared to Judaism, Islam originated with far more fanfare. As we've seen, the

Islamic armies spread their new religion more rapidly than either Judaism or Christianity. This rapid advance has been seen by some Muslims as virtually a miracle in itself. During that first century of expansion, the Islamic wave of conquest must have looked like a juggernaut— an overwhelming force— to the Christians of Europe who were still mired in the Dark Ages. (Back then, Europe was a welter of competing warlords and minor barbarian kingdoms. Nothing substantial had yet appeared to fill the power vacuum left by the Roman Empire's collapse.)

But after capturing a vast territory from the Mideast to Spain, the wars of conquest petered out. Islamic civilization became not an island, but more like an island continent, turned inward upon itself. For a time, most Islamic conflicts would be taking place within that civilization, Muslim against Muslim.

As the Muslim world focused inwardly upon itself, Europe began to emerge from the Dark Ages. In the year 800 a Frankish chieftain named Charlemagne founded the Holy Roman Empire. By the 1090s, medieval European states had gained enough strength to launch their First Crusade, with the goal of liberating Jerusalem. The clash of civilizations was renewed in earnest. The histories of Western Europe and Islam would be forever linked. The ancient capital of Constantinople fell to the armies of Islam in 1453. Then the last Muslim forces were expelled from Spain in 1492. Although certain areas of eastern Europe would remain at issue as late as the [19]First World War, it looked as if the general conflict had been settled. For the most part, the two civilizations would coexist separately. But the animosities which were born in the Islamic crusade (and later European crusades) seem to have left a permanent imprint on the psyches of both civilizations.

---

[19] In 1915, British General Sir Ian Hamilton led an expeditionary force intended (as one of its objectives) to capture Constantinople. The city was not taken and remained under Turkish rule, although the Ottoman Empire itself collapsed as a result of the war. [9:Vol. 5:661-662]

WHERE DOES THIS ALL FIT WITH GOD'S PLAN FOR THE WORLD?

Taking all this as one great picture— knowing as we do, that God is moving history towards the outcome of His choosing— we can ask the question: What does it all mean? For the Western world, at least, the First World War tossed the doctrines of absolute monarchy onto the ash heap of history. World War II and the Cold War did the same for fascism and communism. (After the development of nuclear weapons, the concept of all-out war itself became obsolete.)

But still— we have this seemingly endless tension between the civilizations built on Judeo-Christianity and Islam. And now mankind is in danger of being engulfed by a new conflict, which was thrust to the center of the world stage on September 11, 2001. The widespread availability of nuclear technology makes this a war which cannot be ignored.

In the West, we have a civilization dedicated to certain ideals of individual freedom. Strong, solid economic systems have been developed over many generations. Most of the Western nations are not only free countries, but stable and prosperous democracies. In the Islamic world, we see a civilization where most countries are not prosperous by modern standards. Most of them do not practice democracy; some are monarchies and some are outright dictatorships. Even in the largest Islamic nation claiming to allow democracy— Iran— real power is held by an entrenched group of Muslim clergymen called mullahs.

On one level, we are seeing a dispute between two basic religious views. On another, we're witnessing a struggle between the "haves" and the "have nots." There's no doubt that simple envy fuels the hatred of many who support terrorism. In some Islamic countries, a strong resentment of the West is officially encouraged. Westerners are seen as decadent and hedonistic— given over to selfish pleasures. This is a useful propaganda line for any jihadist who tries to justify the deliberate killing of civilians.

And (unfortunately) there's more than enough decadence in Western society to give such propaganda plenty of traction.

Some Islamic leaders have made the state of Israel a focus for national hostility. In Iran, particularly, a call for the destruction of Israel has been a recurring theme. (As always, any outside focus for hatred that distracts the common herd is good for the ruling elite.)

It's clear that the present war is a world-wide conflict. Many nations around the globe have been attacked by terrorist bombers— including, of course, our own. It may be years before we know if Afghanistan can remain stable after the removal of American combat forces. If the chaos following Barack Obama's pullout of U.S. troops from Iraq is any indication, the outlook is not good.

But God has worked miracles in history before. And there's still that prophecy in the Old Testament, promising a world where men turn their eyes toward peace— where they hammer their swords into plowshares, and never wage war again. {Isaiah 2:4} Also: {Micah 4:3} Certainly, God will keep that promise, just as He kept His promise to restore Israel. It is a vision worth reflecting on.

What kind of world could it be, if the Iranians were to sign a nuclear limitation treaty and then keep their word? What kind of world would we see, if the last jihadist terrorist groups just dwindled into nothingness because war became obsolete? What kind of world will we have in the future?

Perhaps it's already begun. Two great superpowers— America and Russia— opened their borders to mutual inspection, and commenced destroying vast stockpiles of medium-range nuclear weapons. Two great Muslim nations— Egypt and Jordan— have already signed peace treaties with Israel. What will the world be like, once the rulers of other nations come to their senses and choose peace as well? This is the vision.

But we can't allow the vision to become an illusion. We still have that terrible image of Neville Chamberlain waving a scrap of paper back in 1938, and boasting of "peace in our time."

The world seems to be on a threshold— but only God knows what lies across it. It appears that the stage is being set for all three of the great revealed faiths to reach a climax in God's plan. Whatever the outcome, it looks as if events are moving toward a final resolution. Judaism, Christianity, Islam— all three faiths are dedicated to worshiping the true God. But each has a very different view of Him. There is one certainty: Whatever the details of God's plan may be, His overall goal is the salvation of mankind. No matter how much men may blind themselves with pride and hatred— No matter what kind of violence man does to his fellow man— God's plan will ultimately triumph.

WHICH GOD?

The United States is a free country. Every American can decide for himself how to worship. I believe that freedom of faith is not an American invention, but part of God's own design. People in this country can worship whatever they want. It doesn't even have to be a standard god. In the media today, we constantly hear about the latest wonders of technology. Maybe Technology is the highest deity some people can believe in. Mammon certainly has great numbers of worshipers. Sometimes I wonder how many people put more faith in their weekly lottery tickets than they do in a genuine God. But for anyone who looks honestly at world history, it's obvious that there's more. Most people still want to worship a true God— not one that's man-made.

As a Catholic Christian, I strongly recommend the original Church founded by Christ, the modern Roman Catholic Church. Jesus told us just how important it is, to have what He brought for us. {John 6:51-58} There is just nothing like having that kind of spiritual peace and strength.

If anyone is annoyed by my lack of objectivity, I can say only one thing: How can I be objective? How can anyone be really objective, when each of us is guided in part by our own life experiences? If I tried to be completely objective it would be an act of dishonesty. I have no apologies to make for my faith in the God I worship, and in the Church established by His Son.

Followers of Islam claim both Moses and Jesus as prophets. At the same time, they reject Jesus as the Son of God. The rationale seems to be that it's repugnant to accord divine status to a "mere man." But this same rationale is denying that God can even send us His Son. It's denying the power of God to reveal Himself in any way He chooses. The only thing it did for Islam was to reduce the status of Jesus and set Muhammad up as the final prophet. That sounds just a little too convenient for me.

I can't buy into that kind of thinking. God can reveal Himself— and has revealed Himself— in any way He chooses. No one can put limits on God's power. When anyone tries, he's only putting blinders on himself. The Lord of History is not the convenient god of the deists, and He never was.

There are countless churches claiming to be dedicated to Christ. People can follow Him in any way they choose. Or they can pick any type of Judaism they want. Or any type of Islam. The best advice I can give is: Don't put blinders on yourself. Don't close your mind to God, or to faith, or to the rewards they can bring. Perhaps most importantly— don't try to fabricate a god of your own to believe in, simply because that's the most comfortable way to envision Him. I don't think God wants to be "comfortable" for us. I don't think He wants us to just "feel good" about life. If there were an Eleventh Commandment, I really think it would prohibit complacency.

My thinking on this is derived largely from the New Testament. {Luke 12:16-20} In that passage, Christ gave as an example a man who "had it all." The guy decided to build new storage bins for his bumper crops, so that he could live the good life without a care in the world. But God didn't think much of his plan. Instead of a lifetime of ease and plenty, the man was called to meet his Maker that same day. From the message of this parable, it's obvious that God does not condone that type of attitude. Similar warnings are found in the Old Testament. {*e.g.,* Amos 6:1-7}

If you are serious about finding God— and your own eternal salvation—I would recommend strongly that you open your mind to the likelihood that one church may be better than another. Try going to more than one church. Try seeing for yourself which ones are just trying to rope people in, and which ones have something spiritually substantial to offer.

Don't look for a church populated with perfect people. You won't find one. (Although I'm sure there are churches where plenty of people think they're perfect.) Every church has its share of hypocrites, just as every church has its share of sinners. Don't look for people who are trying to be "the best." Look for people who are simply trying to be better.

Truth and salvation may not be that easy to find in this world. But the rewards are worth the effort. Each of us is going to have to spend eternity somewhere. And whether we like it or not, one thing is certain: Eternity is a long, long time.

Chapter 10

THE DIFFERENCE BETWEEN FAITH AND BLIND FAITH

I've talked to enough non-believers to know that they usually don't put much store in the idea of faith. As I've said, we live in a rational society. Scientists pride themselves in seeking verifiable proof for scientific conclusions. Our own legal process claims that guilt must be proven in criminal cases, "beyond a reasonable doubt." In short, our culture teaches us to be skeptics. And skepticism can sometimes be a positive good; for instance, it helps to keep the system "honest." Let's face it— trusting politicians is not always the best way to guide us in how we vote.

But many religions— and Christianity in particular— put a much greater value on faith. We can't forget that in the New Testament, Christ never held out mere knowledge as a key to salvation. Instead, He frequently told others that their *faith* had solved their problem.

In those years when I was an agnostic, I gave very little thought to faith. Once, when I was seventeen, I had a conversation with a custodian at my high school. He was telling me how Jesus freed people who were possessed by demons. I thought that was the most absurd, outlandish thing I'd ever heard. I remember telling him, "Well, that's what you believe." He answered me, "That's not *my* belief." What he was saying was, that's not just what *he* believes, but what countless millions of people believe. But I couldn't understand that. Demons? Somebody actually *believed* in demons? That was way beyond anything I could accept. I was seventeen, and I'd never been taught anything about Christianity. My mind was wrapped in blinders and I didn't even know it.

I think the basic impasse for non-believers is this: Faith is an object of suspicion for them, because very often they confuse it with *blind faith*. Blind faith is the acceptance of something without any doubt or questioning. It's accepting something without really understanding anything about it. I wouldn't recommend that type of faith to anyone. To my thinking, it really isn't true faith at all, but a form of stupidity. It's basically like handing your mind over to something without actually knowing what it is. It's almost like selling your soul— and selling it cheaply.

Going by my own experience, I'd say that a lot of people who look at Christianity with suspicion don't really know much about it. Jesus Himself was not in favor of "blind" faith. (This point was discussed briefly in Chapter 5.) The Samaritans are mentioned a number of times in the New Testament. Back in the first century, they were a separate religious group who followed many Jewish ways, but they had their own interpretation of the Scriptures. In fact, they had (and still have) their own set of scriptures, which is called the Samaritan Pentateuch (corresponding to the first five books of the Old Testament). The Jews of that time did not get along with them, and the feeling was mutual.

In one incident which was noted earlier, Jesus spoke with a Samaritan woman while stopping at a well. She made a comment to Him regarding the place where believers are supposed to worship. (The Samaritans didn't believe Jerusalem was so special for purposes of worship. The Jews, of course, had their Temple there.) That's when Jesus criticized the Samaritan mindset, because they worshiped what they didn't understand. {John 4:22} He went on to say that the Jews *understand* what they worship.

This is an enormously meaningful statement. Jesus Christ, the Son of God, was emphasizing that it's important to *understand what we worship*. Throughout the Gospels, Jesus tells people that *faith* is of critical importance, and virtually the key to eternal salvation. But here, He clarifies what He means by faith. Anyone of our time— including the most hardened atheist— should be able to appreciate this. Even someone who professes scorn for Christianity, and contempt for Jesus, should be able to see that Christ was making a great distinction. He was saying that He doesn't advocate "blind" faith. He was telling us that faith must be accompanied by understanding.

I recall that when I first inquired about the Catholic Church, the priest I spoke with said that I'd have to attend classes and receive instruction. It was necessary, he said, to have an understanding of Catholic doctrines— to actually know what the Church teaches and why those things are taught. I'm not saying that most other Christian churches welcome new people by slapping them on the back and immediately calling them "brother." I don't know how many churches are actually like that. But when I started taking instruction, I soon realized that there's more to Christianity than just sitting in a pew every Sunday.

I don't think much of blind faith. I don't think anyone should. And it's pretty clear that Jesus didn't, either.

I do accept that there are limits to human understanding. For instance, there is only one God. This has been known since the first revelation to Abraham. While the New Testament reveals that God has three qualities— the Father, the Son and the Holy Spirit— there is one thing it doesn't explain. And that is the essence and totality of God. And there's a reason for this. How can any human being grasp that? How can anyone seriously say that they have God wrapped up neatly in one package, and that they know everything there is to know about Him?

It simply isn't possible. No mere human mind can grasp the totality of God. Certainly we can "know" God, as a child knows his parents. But loving God and knowing Him as a Father isn't the same as fully comprehending Him.

Let's face it— the God who created this entire universe and every living thing in it; the God who spoke to Abraham and to Moses; the God who parted the Sea of Reeds for the Israelites and freed them from Egyptian servitude; the God who fathered Jesus Christ and nurtured the seed that grew into a world-wide faith; the God who saved western Europe from the Mongol invasion; the God who decreed the overthrow of the Aztec Empire; the God who saved the American Revolution and ordained the liberation of men's minds— this is a God of literally universal scope, and incomprehensible power. This is a God who far surpasses anything in His creation. For any mere human to really understand Him, would be like (using the biblical analogy) a clay pot trying to understand the potter who formed it on the wheel.

This is not to say that humans are stupid. After all, God made us in His image. In all His earthly creation, there are only two types of beings who have rational minds— humans and angels. No other creatures in this world have the ability to actually think on that level. He gave us minds that have built great ships, immense cities, even civilizations. He gave us minds that have discovered astonishing wonders, like antibiotics and the principles of rocketry— minds that have unlocked the secrets of gravity, the stars and the atom. But even so, we have our limits. We are still creations of God; we're not His equals.

Mankind has made great advancements and achieved great things. But looking at it logically, *there are really no achievements possible without God*. He gave us everything we have. And one of the greatest gifts is our rational minds.

I'm not so narrow, or so bigoted, that I think one has to be a Catholic to be saved. This book isn't a Catholic tract, and nobody should mistake it for one. Christ Himself told His disciples that He had other followers they didn't even know of. {John 10:16} What I'm saying is, there's a vast difference between faith and blind faith. Maybe somebody who literally hates God will try to say otherwise. But anyone with any sense will know better.

Acknowledging God isn't an act of enslavement, but liberation. God has the power to free us from anything, whether it's a drug addiction or agonizing mental anguish. By accepting the fact of His existence, we're not sacrificing our free will, our individuality, or anything else that makes us who we are. On the contrary— we free our minds, making it possible to see far more than we could before.

Genuine faith isn't a form of blindness— it's a cure for blindness. When I was an agnostic, I was locked up in chains that my mind imposed on itself. I couldn't see, because I was too smug in my disbelief to let myself see.

Each of us has the power to put chains on our mind, or to throw them off. All we have to do is think about it and decide: Would we rather live *with* those chains— or *without* them?

Chapter 11

HOW CAN GOD ALLOW SO MUCH EVIL IN THE WORLD?

One of the biggest whimperings we get from atheists, is that no God could possibly allow so much evil in the world. The logic behind that kind of thinking is pathetically twisted. Basically, these people are throwing up their hands and saying, "There, you see how terrible the world is? How could any God allow so much evil to exist? This *proves* there is no God."

In other words, they're posing a question which is supposed to answer itself. And the question is based on complete negativity, accompanied by a massive dose of tunnel vision. *They're totally ignoring anything positive that happens in the world, in order to reinforce their negativity.*

This is one of the greatest handicaps atheists have. Their whole world-view is based on negativity. And to maintain it, they must ignore (or greatly downplay) anything good that happens in the world— anything that might indicate the workings of a benevolent Higher Power. So they *must* have a self-imposed tunnel vision, in order to cling to their precious negative philosophy— which is all they really have left to believe in. But they believe in it deeply, and will react against anyone who questions it. After all, that's part of the atheist's self-made faith.

But still, there must be an answer, even for a question posed by atheists. Why *would* God allow so much evil in the world? Even if a hardened atheist doesn't actually *want* an answer, that still doesn't make it a bad question. And there is an answer for it.

THE QUESTION OF EVIL IN THE WORLD

This is not a new question. In fact, it was dealt with in some of the most ancient parts of the Bible, including the books of Genesis and Job.

For those who already have faith in God, the Book of Genesis basically answers the question. The book describe how God created the heavens and Earth, all the world's animals, and then mankind, whom He fashioned in His own image. It then states that God looked out over His creation, and found it all very good. {Genesis 1:31} In other words, *there was no evil in the world.* How could there be? After all, God had created everything. It may have been a primitive world where dinosaurs and other extinct animals roamed, but this was part of the natural order— the same as modern lions preying on antelope.

When God created the first man (Adam), He gave him something that none of the rest of the Earth's creatures had. God gave him free will. But He forbade Adam to eat any of the fruit from the tree of knowledge. {Genesis 2:16-17} The rest of the story is pretty well known. The serpent (symbolizing the devil) later tricked Eve into eating the fruit, and she talked Adam into it.

As we say nowadays, that's when things went to hell in a handbasket. This was the point where evil was introduced into the world. It is described in religious terms as "the fall of man." It's not a novel idea. Men of faith— far more intelligent than myself— have discussed this same question over the centuries. One who comes to mind was St. Augustine, who lived some 1600 years ago.

MYTH OR EXPLANATION?

Now, by this time any dedicated non-believer will be turning up his nose, snorting in disgust or laughing out loud. *"What is this crap about Adam and the Garden? Everyone knows that's nothing but mythology!"* And in a sense, maybe it is. That passage was written more than 2,500 years ago. There was no Darwin and there were no fossils being studied. In fact, there was no science at all. The people living back then were people of faith. They weren't immersed in an "information age." They weren't interested in nanotechnology or plate tectonics. They didn't care about [20]sub-atomic particles, or landing robotic probes on Mars. They weren't fascinated by a fresh collection of fossils being named as a new species of dinosaur. Those people cared about **truth.**

The question we should be asking is: Was their faith based on falsehood, or reality? Modern genetic research has indicated that all living humans actually *do* have one individual man, and one individual woman, as ancestors. Although it's unprovable, let's say (for the sake of argument) that those two people were not actually named Adam and Eve. Would that mean that God doesn't exist? Would it mean the Adam and Eve story is totally devoid of truth?

In the absence of any modern science, those men were inspired to write something explaining how so much evil came into the world. Obviously, the Genesis creation account wasn't meant to be a scientific textbook. But if we take an honest look at it, we find that it contains a lot of truth.

It was stated that God created everything, including mankind itself. God chose to make people in His own image, and to give them the gift of free will. Soon afterward, the first man disobeyed Him and did evil in His sight. From that point on, evil ran rampant in the world— and, from the earliest written records we have, we can see that this was pretty much the case. (Those ancient cuneiform tablets from the Middle East are filled with tales of war, conquest and destruction.)

So, for people of faith, that question has an answer. Evil now exists because of the rebellious and selfish nature of man himself. This actually does answer the question of evil in the world. *But*

---

[20] One might suppose that the ancients had no interest in sub-atomic particles because such things were unheard of. However, the Atomic Theory originated with a Greek named Democritus who lived around 400 BC. [9:Vol. 4: 6] Ideas regarding the mere physical properties of the universe simply did not impress devout Jews of that era.

only for people of faith. For those who have doubts, something more— such as logic and reason— is going to be required. As a former agnostic, I can appreciate this.

Why does God allow evil in the world? It's not that hard to figure out.

Even with nothing more than a limited human mind, I can still see several reasons why God allows evil in the world. It may sound contradictory or even paradoxical, but they are all centered on love— God's love for us, and our love towards Him. It strikes me that God must love mankind very much, not only to have made us in His image but to also have given us rational minds, along with the gift of free will. All the other creatures of this world are driven by brute instinct— rooting in the dirt for their food, or living by tooth and claw. The only real law animals have is the law of the jungle. Only humans have been given the means to raise ourselves up from the soil of creation.

Of course, in some people, the primitive instincts for survival and competition are still pretty strong. Throughout history, whatever level of technology man has possessed— no matter what heights of civility he has reached— you still find individuals who live by the law of the jungle. Man's cruelty towards man has left a horrifying record. But for those who don't submit to tunnel vision, we can also find a record of hope.

For every ruthless conqueror like Alexander "the Great" or Genghis Khan, we can find an example of decency and humanity. In China, a man now called Confucius developed a philosophy which brought purpose and inner peace to many. In India, a man now called Buddha taught millions to rise above selfishness and violence. In Athens, a teacher named Socrates challenged others to look beyond the evil and confusion that surrounded them.

There was Moses, of course, who brought God's liberation to the ancient Israelites. Then there was the pinnacle of liberation— Jesus Christ Himself, who brought each one of us the power to be liberated from our own failings. It was Christ who actually gave us the means to be transformed. So, in this world with all its evils, we still have choices just as Adam and Eve did. The

God who created the world gave us these choices along with everything else.

This explains a great deal. God wants us to choose for ourselves. He wants to see whether we'll choose to be completely selfish, or to follow His will. He wants to see what each of us will love the most— our own self, or Him. It's a question of love.

WHAT ABOUT SUFFERING?

Of course, there's more evil to be found in this world than just the cruelty of man toward his fellow man. There are things like disease, deformities, genetically-linked troubles— things which cause human suffering. Along with these, we find situations of extreme poverty in many countries. How can God allow all this?

Again, it's a question of love. How much do we love our fellow man? What are we willing to do to help others? Looking at it from my own limited mind, when we see people suffering, it's actually an *opportunity* for each of us— to care for someone else— to do something for someone less fortunate. It's a way for us to find that quality of mercy and charity in ourselves.

I firmly believe that everyone has a share of suffering in life. And it's true that some suffer more than others. I think that for each of us— as we endure our pain in life— it's an opportunity to think beyond the everyday cares and search for answers within ourselves. It's also an opportunity to reach out to God, and to make a connection that we otherwise might find no reason to attempt.

Try to picture a rich man (or woman), sitting in a magnificent home, surrounded by all the comforts of life. This hypothetical person has no physical impairments, no illnesses, no worries about bills or car repairs. Just what do they think about from hour to hour— how to best cater to their appetites? How to make a better show of wealth for their friends?

How many people like that actually know that they need God? Would they have any real reason to think about reaching out to Him? Would they have enough sense (or humility) to know that everything they own is a gift from Him?

It's possible that there really are people like that. What can it be that fills up their minds, other than concerns about wealth, acquisition, and extending their power over others? Except for their own family circle, would they have any reason to even *care* about anyone else?

I'm certainly not anyone's judge. And the Bible makes clear that riches alone are not something evil. {Sirach 31:8-11} But still, in this context, it seems obvious that some amount of suffering is a definite advantage. If nothing else, it draws us closer to the God with whom we hope to spend eternity.

Once you know that God exists, you have to realize there must be a reason for everything. *You immediately lose the easy excuses used by the atheists.* You no longer have the easy cop-out of claiming there are no answers. When asked what governs life, you can no longer plead "chaos."

WHO IS SATAN, AND WHY DOES GOD ALLOW HIM TO EXIST?

For some reason or another, in our culture there's a distinct fascination with evil. Perhaps for many of us, "good" people are somewhat boring compared to scoundrels. Maybe it's because we look at evil individuals, and they simply make *us* look good in comparison. Or possibly (and this is a scary thought), it just might be something deeper in our human nature. Once I was browsing in one of these big chain bookstores, and I noticed something. In the biography section I saw far more books on Adolf Hitler than there were on Thomas Jefferson. What is it in our nature that makes someone like Hitler so interesting? (After all, he was one of the biggest losers in history.)

I have to admit, often when watching a movie, I'll find it really entertaining when there's a villain with a lot of character— a lot of panache. One example that comes to mind was the villain in *Water World,* portrayed by the late Dennis Hopper. But it's not just character that people are fascinated with. For some reason, the most evil personality in the universe is also quite interesting. That would be Satan, also known as the devil.

When *The Exorcist* hit the screens in 1973, theater goers stood in line for hours to be wowed by the prince of darkness. (Although he never even appeared as an actual character.) Back in the 1960s, one enterprising fellow in San Francisco even founded a "church" dedicated to the devil. Apparently he made money off it and lived it up, while he was still living.

In spite of such spectacular publicity stunts, we have to remember one thing: Once we find that God is real, it opens a whole new dimension of reality for us. Because we have to realize that there really are angels and other supernatural beings which do exist. We have to understand that these are a genuine— though usually invisible— part of the actual universe we live in. The Bible doesn't tell us the names of very many angels. We hear of the archangels Michael, Gabriel and Raphael. We also can find references to another angel, named Satan.

I haven't read volumes of literature about the devil. I can't claim to be an expert on the subject. But over the years, anyone can glean information from various sources. And there are some things I've found out.

The Book of Job contains one of the earliest references to Satan found in the Bible. In this book, he is described as one of the angels (called the "sons of God") gathered around God's throne. At this time in Jewish theology, Satan is pictured as a sort of vicious prosecutor. When God asks him his opinion about His good and upright servant Job, the devil challenges Him to test the man.

The name "Satan" comes from a Hebrew word, meaning something like "adversary," or "opponent." The word "devil" is derived from Greek, and means "slanderer," or "accuser." In the Book of Job, we can see how this latter word describes Satan well. There's not very much information on Satan in the Old Testament. In the New Testament there are quite a few references to him. Jesus even went so far as to describe him as "the prince of this world." {John 12:31} In other words, He was saying that the devil has a lot of power here on Earth.

Over the centuries, theologians have developed a fairly strong consensus on the origin and reality of Satan. He is, of course, one of the angels created by God. Many think he started out as one of the most beautiful angels. His original name is thought to have been Lucifer, which in Latin means "light bearer."

Lucifer may have been beautiful, but he had a serious problem. It was his tremendous pride. And apparently it took the form of a rebellious streak a mile wide, because he led a revolt of angels against God's authority. For this, he and his cohorts were cast out of Heaven, and from that time onward he has reigned over Hell. After the revolt he became known as Satan. That's what I would call a "thumbnail sketch" of Satan's origins. I hope that I related it correctly. As I said, I'm no theological expert.

The sudden interest caused by *The Exorcist* generated much new discussion about the devil and his workings. In June 1975 the Roman Catholic Church weighed in on the subject. In a study published that year, the Church reaffirmed the existence of the devil— not as a symbol but as an actual being. (In an earlier speech given by Pope Saint Paul VI in 1972, Satan was described as a "creature of God," but a fallen one.) The study also warned against people letting themselves "fall victim to the imagination," in being too preoccupied with the existence of Satan. [28:11]

Now, in a culture that teaches us to constantly worry about everything from bills to libidos, it might be easy to start worrying about the devil. After all, as a real force in the world, can't he make trouble for anyone? Of course he can. And I have no doubts that he tries as often as possible. But we have to remember that God is infinitely more powerful. Anyone with faith can withstand anything the devil might throw at him. That's worked for me, and I know it'll work for anyone.

But the essential question is— why does God tolerate all this in the first place? Why does He allow the devil to add to the world's evil? Why doesn't God just eliminate him?

Again, it's a question of love. As others have said before, this world is a sort of testing-ground. Each of us is tested, to see where his (or her) heart is. Do we love God most, or do we put ourselves first? Or do we love the things of this world most of all? We can't forget that God gave us free will. If He eliminated His chief opponent, that would deprive men of part of the test. It would be taking away a portion of our choice— almost like a form of coercion. He wants to find out what we love most.

Atheists have no interest in hearing an answer. Where God is concerned, they prefer their own tunnel vision. When they refuse to open their minds; when they refuse to see facts; when they refuse to consider the enormous possibility that they might be wrong, then they can keep *ignoring* the answers. They can go on clinging to the blind faith that there is *no truth*— and there are *no answers*— except whatever it is in this world that they *prefer* to put their faith in.

But the answers are there, and it doesn't take a Newton or an Einstein to figure them out. There may be some mystery as to why there's so much evil and suffering in the world. But that doesn't mean it's an unsolvable mystery.

A philosophy like atheism finds its "answers" in confusion and chaos. In a universe that has no meaning, answers are unimportant. Evidently atheists are more comfortable with that. But once we have the courage to open our eyes and see God behind the scenes, we can see the world as it actually is. And a whole lot more.

Chapter 12

WHAT IS HELL? CAN GOD REALLY ALLOW SUCH A PLACE?

"Hell" is a word that we hear tossed about with relative ease. It's a hell of a situation. That's a hell of a thing to say. It's a helluva this, or it's a helluva that.

But people don't seem to like to talk much about Hell itself. One might say, it's a helluva subject. And so it seems to be often avoided. There seems to be a certain tendency in our nature to avoid Hell in every way we can. We don't like to think about it. We don't really like to talk about it. Maybe it's one of those things people don't feel comfortable discussing.

Maybe that's the reason I'm going to discuss it.

For many, Hell is another of those stumbling blocks to faith, similar to "all the evil in the world." How can God allow such a place? How can any God allow such a punishment for anyone? It's another one of those questions which atheists love to use as its own answer. For an atheist, if there is no God, that means there is no Hell. And if there's no Hell, that must mean there's no punishment in any afterlife. So... while you're here on Earth, "anything goes."

Now that's what I call a comfortable way of thinking. **But is it true?** Back in Nazi Germany, the government had tens of millions of Germans thinking they were a "master race." To the ruling elite, this meant that every act of aggression and every kind of mass murder was perfectly okay.

In the old Soviet Union, hundreds of millions of people put their faith in Marxist communism. This allowed the Bolsheviks to forge an empire which was (to use Kipling's phrase[21]) salted down with the bones of their opponents. In Stalin's empire, uncounted millions were killed in order to "build communism." But the communism prophesied by Marx never arrived. It was nothing but an empty promise, used to justify an iron tyranny.

Nazism attempted to make one man into a god. Communism cultivated a faith in a future heaven on Earth, while denying any life beyond this one. Each system created its own hell in this world, while denying any punishment in the next. In essence, both of those ideologies were saying, "There is no God above, so there's nothing to fear for the crimes we commit here."

But— as we've seen— there are obvious proofs in history that God *does exist*. Not only this, but we can see that He is a "proactive" God, intervening in human events when necessary. What does that say about ideologies such as Nazism, communism and atheism? Simply put, it shatters them. The overriding reality of God simply destroys any man-made belief system which attempts to diminish Him. It proves that they're not only valueless, but self-destructive as well.

And once God's reality is acknowledged, we have to realize that all those other things the Bible teaches can no longer be so easily dismissed.

WHY HELL?

There's a popular trend these days, even among many pastors in many churches, to describe Hell in symbolic terms. It's simply a separation from God. It's simply a state of loneliness. It's simply a psychological self-punishment of some sort, where we "create our own hell." Another popular cliché is that Hell is right here on Earth. (I was once acquainted with a fellow at work who was actually a Satan worshiper, who said he believed that.)

These are all somewhat trendy modern views, which greatly appeal to people living in a culture which shuns religious "mysticism" in favor of rationalism. If our culture teaches us

---

[21] The imagery is from a poem by Rudyard Kipling, titled "The Sons of the Widow."

anything, it tells us to be rational. However, not everything in this universe is going to conform to our preconceived "rational" ideas. God certainly has no need to. (He's the one who *created* this universe.)

No matter what kind of culture we're raised in, we must recognize one fact of life when visualizing God. We can't expect Him to conform to *our* views and desires. He is not some new boyfriend or girlfriend whom we'd like to "train" to behave as we want. He's not some doting grandmother who's going to spoil us and cater to our every whim. If we have the courage to accept the existence of God, we *have* to accept Him on His terms. It's as simple as that. After all, He is God, and we aren't.

This doesn't mean that He's standing over us with a whip, ready to beat us into submission every time we step out of line. We have to remember that He's a loving God, who wants each one of us to find eternal salvation. He's a Father, not a slave driver. And He did give us free will. He's not going to force anyone to worship Him, or even to do His will in this life. He gave us that choice. He wants to see where our hearts are.

The sad truth of the matter is, that not everyone chooses God.

We can be honest about it. We all have our own goals and desires. And many of those are for ourselves. It's only natural to want joy and happiness in life. And there's no doubt that God wants us to be happy too. After all, He was the one who placed these yearnings within us. But this doesn't mean the "happiness" felt by a heroin addict as he injects a new dose of his favorite drug. It doesn't mean the "happiness" felt by a serial killer, when he finds a new victim on whom he can vent his monstrous hostilities. I think it's safe to say, God wants a *genuine* kind of happiness for us— one that increases our inner peace and brings us closer to Him. Not one which drags us down and separates us from Him.

As we know, however, there are some who choose those other paths in life. Some people choose to seek their rewards in doing evil. And our God— loving parent that He is— is also a God of justice. God allows people to reject Him, if that's what they choose. But in rejecting God, they also run the risk of losing Heaven and its rewards. Just as Lucifer did. And that's their choice. A God of love will not force Himself on us. And that same God— who is also a God of justice— won't allow a creation where there are no consequences, or a universe where evil receives the same reward as faith.

WHAT IS HELL LIKE?

The Old Testament doesn't say much about Hell. From what I've read, the ancient Hebrews thought that most (if not all) people went after death to a place called Sheol. It was seen as a dark world of shadows, situated under the Earth. Many Middle Eastern peoples believed this in ancient times. The Greeks, of course, had their own version of Sheol called Hades.

During His mission on Earth, Jesus described Hell in much more vivid terms. He consistently described it as a place of fiery torment. In one parable, Christ warned that an uncharitable rich man who enjoyed the good life on Earth, while ignoring the sufferings of others, received as his punishment an eternity in flames. {Luke 16:24}

In other places in the New Testament Christ refers to Gehenna, which is the word He used for Hell. It was a reference to an actual location near Jerusalem, called the Valley of Hinnom. Centuries earlier it had been a place of ritual infant sacrifice. {2 Chronicles 28:3} In the first century AD, however, the Valley of Hinnom was being used as a refuse dump. Fires were usually burning there, to consume the tremendous amounts of refuse brought by residents of Jerusalem. So the very mention of Gehenna painted a picture of fires constantly burning. And this is consistent throughout the New Testament. {*e.g.*, Matthew 25:41}

This was the way Jesus Christ described Hell. And— being the Son of God— it's a safe bet that He knew what He was talking about.

A DESCRIPTION FROM A MODERN SOURCE, AND A WORD OF CAUTION

There is also one modern description of Hell, which countless millions believe to be from a reliable source. There are others who scorn it, simply because of that source. Unfortunately, some people have a sort of a knee-jerk reaction against anything that comes out of the Catholic Church. There may even be some who feel that the wars of the Reformation are still being fought. (I don't say this as a judgment, simply as an observation of an unpleasant reality.)

I can understand such a mentality in a hardened atheist, whose beliefs are petrified into unbelief. I can see how a person who actually hates God could also hate the Catholic Church. But I can't understand such a mindset in other Christians. Catholics and Protestants believe in the same God. They recognize God in the Father, Son and Holy Spirit. They all acknowledge Jesus Christ as Savior. And that Savior told us to love one another.

But still, there are some whose faith seems to be partly fueled by animosity. This is one of the great blights on Christianity which remain from the days of the Reformation wars. After some 500 years, it still reflects badly on the followers of Jesus.

But once we know that God is real, any limitations which we may have once put on Him must be discarded. God can communicate with people in any way He chooses. Many churches acknowledge this. One of them is the Catholic Church. This isn't a statement contrived to bend anyone toward a certain Christian denomination. It's simply an historic and doctrinal fact. In ancient times God sent prophets to warn His people. When He sent Joan of Arc to save her country, people of faith listened. What's so impossible about the idea that He can send the mother of His Son?

AN AMAZING EVENT IN A REMOTE CORNER OF EUROPE

In 1917, the First World War was raging in Europe. But in Portugal— tucked away on the Iberian Peninsula next to Spain— things were relatively quiet. Portugal had sent men into the war to fight against Germany, but the fighting was far away.

The Portuguese government at that time was socialist in its outlook and strongly anti-clerical. The old monarchy had been overthrown in 1910, and the new government was both anti-monarchist and hostile toward religion. In particular, the new regime had taken harsh measures to harass and suppress the Catholic Church. This was the political climate in Portugal in 1917. However, all of that meant very little to three young children who were herding sheep in the distant countryside. Little did they know, that their simple lives were about to radically change.

On the 13th of May that year, an amazing sight appeared to them. One of the children described her as a beautiful Lady who radiated a dazzling light, even in the afternoon sun. [11:174] Eventually, this supernatural being made it clear to them that she was the Lady of the Rosary. [11:182] For the children— and for countless others— this event was destined to have an enormous impact. Because the "apparition" was now identified as the Virgin Mary herself, the woman who in her earthly life was the mother of Jesus Christ, and who is recognized as the greatest saint in Heaven.

The Lady promised to appear again to the children, on the 13th of each month. And, indeed, she did. From the start, the children's parents were stricken with fear. Government officials started harassing and intimidating the children. The local Catholic priest was terrified, and did all he could to get them to retract their claims. Everyone was fearful of retaliation from the government.

The Lady kept appearing to the children each month. In July, she told them that there would be a public miracle, to demonstrate the truth of what was happening. [11:178] And, in fact, at her last appearance on October 13th, the huge crowd of onlookers saw something that astounded them. Many of them thought it was the end of the world. But more momentous than this— more stunning than the political turmoil that accompanied these events— were the things that the Lady told the children. She revealed to them a number of secrets, which included information on major events which would occur in the future. (More on this will be discussed in Chapter 19.)

A GLIMPSE OF THE REAL HELL— NOT A PRETTY PICTURE

Along with these prophecies, she showed the children something which transformed them. It was a glimpse of Hell itself. On the 13th of July that year, the Lady opened her hands, and rays of light seemed to penetrate the surface of the Earth.

These were just children, the oldest only ten years of age. Their faith wasn't blind faith, but the trusting faith of children. The love and kindness radiating from the Lady of the Rosary was proof enough for them. But what they saw now affected them tremendously. From that day on, they greatly increased the time they spent praying. Years later, the last surviving member of the three, Lucia dos Santos, described what they were shown. When the rays emanating from the Lady penetrated the ground, the children saw a vision of what was below. And what they saw was a vast "sea of fire."

Tossed about in the flames, they could see "souls in human form". They looked transparent, like burning lumps of coal or wood. Along with the human souls were other figures displaying a "terrifying and repellent likeness to frightful and unknown animals..." These were identified as demons, "black and transparent" as were the human souls. [11:178] All these figures were being churned about helplessly in this ocean of fire, and were letting out "shrieks and groans of pain and despair".

The glimpse given to the children lasted only a moment. But the sea of fire was a thing of eternity. For the souls that were lost in that ocean of flames, there would never be an end.

This coincides with the way Jesus described Hell— the fires of Gehenna. Not quite the same as the comfortable, well-reasoned pictures of a *rational* hell being pushed by so many of our modern "experts." But this was what the Son of God was talking about, not them.

WHAT ARE WE TO THINK OF THIS?

It's curious, that people are so fascinated by the supernatural. Books like *Angels and Demons* will sell like hotcakes. Dark conspiracy theories revolving around corrupt priests entertain the multitudes. Everyone likes a good thriller. And if angels, the devil, or even God can be made part of the entertainment, so much the better. But the idea of a real Hell isn't so entertaining. The idea of a real God, who actually exists, who actually does watch over the world, caring for each of us— somehow, that just isn't part of the "fun." What is it, exactly, the problem that people have with reality?

The truth is, reality isn't so bad. Think about it. What would be worse— to have a world where no God exists, where chaos reigns and life has no meaning? Or to have a God who listens to our prayers and helps us with life's challenges? Is it better to have an eternity ahead of us where death is the end— nothing but annihilation? Or an eternity available to us that can be spent in a paradise? That's the way Jesus described Heaven.

At the final moment of our life, each of us will have to accept eternity. But those who choose God should never have any dread of Hell. It's real— just like man-made prisons are real— but we don't have to go there. Hell is only for those who reject God and waste the life that He gave them. For those who open their minds— who break free from the blinders— who have the courage to take that "leap of faith"— the rewards are far greater than any ordeal in this life.

Chapter 13

A PERSONAL BRUSH WITH THE SUPERNATURAL

For some time, I've been mulling over whether to write a chapter about this. It concerns some personal experiences I went through earlier in my life. By recording this, I realize that it will bring scoffing and jeers from the skeptical. It may even give some a pretext to question my very sanity. Exposing one's self to ridicule is something only a comedian could enjoy. However, a lot of good people have been ridiculed for being witnesses to their faith. I'm not writing this to make myself look perfect, but to draw others to faith in God. And so I've decided to record this incident. I think God is worth the risk of a little ridicule.

This happened to me a couple or three months prior to my 26th birthday. After several years of being an agnostic, I'd finally found that God is real. After that I'd spent several more years trying to center myself spiritually, without attending any church. But I couldn't find the spiritual strength— or the inner peace— that I craved. Finally, I'd decided to try the Catholic Church. After some time attending church regularly and taking instruction in that faith, I was baptized by Father David E. Hoover at Sacred Heart Church, Pomona, California. I kept on going to Mass and started taking Communion.

I think it was in March, the month following my baptism, that this happened. It might have still been February. It was totally unexpected. It couldn't have taken up much more than an hour of my life, maybe less. But it was an experience that indelibly stamped my consciousness with the truth of God and His universe. It left no doubt in my mind that it's all real.

Being a student in college, I had unfortunately slipped into the bad habit of drinking excessively on weekends when partying with friends. I had graduated the previous June, and now I was taking some graduate classes. My best friend, who had lived in another state for years, was visiting the area while on leave from the Air Force, as I recall. He and another friend and I had spent some time hanging out together. Then, when his leave expired, he left to go back to his base.

It was shortly afterward that everything happened, perhaps even the day after he left— I remember that it was a Saturday. I was in my bedroom working on a crayon drawing for an art class. It seems sort of juvenile now as I think about it, but that was the assignment.

I had just gone to my first confession, earlier that same day. There had been nothing extraordinary to confess, but it had been my very first confession. And now I was sitting on my bed, working on this crayon drawing for an art class. Suddenly, I had a very restless feeling. I couldn't sit still and work on the drawing. I stood up next to the bed. I realized that I wanted to go do something.

I wanted to go out dancing. There was this dance place called "The Posh" out in Cucamonga. (The name of the town had become something of a punchline for comedians, so later they changed it to "Rancho Cucamonga.") It was about a half-hours' drive from where I lived. I went to my wardrobe, put on some of my best clothes, and got in my car and started driving.

A few minutes later I was driving up Garey Avenue (or maybe it was White Avenue) toward the freeway, when I realized that something was unusual. I had a strange feeling— one that I couldn't remember ever having before. Driving up the street at that moment with the window down, I felt a strange exhilaration. It was a kind of wild feeling. I felt as if I wasn't driving, but *flying*.

And I noticed something else. All the street lamps seemed to be giving off a yellowish light. The whole street looked slightly unreal, as if it were tinged with a shade of dirty yellow. Everything just looked a little weird. I got on the San Bernardino Freeway and headed east, toward the offramp that would take me to Cucamonga. As I drove along the freeway, I saw that all the lights were still glowing yellow. It looked almost as if there was a hazy, yellowish fog enveloping everything in sight. The lights, even the freeway itself had that same eerie tinge.

The feeling of exhilaration was getting more focused. I started thinking about The Posh, and all the women who'd be there. I started thinking that I'd pick one up, take her home, and then have a really *swell time*. (The actual words going through my head must have been much cruder.) I was really enjoying this line of thought. But then I realized something. That wasn't the way I lived. Maybe I didn't qualify for sainthood, but I definitely wasn't the type of guy to be looking for superficial relationships. ("One-night stands" were not my thing.)

And I realized something else. I had just gone to confession— my first confession. Here I was, a newly-minted Catholic, and I was gearing myself up to act like a total *slimeball*. I could sense that something was happening here, something beyond my experience. And it scared me. I didn't know what was going on. It was as if I was under some type of compulsion.

Unable to turn back and unable to think of anything else, I started praying the Our Father— the Lord's Prayer. I may have been praying it without speaking. When I came to the words, "Thy will be done," I focused intensely on them, meaning every word of it. In that moment, I was putting my total trust in God. There was nothing else I could do.

In that same moment I witnessed the most astonishing thing in my life. Directly ahead of me, at about a 45-degree angle upward, I saw the glowing figure of a crucifix. It was more like an outline, a little indistinct, but clear enough to distinguish from a simple cross. The crucifix appeared only for an instant and, like everything, it was tinged with yellow.

In that same instant— or maybe a millisecond later— I saw something else. Without turning my eyes, in the upper right area of my peripheral vision I saw something like a black dot, which immediately shrank into nothingness. Along with it there was a fleeting sound, which was like a silent "whew!" Or maybe like the sound of something whizzing by. The sound itself lasted only an instant, and was gone after the dot vanished. These two visual events lasted less than half a second. But they packed a hell of a jolt. I remember my astonishment at that moment. "What was THAT!!?"

I don't remember pulling the car over; I'm pretty sure that I just kept driving. But immediately after all this, I saw that the lights, the freeway, everything else no longer had that yellow tinge. Everything now appeared normal. I noticed one other thing: I no longer had any compulsion to go to The Posh. It was as if some driving force inside me had suddenly vanished. I felt relatively relaxed and normal, though somewhat shaken. Instead of going to the dance hall I went to Fontana where my grandmother lived, just a little farther east. I stopped by and spent some time at her place. She was good company.

TRUTH IS STRANGER THAN FICTION

It may have taken a little while before I realized what had happened. But the truth of it stunned me almost as much as the event itself. It had been a damned demon.

That moment back at my place, when I suddenly became restless and stood up, must have been the exact instant that it entered me. Everything between that moment and the vision of the crucifix was immersed in compulsion, mindless exhilaration, and— as soon as I could notice it outdoors— bathed in that same weird yellow glow.

It may have been a couple of days later, that I had another instruction session with Father Hoover. (I was still preparing for Confirmation.) I figured that a priest would understand, so I told him what had happened. His initial reaction was surprising. He made soothing sounds, saying "Yesss...," as if to mockingly humor me. Obviously, he was expressing his skepticism in the bluntest way he could, without being too obviously insulting.

It angered me. Without raising my voice, I let him know it. He could tell that I didn't appreciate his reply. I told him that I thought Satan had sent that thing to destroy me, just as I was starting out on my path to spiritual strength and salvation. I'll never forget Father Hoover's reaction when I said the devil's name. He jerked his head around, as if looking over his shoulders to see if the devil would appear. By this time he evidently was taking me more seriously. Quickly losing the mocking tone, in very circumspect terms he acknowledged that there are "evil influences" in the world.

THAT WASN'T THE END OF IT

Not long after the possession incident, another unexpected event took place. It wasn't quite as dramatic, or as obviously supernatural as the possession had been. But it was every bit as real. It was unlike anything which I'd experienced before. It seems like it wasn't more than a week or two— perhaps only a few days— after the possession occurred. I remember that I was laying in bed; maybe I was taking a nap at the time. I don't remember what time it was, but it may have been in the afternoon. But I don't think it was any normal type of sleep. It wasn't like a dream at all. It was all very sharp and vivid. I felt as if I was floating, horizontally, and I was surrounded by darkened clouds. I couldn't see anything else. Suddenly, I noticed a falling sensation, and it seemed to be picking up speed. I don't remember any sound accompanying it. As I fell, the clouds appeared like a great canopy above me, but no longer surrounding me.

Along with this falling sensation, I could see that I was falling farther and farther from the clouds, which were now way above me. It occurred to me that if I kept falling, I would die. Now I was afraid, caught up again in an unknown vortex of events and feeling helpless. Again, I started praying the Our

Father, concentrating as hard as I could on that phrase, "Thy will be done..." At this point my descent halted, and I could see the clouds above me becoming closer. I was rising back toward them. When I reached them, I was finally able to open my eyes. I was back in my bedroom, as if nothing had happened. But I knew that something had.

Perhaps a day or two later, the same thing happened again. It didn't seem as pronounced as the first event. But I recall that it was identical. Again, I told Father Hoover about it. Whatever his reply was, I don't remember it. (Lord knows what he was thinking by that time.) He may have discussed it with another priest at the church, because during a sermon at Mass shortly afterward, the other priest said something about "the void." I don't remember the context of it. Years later when I described these events to someone, he considered it an "out of body experience."

I'm glad to say, those were the only occasions in my life when I experienced such direct Satanic attacks. Shortly after the possession thing, I'd prayed hard that it never happen to me again. Life can be difficult enough without having to go through supernatural ordeals.

WHAT DOES IT ALL MEAN?

These events took place soon after I had joined the Church. They were obviously more than a coincidence. It's highly ironic, that the demonic possession incident became one of the turning points of my spiritual life. (Once you've experienced something like that, you can never fall into unbelief again.)

When those things happened to me, I hadn't been drinking and I hadn't been taking any drugs. (I've never taken LSD, or any other hallucinogenic substance in my life.) I wasn't in any kind of trance. They happened, just as I've related them here. And I'm very glad that this particular bit of history never repeated itself.

What does it mean? It seems obvious enough. Either I'm the world's biggest liar, or it means that all that stuff in the New Testament is real. It means that demons do exist. It means that the devil does use them, in his quest to ensnare as many victims as he can. It means that we're all part of the same universe, and this universe contains more than we might have realized.

A GOD WHO RIDES THE CLOUDS WITH MAJESTY

There was one other supernatural event which I witnessed soon after I joined the Church. It happened some time after the possession incident, perhaps as much as a year or so later. I can't remember the exact month and year, but it was during this time. It was a difficult moment in my life, a time of temptation. I was attracted to a young coed who was attending the same junior college as myself. She was going steady with a friend of mine. They may have been actually engaged by then. But suddenly she was showing a distinct interest in me. I was just as interested in her. And so I'd been giving her a lot of thought.

This was one of those situations where God has other plans— and lets us know it.

I was still going to Sacred Heart Church in Pomona. I recall that the church building was on the west side of the street, facing east. I think it was late in the afternoon; I was heading toward the entrance of the church, going to Mass. As I went up the steps I turned and looked over my shoulder, toward the southeast.

And then I saw something that I'd never seen before. It was a huge thundercloud— like a self-contained storm front— looming up toward the church. It was close, I'd say less than a half-mile away. The cloud formation was dark, and it appeared to reach high into the sky. Accompanying it were flashes of lightning, which if I recall correctly were visible inside the cloud, and also on the outside. It looked like something out of *Raiders of the Lost Ark*— an incredible sight. I could tell that the entire storm cloud was heading toward the church. Not thinking much of it at the time, I went inside and sat down. Father Hoover was celebrating the Mass. Soon, the immense cloud was actually enveloping the church building.

And this is where the supernatural character of this event was clearest. When Father Hoover was delivering the homily (the sermon), the flashes of lightning lit up the building at those exact moments when he was emphasizing something important. It was as if the thunder and lightning were actually entering the homily, becoming part of it. The overall effect was stunning, to say the least.

For the life of me, after so many years I can't remember a word of that homily. But what I do remember was that God Himself showed His presence that day— not only in the Eucharist, but in the power and majesty of the Father as well. It was another of those experiences that I'll never forget, nor want to forget. In future years there would be other occasions in my life that lightning storms appeared at significant moments, when they could be taken as distinct warnings. But none of them were as vivid and powerful as that Mass where God the Father added His voice.

I recall that after the Mass was over, the storm had passed over the church, continuing on its way. Left indelibly on my mind was that picture of the God of Heaven, who rides the clouds in majesty and gives voice from His throne over the world. This type of imagery appears in the Old Testament. {*e.g.*, Psalms 18:10-14, also 104:3} Scholars have found similar phrases in ancient Canaanite tablets. [1:538 (footnote for Psalms 68:5)] Sometimes skeptics mention such inscriptions, as if to paint these biblical Psalms as mere borrowings from ancient pagan mythology.

In this modern world, filled with the inventions of men, it does seem easy to dismiss such events as myth. If I hadn't seen it with my own eyes, I might be skeptical myself. But I did see it with my own eyes. And it was no myth. Those Canaanites knew a supernatural event when they saw it. They just didn't know the God they were witnessing. They thought it was one of their pagan deities; but they were seeing the real article. The awesome presence of the God who created all of nature remains with us— just as He was in ancient times.

I recall that not long after that, my interest in the coed faded. Like most such romantic sparks, it cooled and vanished. But the memory of that Mass has never vanished.

SOMETHING TO CONSIDER WHEN SEEKING GOD

These factual events I've described have implications for anyone. It may seem a little frightening, but it should bring much more hope than fear. When you choose to seek God— and your own salvation— there will be obstacles. The devil is a supernatural being. He remains an angel of sorts, with the power to create trouble, to influence people and tempt them. Once you make a decision to seek God and belong to Him, the devil *will try* everything he can to discourage, distract or divert you— anything that might steer you off course. The "prince of this world" will use this world (and all his snares) to try to drag you down. Putting it simply, he wants to trick you into giving up. That's really the only way he has to win.

But God is far more powerful— His power actually is unlimited. Even in the middle of a demonic possession, the Lord heard me when I called on His name and I was saved. Not only that, but God the Father showed the reality of His presence on that occasion during the Mass.

Don't ever fear the troubles you'll inevitably go through on your journey to faith. Nobody in this world is immune to them. But when you choose the true God— and true salvation— you'll find that He *will be there* to help you through it.

Chapter 14

WHAT THE HELL IS SIN, ANYWAY?

The idea of sin is not a popular one these days. The very word "sin" conjures up pictures of black-clad Puritans going around in their funny hats, pointing their fingers at everyone else and pinning scarlet letters on people. Sin itself is another of those things people don't usually care to talk about. But what is it, exactly? And what makes it wrong?

The concept of sin is simple. I think a good definition would go something like this: Anything that threatens to harm your soul is a sin. Anything that doesn't harm you spiritually is not. That sounds pretty simple. It just about makes each one of us his own dictionary. We can define for ourselves what's best for us. Except for one minor detail.

There is a God. And He does all the major definitions. Like the Ten Commandments, for example.

People don't always like that idea. After all, we're in this big, bad world and having to deal with it. We've gotten through puberty, through school, and some of us have "grown up fast" in the military or on the streets. Most of us are over 21. We can make of up our minds for ourselves. *We don't need to hear no stinkin' sermons!*

But maybe we do. Maybe we do need some outside help. Maybe we do need this God in Heaven, this loving Parent who's made rules for His children. Maybe without any rules, and without any self- control at all, we could *all* go to Hell. According to what Jesus said— and to what those three shepherd kids in Portugal were shown— there's plenty of room there for everyone.

When you think about it, this is without doubt the single most important life-issue facing each one of us: Where do we want to spend eternity? No one likes to think about the moment when we'll draw our last breath. But each of us will some day have that moment. I'm no expert on sin. But I'll never forget what one priest said years ago, during a Mass. "If you ever want to find a bunch of sinners," he said, "you'll find us sitting right here in church." He said this not as a joke, but in a very matter-of-fact way.

A lot of people have a favorite excuse for not attending any church. They dismiss all those who do as nothing but a "bunch of hypocrites." But by not going, they're only reinforcing their own ignorance. I'm sure that *every* church has its share of hypocrites. There are always going to be some individuals who actually think they're perfect. But the vast majority of people sitting in the pews are ordinary folks who know they're weak and sinful— and who want to do better.

Hypocrites say they're "above sinning." But people who are honest with themselves know better. The Bible says flat-out, that anyone claiming he's never sinned is trying to make God into a liar. {1 John 1:10} And this rings true. We've all made mistakes. We all have human weaknesses, emotional baggage and/or failed dreams that make each of us less than the person we'd like to be. I'm no exception, and neither are you.

WHAT DID JESUS SAY?

This may come as a surprise to some, but Christ Himself said He came for sinners, not for the self-righteous. {Mark 2:17} Jesus said very simply, that "healthy" people (those who think they're perfect) aren't the ones who need a doctor— *He came to help those who do.*

And He lived up to those words. During His mission on Earth, Jesus scandalized the "polite society" of Judea by associating with those very people whom the hypocrites scorned. He would talk to tax collectors (who everybody hated), to the sick (who were believed to be punished for their sins), and even to women with low reputations.

The religious aristocracy of the time, the priests and religious lawyers, were horrified by this troublemaker who associated with the very people they condemned. You just didn't do that in Judea! You were either one of the elect, one of the humble folk who observed all the rules (and kept his mouth shut), or one of the scum of the Earth who didn't! The latter group, of course, was defined by the first. And no inter-group socializing was allowed.

WHAT MAKES US "SINFUL?"

The question of man's sinfulness wasn't just an issue back in biblical times. Some 1600 years ago, there was a monk named Pelagius. He was born either in Britain or Ireland, around 360 AD. About the year 400 he began expounding a new theological view. He declared that all people are born inherently good. He asserted that no one is naturally disposed toward sin. Going by that, he said, babies have no need of baptism. The concept of Adam's "original sin" was invalid. And every human being is born with a soul which is immaculate— free from any taint of sin.

This teaching, of course, went against just about everything the Bible says about human nature. Jewish theology had taught from the beginning that Adam's sin had tainted all humanity. And Christ reaffirmed this, when He accepted baptism Himself in the River Jordan. (Being the Son of God, He of course didn't need to be baptized. But to emphasize its importance, He accepted baptism just the same.)

But this idea pushed by Pelagius— the idea that babies (and people in general) are naturally disposed toward goodness— got quite a bit of traction. And it's even *more* popular today in our modern society. And, one has to say, it *is* an attractive idea. Back in the 1920s, the demoralized German people really liked it when a certain rabid politician started telling them they were the "master race." And who among us nowadays wouldn't prefer to be called "good," instead of "sinful?" One must admit, it can be quite a boost for the self-esteem.

But is it true?

One day Jesus Himself had this fellow come up to Him, and who address Him as "good teacher." Now, Jesus immediately knew flattery when He heard it. And so He asked the guy why he was calling Him "good?" He added that only God is good. {Mark 10:17-18}

That may be the best rule-of-thumb we've ever had for this particular question. In other passages, Jesus makes occasional references to "good" people, as opposed to evil people. But here He makes a point to a would-be flatterer. *Only God is totally good*. And if we take an honest look at ourselves, we can see how true that is.

Deep at heart, I'm a selfish individual. I may help someone else out when I can, and I may send a few bucks to a charity now and then. But in my heart and mind, I'm usually thinking about my own goals in life. That, in itself, is no big sin. At least I don't think it is. Just about every human being, I'd say, is like that— or at least we start out like that. In other words, we are essentially selfish in our outlook. Not always, but usually. After all, it's just part of the human condition.

And that's what this issue is about. Human beings are born with all the necessary instincts for survival. A baby wants nourishment, and will cry his head off until he gets it. Certainly, that's not in itself a sin. So it stands to reason that selfishness alone is not sinful. But it is a natural trait.

Let's be honest. People are born selfish. And weak. And all those instincts ingrained in us can later work to make our lives miserable. Our appetites, our ambitions, our tendency toward hostility— all these forces, and many others, work against our conscious desire to do good.

Pelagius was wrong and Jesus was right. People need baptism, to help free us from original sin. And— I can't speak for everyone else— but I not only need baptism, but also confession, going to church regularly, and a little daily prayer to keep everything from dragging me down. If I hadn't started going to church, I doubt very seriously that I would've survived my college years.

It may be even *better* to emphasize our weakness, rather than our strengths. Pride is counted as one of the Seven Deadly Sins. (They're called "deadly" because they can lead to worse behavior, and ultimately to spiritual death.) After all, pride was the sin that led the angel Lucifer to rebel against God in the first place. How many of us ordinary humans are immune to pride?

FAITH IS MORE THAN JUST WORDS: IT'S ALSO A MATTER OF CHOOSING DIRECTION

There's another aspect to sin. As we saw in Chapter 7, God has a plan for this world, and He has a plan for each one of us individually. In other words, God has His own will. What if our own ideas don't correspond with His? There, as Shakespeare might have phrased it, is "the rub." And this is without doubt the greatest challenge of faith. Because this is where each of us must make a decision. Putting one's faith in God is more than simply a matter of words. Much more. It is actually a total commitment of one's life. It mandates a radical change in our outlook, our priorities, and our behavior.

What's going to be our main priority? Do we want to seek God and find Him? Or would we rather shunt Him off to one side and leave Him there as an afterthought— something to be considered only when it's convenient? Will we try to build our lives on God's precepts, living as He wants us to? Or— instead of putting God first— will we prefer to follow our own whims, chasing after our favorite pleasures, catering to our personal addictions? In other words, *what will we actually choose to center our lives on?*

This is the challenge we face in our relationship to God. In modern terms, we might describe it as the litmus test of faith. Are we going to put our own desires first, or live our lives within the will of God? This isn't some novel idea of my own. Jesus Himself summed up the essence of living one's faith: not in calling Him "Lord, Lord," but in *actually doing the will* of the Father. {Matthew 7:21}

NO ONE EVER SAID IT WOULD BE EASY

This is not an easy rule to live by. I remember when I was taking instructions to be a Catholic, the instructor said that one of the hardest things to do, is to say to God, "Let Your will be done, not mine." And he was right. When I pray, I want all my prayers to be answered with a yes. And I suppose just about everyone does. But the truth is unchanged. If I go against what God wants, I'm sinning like anyone else. And sooner or later, I'll have to come around.

I think that in most cases where we let sin take over, pride must be a factor. And this is where a lot of us have a problem. Our culture teaches that pride can be a positive good. Have you ever seen those bumper stickers on vehicles with the slogan, "Power of Pride"? On television, in movies, we're constantly shown that being "assertive" is the way to be. Being strong, confident and even a little pushy is presented as a good character trait.

And I'd say that there are times when this is not entirely wrong. Pride is not the same thing as courage. When you're in the right, standing your ground when threatened is not what I would call a sin. On the contrary, in a situation like that, I think it would be a sin to give in.

However, pride is real, and it shouldn't be confused with courage. If we let it take over, it can turn us into a whole different person. If someone is so sure of himself, so convinced of his own strength or perfection, that he can look himself in the eye and say there's no more room for improvement— isn't he in danger of missing something? Isn't he forgetting that without God, he would have *nothing?* And when one starts leaving God out of the equation, isn't he doing so at his own great peril?

THE PREDESTINATION FACTOR

There was another major issue in that controversy involving Pelagius. It was about the idea of predestination. When I was an agnostic, I had almost as much scorn for this concept as I did for the notion of demons. I'd been raised in a culture steeped in *rugged individualism.* How could anyone actually believe there's such a thing as predestination? (Surely, each of decides his own destiny!) Like Pelagius' doctrine of inborn human goodness, this is also an attractive idea. But again, the question is worth asking: Is it true? Or— could some aspects of our lives actually be "programmed" in advance?

Some years ago, I read an old *Reader's Digest* article about a scientific study done on sets of identical twins, some of whom had been separated soon after birth and then placed in different adoptive homes. [Source No. 35] According to the article, that study revealed some amazing things. Many of the twins had developed incredible parallels in their lives— including details which closely mirrored the lives of their siblings. Not too surprisingly, many of them had similar school records and shared the same interests as their counterparts. However, some of those separated twins had given their children the same first names. In one case, twin brothers had married women with the same first name, then eventually divorced. When they remarried, their wives again had the same first name. These brothers "both favored the same St. Petersburg, Fla., vacation beach." [35:78] This might not sound like much of a coincidence, but at the time both men were living in Ohio— in cities some 70 miles apart.

Now, neither of these men knew he even had a twin. Some of the other sets of twins were also unaware of each other's existence. And yet, there were amazing instances of duplication *in some of the smallest aspects of their lives.* That study proved one thing: There are many more factors in our psychological make-up which are genetically influenced, than had ever before been imagined. Who can predict how much more will be discovered with further research?

Genetic programming. Could it really be that (as Shakespeare said) the fault lies not in the stars, but in ourselves? If it can influence our choices of spouses and careers, what else can it determine? Certain diseases, such as cancer and Alzheimer's, are known to be genetically linked. Tendencies toward certain behaviors, such as alcoholism, have also been found to be genetically based. How many other behaviors are influenced by our genes? Can they push some people toward conventional living, and others toward criminality? Do they make some of us prone to the temptation to make weak moral decisions, but give greater strength to others? *Is genetic "programming" actually the scientific equivalent of predestination?*

This is simply a hypothesis. But now that the human genome is being mapped, how many future discoveries will illuminate the mysteries of our own genes? How many aspects of human character have yet to be identified in the vast realm of the chromosome? There's another thing to be considered: Who actually determines which genes we inherit from each parent at the moment of conception? Can that be anyone other than God Himself?

In our innermost physical being—in our very genes—the power of the Creator can be seen, just as in the infinity of the universe. St. Augustine knew nothing of genes and chromosomes. But he did know that men and women often display little control over their own lives. He called it predestination, and saw in it the will of an all-powerful God. Through the study of genetics, modern science has just begun to understand what that means.

Sin— in any guise— isn't just a concept or an abstraction, but a fact of life. In this world, with all our human drives and weaknesses, it is simply an inescapable condition that makes the goal of salvation even more challenging. Again: Pelagius was wrong, and Jesus was right.

I haven't spent years studying the philosophy and theology of sin. But like most of us, I've spent my whole adult life struggling with it. Life might be very simple, if the stereotyped Puritan idea of sexual sin were the only thing we had to worry about. But that's not what I'm talking about. I'm talking about everything—from the Commandment prohibiting murder right down to the sin of mindless anger, which can drag someone down as surely as any addiction. If someone keeps his own mind in turmoil without any purpose, what else can that be but a sin against himself? Pride might label it as a strength; but a mind trapped in chains of anger and frustration is anything but strong.

Some clichés are really true. We're all sinners. "Only God is good." Jesus Christ said so, and that's good enough for me.

I'd say that most people are honest enough to admit they have their weak points. Honesty, perhaps, is one of the great redeeming qualities that we can possess. Because if anyone is honest enough with himself to admit he's not perfect, at least then he has something to build on. If someone is too proud— or too petrified in their mind— to admit there's a God, then admitting to the existence of sin is the lesser of his problems. Like Jesus said, only the self-righteous are the ones who think they don't need any doctor. All I can say to them is, I wish them luck.

Chapter 15

A SMALL DISAGREEMENT REGARDING THE END OF THE WORLD

One of the biggest obstacles dividing Christian denominations is doctrinal disputes. One church will say that drinking, smoking or gambling to any extent is a sin. Others say such things aren't so bad, if done in moderation. One church will say that you can communicate with saints in Heaven by praying to them, and another will scorn the very idea of it.

We're all aware of such disagreements in the modern world of Christendom. And to those who aren't believers, what a jumble of confusion it must seem! No wonder some people find it so easy to reject Christianity. Many of them are already predisposed to see it in a negative light, and when they look at the state of Christianity today, they see only the things they expect to see. They feel negative toward it, and so they see only what's negative.

Perhaps the most contentious book of the New Testament is the Book of Revelation—the last book of the Bible. Unlike any other New Testament book, it's filled with symbolism, descriptions of visions, and even some arcane topics that are challenging to understand.

Its main subject is just as challenging. Because the Book of Revelation deals with the End Times— things like the Second Coming of Christ and the end of the world. This is a book unlike any other in the New Testament. And this is what makes it interesting on a number of levels.

WHAT KIND OF BOOK IS IT?

To understand the Book of Revelation, it's important to keep in mind the era when it was written. From about 200 BC to about 200 AD, there was a type of writing which was popular in literary circles. It was called apocalyptic literature. "Apocalypse" is a Greek word, meaning something like, "to uncover," or "to reveal." Apocalyptic literature dealt with hidden things, and questions such as the final triumph of God in the world, and even the very end of the world we live in. For people of faith, the Book of Genesis explained how the world began. Apocalyptic literature was written to reveal *the end of history*.

One must remember that in the first century AD, there was no New Testament as we know it. This is the time when the Gospels were being written down by the apostles— the men who had actually worked with Jesus. At the same time, some of the apostles were also writing epistles (letters) to various churches around the Mediterranean. As these Gospels and epistles were being written down, they began to circulate— often one at a time— among the Christian faithful.

However, there were also fake books being written by people who had never seen Jesus. Some of them were undoubtedly written with good intent, to help strengthen people's faith. Others may have been written simply to "cash in" on the demand for authentic writings. Among the many books (authentic and spurious) which were circulating at the time, were some apocalyptic books.

There are several examples of apocalyptic literature found in the Old Testament, in the books of Ezekiel and Daniel, for instance. Some of the apocalyptic works circulating in the first century were Jewish, and some were written for that new group of messianic Jews who came to be called Christians.

The early Church was scattered around the Mediterranean, but it was still very well organized. The bishops who were governing the Church realized that something had to be done, to separate the genuine gospels and letters from the fake ones.

Thus began a process of review and examination, which wasn't completed until about the 5th century. Eventually the New Testament took on the form that we now have. [18:72]

We have to remember, also, that during the first three centuries of Christianity, the Church was rocked by periodic persecutions. During those persecutions, vast numbers of Christian documents were confiscated and destroyed; and vast numbers of people were arrested and destroyed along with them. The process of sorting out the genuine writings was not made any easier by all this. But eventually, the Church leaders were able to clarify the issue.

After the long period of examination was finally completed, the Book of Revelation was found to be the only Christian apocalyptic book which was authentic— having been written by, or under the authority of St. John, one of the actual apostles who had been commissioned by Jesus.

VISIONS AND SYMBOLS, AND WHAT THEY MEAN

As mentioned already, back in the first century apocalyptic literature was well-known in literary circles. Scholars knew that such writings were filled with symbolism, just as modern readers know that novels are fictional. This usage of symbols to describe events was understood by those who read it. But unlike fiction, the symbols in apocalyptic literature represented realities. You might say that it was a type of literature where great truths were presented in almost a "fictional" way— using a lot of symbols and imagery to disguise the realities contained in it. For anyone not familiar with such literature, the actual meaning of it would be hidden.

There was a reason for this. In the Book of Revelation, one of the main themes is the future destruction of the Roman Empire— an event which was related triumphantly. At that time, anyone caught with literature openly describing such a scenario would be quickly and harshly dealt with. In other words, reading that kind of stuff could get you killed. With symbols, at least, one could tell the authorities that it meant something entirely different. That may have saved quite a few lives.

Many biblical scholars think the Book of Revelation was written in the mid-90s AD. This would place its authorship during the reign of an emperor named Domitian. Domitian was a very religious individual. But his religion was pagan—focused largely, in his case, on the Roman goddess Minerva. He enforced his views rigorously. When some of the Vestal Virgins were found guilty of immorality, he ordered them buried alive in accordance with ancient custom.[36:63]

When too many people in Rome began believing in a new kind of Judaism (Christianity), Domitian decided to deal with them as well. It was in his reign that a second persecution of Christians took place in the Roman Empire. The first, of course, had been under the emperor Nero some thirty years earlier. It's difficult for the modern mind to picture what a persecution was like in those times.

When Hitler ordered the genocide of Jewish people in the 20th century, the murders were carried out in secrecy. Under Nero, Christians were killed for *the entertainment of the population.* In the arena at night, many victims were tied onto elevated poles and covered with pitch— then set on fire to serve as human torches, so that the crowd could watch the others being slaughtered on the ground.[3:365 (Tacitus: Book 14)]

At heart, Domitian was no better. With his rigid paganism and disregard for human life, he sought out as many of these new "enemies of the state" as he could. Anyone refusing to sacrifice to the emperor's divinity was rounded up and accused of "atheism." Even two members of the imperial family, a Roman consul named Flavius Clemens and his wife, were executed and banished respectively. [36:63-64] In the Roman Empire, no one was safe. At that time many Christians could remember the horrors they'd suffered under Nero. There was a legend circulating which said that one day Nero would return, to persecute the Church again. When Domitian began rounding people up, it must have seemed a fulfillment of prophecy. It was with this in mind, undoubtedly, that the writer of Revelation gave us the image of the beast with the number 666.

In the 13th chapter of Revelation, a great beast is described— a beast with a mortal wound which had healed. The beast forced all men into submission, and compelled them to be numbered. In verse 18, the beast itself is given the number 666. In ancient times there was no science as we know it. But certain areas of knowledge, such as astrology, were studied with great interest. They were the "sciences" of their day. One of these areas was numerology. Putting it simply, numerology was the idea that numbers held special meaning. In some cases, things such as alphabetical letters could be assigned numbers— such as a "1" for "A." The letter "B" would have a value of "2," etc.

The writer of Revelation stated that anyone using a little ingenuity can understand the meaning of the number 666. {Revelation 13:18} The name of the emperor Nero, when written in the Hebrew alphabet, has letters whose numerical values add up to exactly 666. [1:1243 (footnote)] The symbolism is obvious. The beast whose wound had healed represented Nero himself. And now he was back— in the guise of Domitian— trying once more to destroy the people of God.

On one level, the entire Book of Revelation was written to give courage to those suffering under this second persecution. It prophesied the ultimate return of Christ in glory and the inevitable fall of Rome— described as the great whore "Babylon," which was situated on seven hills. {Revelation 14:8, 17:9} The Christians living in those dangerous times needed that encouragement. The Book of Revelation was meant to provide it. But there was far more to it, more than even the author may have anticipated.

As with the other books of the New Testament, the Catholic Church found the Book of Revelation to be divinely inspired. The Apostle John, who wrote it, was not just writing for himself, but for God. And the vivid symbols he used in that book continue to ring throughout the ages.

Revelation depicts a society where the state has regulated everything— forcing men to take numbers, and turning the government itself into a sort of dehumanizing beast. This is not exactly a situation unique to the Roman Empire. Every totalitarian regime in history has shown similarities. (Tyrants tend to behave like tyrants.) And many times, people have found themselves being persecuted for their faith. Not only for the people of the Apostle John's time, but for every generation, Revelation is like a lamp that helps illuminate a darkened world. Throughout the centuries, it has provided hope for every Christian who's been threatened because of his faith.

WHY DOES REVELATION DIVIDE SO MANY CHRISTIANS TODAY?

There are basically two ways to interpret Revelation— either literally or symbolically. And as we've seen, it was inspired to be read both ways. Not only did it give courage to those Christians who were suffering under Domitian, but its timeless messages have encouraged countless Christians of later generations.

But the western Roman Empire fell a long time ago. There are a great number of people today who don't give a hoot in hell about such "ancient history." In other words, a lot of people don't realize the original meaning of the Book of Revelation, as it was written for Christians of the first century. When some people in more recent times have read the book, they've read into the symbols a prophetic description of specific *modern* events.

As an example, one passage in Revelation explains that ten horns found on one of the great beasts represent ten kings. {Revelation 17:12} Not too many years ago, after the European Common Market was formed, the number of countries in that organization reached exactly ten. Some people started saying that those nations were the "ten kings" referred to in Revelation. This meant, of course, that the End Times must be imminent. After more countries joined the Common Market, the hoopla subsided.

As another example, we have several references in Revelation to the period of exactly 1000 years. (Another instance of the use of symbolic numbers.) Toward the end of the 1990s, quite a few people were predicting that a "Y2K" (Year 2000) disaster would cause computers and communications satellites to crash worldwide, destroying our modern technological base and thus fulfilling the "end of the world" prophecy.

This "thousand year jitters" isn't a new thing. As the year 1000 approached back in medieval Europe, some people started getting agitated, thinking that the world would end right then and there. Of course, at that time computers and satellites were not part of their concern.

But here we see the danger of trying to apply a literal interpretation of Revelation to a specific point in modern history. The Book of Revelation has probably produced more false prophets than any other portion of the Bible, even though many of them were undoubtedly sincere.

WHAT DOES THE BIBLE ACTUALLY SAY ABOUT THE END TIMES?

The Book of Revelation, of course, has much to say about the End Times. And as an inspired book, it's all true— even in its original, first century context. After all, the Roman Empire did fall. And when that happened, it must have seemed to many like the end of the world.

Jesus Himself had promised that there were some then living, who would witness the coming of the Kingdom of God. {Mark 9:1} But regarding the End Times, Jesus also cautioned His followers not to be overly enthusiastic. He warned them time and again, that false messiahs and false prophets would appear. {Mark 13:21-22} Christ understood well that people with the best of intentions could be taken in, if they allowed their hopes to run wild.

Also, in the 2nd Epistle of Peter, believers are cautioned to have patience in anticipation of the return of Christ. {Chapter

3, verses 8-9} In the Lord's eyes, we're reminded, a thousand years is as one day. Even in those early years of Christianity, it was becoming clear that the End Times are not something to be thought of as here and now. The early leaders of the Church, including St. Peter, could see that God's plan for mankind covered not just one generation but the whole expanse of history. They understood that God's people have not only a glorious past, but a vast and beautiful future. They knew that spiritual events can be distinguished from worldly events— and that Christians possess a faith which transcends worldly troubles.

Those who are baffled by the Book of Revelation love to debate about whether it should be taken literally or symbolically. But what some of these people are missing is the idea that it speaks to all generations of Christians— on *more* than just one level. Perhaps the most telling part of the Book of Revelation is the passage that foretells the aftermath of the great battle of Armageddon. It describes a new Heaven and a new Earth— not the physical destruction of the old. Instead of being a book of doom and gloom, Revelation reveals the completeness of God's triumph over the forces of evil. *In this world and the one to follow.*

Those who despise religion love to say that the Bible contradicts itself. But for anyone who isn't thinking with their blinders on, it can be seen that the Scriptures are extremely consistent. They contain truths which are meant not to demoralize people, but to sustain them.

In the last analysis, the Bible's teachings are— like Jesus Himself— not sentences of condemnation, but keys to salvation. They help us to *escape* the things that can drag us down to Hell. They offer hope and strength for all believers, of every generation and every century. And this is what inspired words from God can be expected to do.

Chapter 16

PROTESTANTS AND CATHOLICS, MORMONS AND WITNESSES

The world can be a confusing place. And nowhere is the confusion more damaging than in the sphere of faith. We have a modern world where it's generally agreed that there's one true God. Yet Christianity, Judaism and Islam all disagree on what type of God He is. We have a country where most people call themselves Christians. Yet there are numerous major churches, hundreds of smaller denominations, and thousands of different doctrines revolving around the Christian faith— many of them wildly at odds with each other.

Back when I was an agnostic, I saw all this through my adolescent eyes and shook my head in disbelief. Whenever the devil looks at it, he must be rubbing his hands with glee. How can anyone make sense out of it all? How can we even *find* true faith, when Jesus seems hidden like a needle in a haystack of conflicting views?

He gave us the answer Himself: For man, some things are impossible. But with God all things are possible. {Mark 10:27}

There are answers. Genuine truth exists. And if we look for it, we'll find it. But to do so, it may be necessary to pull away from our TV sets, quit worrying so much about our finances, and maybe even get rid of a few bad habits that can hold us back. Finding God may be a goal that has its challenges, perhaps even a few sacrifices. But I can't think of anything more important, than where I'm going to end up spending eternity. Sooner or later, each of us has an eternity waiting for us. Nobody stays around to celebrate his 500th birthday.

ONE SAVIOR, BUT TEN THOUSAND CHURCHES?

Off the top of my head, considering all the Christian churches to be found in the world, I'd say that ten thousand is as good a guess as any. The exact number is constantly changing, and really isn't that important. The important question is: How did it get to be this way?

Religious confusion is nothing new to mankind. Three thousand years ago, there were countries such as Egypt which claimed to worship a thousand gods— and they were proud of it. (In India, the Hindus may still have that many.)

The world's first successful monotheistic religion— Judaism— was far from unified. The Samaritans were practicing a separate form of Judaism centuries before the birth of Christ. Even earlier, after the First Temple was built by Solomon around 960 BC, the Jewish faith experienced numerous divisions— many of them involving relapses into worship of the pagan gods embraced by the nations bordering Israel.

As we've seen, in the years before Christ's birth, opinion was sharply divided on what type of Messiah Israel should expect— a conquering liberator who would free Jerusalem from foreign rule, or a spiritual Savior who would save men from their sins. Even after Jesus Himself revealed the answer to that question, the divisions continued. Two major revolts against Rome brought disaster for the Jewish people. (These have already been noted in Chapter 9.)

It is not my purpose here, to sum up the entire history of Christianity. How could anyone sum it up? However, since it's important to have some idea of the development of Christianity as it is today, I will try to present a very brief picture of these events. I think it's a subject that's worth a few pages.

After Jesus' death and resurrection, the Church which He established remained organized. The original apostles selected others to help bring the word to surrounding peoples. In a miraculous appearance to St. Paul (who was originally named Saul), Christ Himself commissioned him to be an apostle. Paul was without doubt the most active of them all, traveling through much of the Mediterranean region and converting countless numbers of people.

In the first years of Christianity, the new faith was simply considered a part of Judaism. Only after several decades were its followers being called "Christians." By the 2nd century, people also began referring to the Church as "catholic," a Greek word which simply means universal. In these earliest generations of Christianity, the Church remained essentially unified. As mentioned earlier, Christ had told His apostles that He had other followers whom they were unaware of {John 10:16}; but the New Testament provides no specific information on them. Some scholars think Jesus was referring to the Gentiles, who would later be accepted by the Jewish Christians. {Acts 11:1-18}

Controversies within the Church, however, started appearing early on. There was a particularly thorny issue over whether Gentile (non-Jewish) converts should have to follow traditional Jewish laws. (The first Christians in Judea were all Jews, and used to observing them.) It was finally decided that Gentile converts would not have to follow Jewish law. {Acts 15:5-20}

Aside from this, there were a few petty jealousies over leadership in the beginning, but nothing too serious. (Much of this information on the formative Church is found in the New Testament Book of Acts.) The chief of the apostles, Peter, eventually traveled to the capital of the Empire at Rome and became the bishop there. Another apostle, James, became bishop of Jerusalem. Both were later martyred for their faith.

In spite of the terrible persecutions that occurred from time to time, the Church was stable. But it was inevitable that there would be differences. One of the first serious divisions occurred when a separate group of Christians, called Gnostics, arose in the second century AD. These were basically a bunch of spiritual snobs who held that salvation comes through possession of secret knowledge, rather than by faith.

The military tyrants who ruled the Roman Empire were constantly wavering between toleration and persecution— a choice which often depended on the political climate of the moment. For some of them the very existence of the Church seemed a threat. Many of the early popes (bishops of Rome) were hunted down and killed. [Source No. 32] After having Pope Fabianus executed in the year 250, the emperor Trajanus Decius was quoted as saying, "I would far rather receive news of a rival to the throne than of another bishop in Rome." [36:157]

The persecutions pretty much ended with the reign of Constantine. As noted in Chapter 6, the Edict of Milan in 313 guaranteed religious freedom for Christians and pagans alike. From that time onward, the Church was able to grow in relative peace. However, controversies continued to spring up in the Church from time to time. Perhaps inevitably, some schisms, or divisions, occurred. The Egyptian Coptic Church refused to accept the teaching of both the divine and human natures of Christ, and broke away from the Catholic Church in the 5th century. [9:Vol. 4:519] In 1054, following a period of doctrinal disputes, the Eastern and Western churches were divided. The Eastern Church is known today as the Eastern Orthodox church (actually a number of churches). The Western Church remained unified under the authority of the popes, and continues to be known as the Catholic Church.

Other notable events were taking place. After a long period of decline, the western Roman Empire fell to Germanic invaders in the year 476. The eastern half of the Empire, centered at Constantinople, withstood Muslim assaults until 1453. Through it all, the faith established by Christ continued in strength. A number of the Muslim states established in the 7th and 8th centuries tried to extinguish it in the Middle East. But even in that region Christianity still survives, such as in the Coptic Church of Egypt.

THE EMERGENCE OF RELIGIOUS FREEDOM

It is an unsettling fact, that for *most* of human history individual freedom has not been a priority. In fact, it was usually a concept which was not even considered. Truth be told, most of man's energies were spent in conquering his fellow man, and bending the conquered to his will— *not* in respecting his rights.

The Edict of Milan, which granted religious toleration to the Roman Empire in the year 313, was not destined to be permanent. Some fifty years later, the last of the pagan emperors, called Julian the Apostate, tried again to subdue Christianity. He did not succeed. It was ancient paganism's last gasp. In the year 380, the emperor Theodosius I declared Christianity— as defined in the Nicene Creed— the official religion of the Empire. In 391 he ordered all non-Christian temples to be closed. Then it was the turn of the pagans to be suppressed. [36:272-273]

For the next thousand years, Catholic Christianity was supreme in western Europe. The faith established by a Jewish carpenter named Jesus had conquered an empire of pagan gods.

But it was a world still ruled by the sword. After Europe was overrun by tribes of Germanic barbarians, the Church at Rome sent out missionaries to convert them to Christianity. Throughout the Dark Ages, petty monarchies rose and fell. A political entity called the Holy Roman Empire, founded by Charlemagne in 800, helped to restore some stability; with that, the Dark Ages finally ended. Gradually Europe saw the birth of a number of permanent nations, such as France, Spain, and later Germany and Italy. A unified state emerged in Britain, dominated by the English. In the East, the Orthodox nation of Russia grew into a power to be reckoned with.

Western Christendom was finally a stable entity (religiously if not politically), now civilized and to a degree unified by the Catholic Church. The popes— once hunted down by pagan emperors— now governed not just the Church but some secular territory as well. The monarchs of Europe, enjoying the worldly fruits of this stability, acknowledged the authority of the Church. Medieval Europe was not what we would call a bastion of individual freedom, but by any measure it was a great improvement over the virtual anarchy of the Dark Ages.

A SECOND MAJOR SCHISM FOR CHRISTIANITY

The medieval Crusades brought many of the European monarchs together in common cause. Principalities grew into nation states. Through it all, the Catholic Church continued as a unifying force for most of Europe. But this framework of stability in the West was not destined to last.

In the early 16th century, a German priest, disgusted by what he saw as greed and corruption in the Church, openly denounced it. (The Catholic Reform— the Church's own effort at self-reform, which had started before this— had not been making much progress.) Martin Luther's defiance caught the attention of some of the German princes, who sided with him. It was, after all, an opportunity for them to gain more political independence from the popes. The wars of the Reformation which followed destroyed uncounted lives, perhaps millions. Finally the Peace of Westphalia, signed in 1648, put an end to the horrendous Thirty Years' War. From then on, western Europe would be a place where Protestant and Catholic nations could generally co-exist. Wars were still being fought, but at least with less carnage than the Reformation wars.

The Protestant Reformation wasn't intended to be a revolution in individual liberty. But the very concept of religious freedom seized men's imaginations. Dissenters were appearing everywhere, looking for a chance to say and believe whatever they wanted. In the 1640s, Puritans in England rebelled against the Anglican tyranny set up by Henry VIII and fought their way to power in a civil war. In 1649 Charles I lost his crown as well as his head, and England became briefly a republic.

Dissenters of every stripe emigrated to the British colonies in America. And here, almost unconsciously, began a new experiment— one where toleration would become not the exception but the rule. When the American Revolutionary War ended, a number of states still had official state religions. Within a few years that practice was abandoned. It was now a country where anyone could worship as he chose— something which, if not quite unprecedented in the world, was still a novel concept.

THE TURNING POINT

While the development of the religious liberty idea went on for the better part of three centuries (from the start of the Protestant Reformation to the adoption of the U.S. First Amendment in 1791), the main turning point occurred early in that process. As Martin Luther was developing an ideology to justify his stand against the Church, he realized that he was actually discarding all allegiance to the Catholic Church's authority. This, in itself, was simple enough. But it presented a serious theological problem.

The Catholic Church had been virtually the sole authority in Western Christendom since the very first generation of Christianity. The Scriptures of the New Testament hadn't even been assembled for the first few centuries. (As noted before, Jesus Himself had not written anything down.) Therefore, for all those centuries, the Catholic Church had been *the* authority. It had built a strong network of believers throughout the old Roman Empire; it had sent out missionaries to convert the barbarians; it had kept Christian civilization pretty well unified for the first thousand years, until the schism of 1054.

The problem was, when Luther renounced the authority of the Church, what was left? His own word? Was he to be a new pope? Such a claim would have seriously damaged his credibility. Luther knew better. The only real authority, he told his followers, was the Bible— the inspired word of God.

This was the great turning point in the development of religious liberty. And it was a turning point not just in theory but in actuality. Throughout the 16th century, numerous new editions of the Bible were printed in various languages. It was becoming available to the literate peoples of Europe as it had never been before. The recently-invented printing press was now helping to bring about the liberation of men's minds. And not only the minds of Protestants. At about the same time, the Catholic Church began to authorize printed copies of the Bible for the people.

In fairness, it's important to note one thing: The reason the Catholic Church had fulfilled the role of sole interpreter of the Scriptures in the first place, was so that the (mostly illiterate) populations of believers would not interpret them wrongly, or be swayed by false teachers who did. Because the Bible is the written word of God— and one of the keys to salvation— men's souls actually depended on its interpretation, as they still do. After all, anyone taken in by a heresy could find himself in serious danger of final damnation.

When we think about it, this was (and is) an extremely valid line of reasoning. Jesus Himself warned about this, when He denounced the "lawyers" of the ancient Mosaic law for their false teachings. {Luke 11:52} For all its supposed faults— including those priests who were taking money for indulgences— the Catholic Church was indeed trying to safeguard the souls of the faithful.

A VICTORY FOR FREEDOM, BUT WITH A "DOWN" SIDE

This revolution in religious diversity changed the cultural landscape of the West forever. It ensured that from then on, not only religious doctrines but political doctrines (such as monarchy itself), would be open to question. Great thinkers like Thomas Hobbes, John Locke and Jean-Jacques Rousseau analyzed the dynamics of power and blessings of liberty. In the minds of men, the seeds of a hundred revolutions had been planted.

And those revolutions came. From the revolt of Dutch provinces against Spanish rule in 1567 to the collapse of the Soviet Empire in 1991, upheavals against tyrannical regimes shook the foundations of the West. In the Middle East the aftershocks continued, with the flowering in 2011 of the Arab Spring— a cry for freedom which may be heard again in future.

For the first time in modern history, ordinary men were learning that they could acquire freedom. But, as with nearly every "good thing," a number of consequences came with it. The consequence that is of particular interest here, is the result of Martin Luther's decision regarding the Bible. The freedom to read and interpret the Bible brought with it a multiplicity of ideas, on a scale unseen before in Christianity. Suddenly anyone could come to his own conclusions about what the Scriptures meant. One of the fruits of religious freedom was doctrinal anarchy.

This explosion of contending views might be compared to the confusion of languages which struck those people who had built the Tower of Babel. {Genesis 11:5-9} Mankind had, in a sense, constructed a new edifice built on the principle of freedom of conscience. And the result— for better or worse— was a vast landscape of conflicting doctrines.

The entire history of the Western world can be seen, in one view, as a series of events destined to unchain men's minds. And this has set the foundations for our modern society.

THE RELIGIOUS LANDSCAPE OF AMERICA TODAY

We live in a country which claims to uphold individual freedom. As an American, I'm grateful to God for that. And I fully support the principle of religious freedom— without any reservations. The only "down" side is trying to sift through the confusing jumble of ideas which now exists. Would it be better to eliminate all such confusion and go back to one culture, one Church and one interpretation of Scriptures? Even if it were possible?

Never. The "cure" would be far worse than the disease. My ancestors fought in the Revolutionary War, and I cherish the Constitution and Bill of Rights. If I live to be 90 years old, I'd rather be in the front lines fighting anyone who tries to destroy them. And I *don't* mean that symbolically.

Of course, that still leaves us the challenge of sifting through all the conflicting schools of thought which freedom has generated. In today's world we have Catholics, Baptists, Orthodox, Lutherans, Mormons, Jehovah's Witnesses— and a thousand other views and voices. (This is just considering religions which count themselves Christian.) And nearly every one of them will give you a different interpretation of the End Times. This is not a statement of condescension, but fact. Once the Bible had been held out as the ultimate authority in such matters, a multitude of churches (and doctrines) was going to be the inevitable result.

Quite a few modern churches pride themselves on being Bible Christians. (Which, in principle, I would describe as a good thing.) Some of these churches have a doctrine that everything in the Bible should be taken in a *literal sense.* However, that's a little self-contradictory, because (as others have pointed out before) nowhere in the Bible does it say that. In fact, in a number of instances the Bible itself explains certain imagery which is used. {*e.g.,* Matthew 13:18- 23, and Revelation 17:9-12}

There are other factors contributing to the confusion of conflicting views. Due to the description of Armageddon— the ultimate battle between good and evil found in Revelation— a lot of false prophets have spoken up over the centuries. Every once in a while, we hear about another "end of the world" scare, such as the Y2K thing in the late 1990s. (More recently, the "prophecy in the Mayan calendar" was making money in theaters, pushing 2012 as the Big Doom Date.)

But in the actual Book of Revelation, it says only that the empire of pagan Rome (called "Babylon") would fall— nothing about the world being physically destroyed. Instead of world-wide destruction, the book describes a new Heaven and a new Earth after Armageddon.{Chapter 21, verse 1} This seems to create less of a sensation, apparently, than prophecies of destruction.

There are some who may actually prefer the "doom and gloom." When seen as entertainment, that type of thing has been lighting up screens for decades. For the Hollywood fantasy factory, it looks as if the last book of the Bible has no better purpose than to popularize disaster movies. (Apparently happy endings just don't sell as many tickets.)

THE BOTTOM LINE

Again, any way you slice it, the Bible is the written word of God— divinely inspired and without error— in the way it was intended to be read. I have no problem with that. God can move history in the direction He chooses, and He can communicate with men in any way He chooses. (After all, He is God.)

As the inspired word of God, it's obvious to any Christian that the Bible stands head and shoulders above any other literature in the world. Personally, for anyone starting on the path to faith, I would recommend a Bible in modern English, translated directly from the original languages. Not only do these newer translations benefit from knowledge gained from the study of recently discovered ancient documents (such as the Dead Sea Scrolls), but the use of modern English makes it more understandable. Also, many editions include footnotes to help explain obscure phrases.

My purpose in this chapter is definitely not to "put down" any particular church, or group of churches. I think the Mormons do a fabulous job of turning out clean-cut, clean-living young people. I can't help but respect the zeal of Jehovah's Witnesses, in reaching out to others to spread their faith. And I've always greatly admired the way the Southern Baptists stick to the moral teachings found in the Bible.

As a Catholic, of course, my allegiance is to that Church which Christ founded. The Catholic Church not only has all seven sacraments instituted by Him, but also provides the Lord's body and blood, just as He mandated. {John 6:53-57} Even if I could depart from the Catholic Church and join another, I know throughout my entire being that I could not find my salvation elsewhere.

But I also know that God didn't make us all the same. If He wanted that, He could have made us clones. But He didn't. We all have our individual journeys to make in this world. I don't expect everyone to choose the same path. But at least we can understand how there came to be so many paths. I doubt very much that all of them lead to the same destination. After all, there is such a thing as Hell. But we— as individuals— have to find out for ourselves. Each of us still has that precious gift called free will.

That's part of the challenge of being a Christian in today's world. We can't let conflicting views discourage us. We can't just give in to confusion and quit— the stakes are too high. Nothing can be more important than our eternal salvation.

But using our intelligence that God gave us, we can find the answers. The Lord Himself said it: If we seek, we will find. And once we find the faith to trust Him, nothing can keep us from our goal.

Chapter 17

DARWINISM VS. CREATIONIONISM

I get a kick, sometimes, seeing those little metal thingamajigs on the backs of cars that show a Christian fish symbol with feet, with the word "Darwin" on it. Their message is simple. These smug sophisticates are telling anyone who'll listen that Christianity is "disproved" by Evolution. In other words, it's one of those little symbols of atheism which those true believers (in non-belief) love so much.

Not only that, but it's a nifty little reinforcement patch for their blinders.

Evolution is, of course, the theory proposed in the 1850s by Charles Darwin and Alfred Russel Wallace. This theory teaches that species change over time by a process of natural selection. Simply stated, creatures having characteristics which give them an advantage in the struggle for survival tend to pass those characteristics on to offspring. Creatures which are not so successful in surviving don't have as many offspring. So, by natural selection, even entire species (which fail to compete) can go extinct. Other species improve over time, and occasionally one will transform into an entirely new species. This would explain the fossils of primeval birds resembling small dinosaurs, and of ancestral whales which were obviously land animals.

Militant atheists love the Theory of Evolution, because they like to think it disproves the Bible, and (by implication) even the existence of God. More than that, they think it makes them superior to anyone who believes in God, by virtue of their scientific minds. To their thinking, anyone who believes in the Bible is mired in primitive superstition.

There are a number of flaws in that type of thinking, but the biggest flaw is this: The Theory of Evolution doesn't disprove God, or the Bible, or Christianity or Judaism for that matter. All it does is provide a serious stumbling block for those who subscribe to the doctrine that every word in the Bible must be taken literally— a doctrine which (as mentioned before) is stated nowhere in the Bible.

But this is a legitimate issue. I know. Because years ago, when I sat in catechism class back at Sacred Heart Church in Pomona, the first question I asked was about the Catholic Church's views on the Theory of Evolution. I had read scads of materials on paleontology and anthropology, and so I'd already accepted evolution as a scientific fact. But at the time, the issue was still murky enough that the class instructor had to go ask a priest who knew about the subject. The answer he came back with was quite interesting.

He found out that the Church held that Catholics could accept creationism, or Darwin's Theory of Evolution, or both. The basic position was, that the creation of the human soul was a separate and distinct event from the creation of the human body. In other words, from a religious standpoint, it was the creation of the *soul* that actually counts. Later, I found that this was outlined as a Catholic teaching in 1950 by Pope Pius XII, in the encyclical *Humani Generis.* In 1996 the late Pope Saint John Paul II went even further. He officially stated that evolutionary theory is more than just a hypothesis; in other words, the Catholic Church accepts it as valid.

It made perfect sense to me, and it still does. God is still God. He could create this world— and all the living things in it— in any way He saw fit.

Maybe it's true that man's distant forerunners were australopithecine apes. From the fossil record, it's quite evident that at least four or five million years of evolution *did* precede the appearance of the modern human form. But when God the

Father placed the spark of humanity in one of those early humans and give him a rational soul, *that* was the actual creation of man. That was the decisive moment in prehistory when man became more than an animal.

Basically, the atheists who use Darwin as a bludgeon against Christians are stumbling into the same error that those 17th century churchmen did, when they used the Book of Genesis as a bludgeon against Galileo. These people are mixing up science and religion.

And— more to the point— they're grasping at straws. Do they actually think they can do any harm to a faith that's withstood centuries of persecutions and wars, simply by touting a scientific theory that isn't even proved? And which (because of the fragmentary fossil record) can never really *be* proved?

But this is just one of many flaws in the atheist mentality. It's understandable that these people would have to grasp at any straws available. The great revealed religions have miracles, saints and thousands of years of history to support their teachings. What does atheism have? Madalyn Murray O'Hair and her martyrdom over a pile of gold? A few droning "intellectuals" whose only real goal is to make a pile of their own, by writing books contrived to kill other people's faith?

No wonder Darwin is so important to these people. He handed them what they thought was a victory. But the only thing really proved by Evolution, is that the workings of God are so far beyond human comprehension that it took five millennia of history before men could even *begin to understand* this aspect of creation.

What modern science reveals is a God who spans *eons of creation,* not the pathetic 5,600 years estimated by Bishop Ussher.[22] Who could have guessed in the 17th century that the Earth was formed more than four billion years ago? At the time Genesis was written, who could've possibly known that countless extinct species preceded man? (When the ancient Greeks found

---

[22] James Ussher — (1581-1656) Anglican bishop who asserted, after calculating the estimated time spans of generations listed in the Book of Genesis, that the world was created in 4004 BC. For a time he also served as archbishop of Armagh, in northern Ireland. [9:Vol. 12:214-215]

oversized fossil bones in the soil they thought they were the remains of mythical giants, and enshrined some of them in their pagan temples.)

The way I see it, every Christian should thank God that Darwin opened our eyes to the infinite scope of our Creator. Because of his and Wallace's Theory of Evolution— and the countless scientific discoveries since it was published in 1859— we now have a view of God's creation that was never dreamed of. In the Old Testament, the Book of Job shows us a God who laid the foundations of the Earth and set the very stars in place. {Job 38:4-8, 31-33} Three thousand years later, thanks to the discoveries of men like Galileo and Darwin, we can more fully appreciate the truly inspired nature of that book.

Chapter 18

THE CHALLENGE OF TRUTH

"Truth" is an interesting word. It's one of those words which seem to generate their own sense of reverence. Like "freedom," or "destiny." Somehow, we all have a certain sense about truth. There's something special about it. It's a sense which seems to be naturally ingrained in us. Like love, like friendship, truth is something that we all need in our lives. Because without it, there's something very much like chaos. Without any truth, life seems to lose some of its purpose, some of its meaning.

Often, we have a tendency to correct an error if we see it or hear it. The rational mind seems to have a natural intolerance for errors. It's as if we're recoiling against chaos. Most of us don't like it when something is "wrong." We like things to be *right*— as they should be. Truth, it seems, is one of those attributes which God has placed within us, which we cannot really live comfortably without. The ancient Egyptians had a great reverence for this sense of rightness and order. They called it Ma'at, personified it as a goddess, and saw it basically as the foundation of all civilization.

But, realizing that the quality of truth is so crucial, how do we go about seeking it? How can we see past all the layers of commercialism, political posturing, shallow entertainment, etc., to get to the core of it? How can we find *real* truths nowadays? How can we even discern them from the clever deceptions all around, which are masquerading as truth?

One thing is certain: In today's world, it won't be all that easy.

We live in a society that's not geared towards truth. In Chapter 8 we glimpsed the enormity of the challenge. We have a political structure where the Congress is strongly influenced by Big Business. We have an entertainment media which constantly blurs the lines between clean living and immoral lifestyles. We have an incredibly wealthy country, where thousands of homeless people are living on the streets. And the contradictions don't end there.

Even in the churches we can find confusion. There are countless different churches and synagogues, with countless different doctrines. Once we start looking for truth in this society, we find a thousand different sources claiming to give us the truth!

FINDING A TRUE PERSPECTIVE

As we've seen, Jesus Himself described Satan as "the prince of this world." Christ knew very well that this world is the devil's playground. He knew that the devil isn't going to make salvation easy for us. After all, Satan has his own agenda. He wants our souls, and he wants to torture us for all eternity. But we can't forget one thing: God is far more powerful than any angel—especially the angel of evil. When we have God's help, we can overcome anything. As Jesus said, for Him, all is possible. {Matthew 19:26}

It's important that we look around us and see the obstacles. For one thing, there's the entertainment media. We have an entity here, that wants to consume every possible bit of our thinking. If the cable and satellite TV industry had their way, we wouldn't do anything else except watch that tube every hour of the day. And why not? This is what they get paid for. They charge the corporations vast sums of money to advertise their products. Then they charge the public for the privilege of watching those wonderful commercials. For the entertainment industry, it's a "win-win" situation— and it's all about the money.

I'd say one of the best things anyone can do for himself is to drop cable TV. Instead of keeping the magic box on during every waking moment, we can actually spend some of those waking moments thinking. This doesn't mean we have to live without entertainment. When we feel like sitting back and watching something, there are countless movies and TV shows on disc. (When you think about it, videos are to television what methadone is to heroin. They help us to "kick the habit.")

By dropping cable, we're not only saving forty to a hundred bucks a month, but we're no longer a slave to our TV sets. Those things are no longer commanding our attention during most of our free time. They're no longer saturating our brains with garbage and commercials. We're actually achieving a whole new level of freedom. There is simply no substitute for a peaceful mind. And don't forget— a peaceful mind is a mind that's capable of thinking.

If you have the courage to drop cable or satellite, you will receive numerous ads trying to get you back on the drug. You'll probably receive calls from cable and satellite TV advertisers. Cable guys may knock on your door, asking why you don't still subscribe. (This has actually happened to me several times.) They'll have innumerable smiles on their faces. They'll offer countless *fabulous* deals.

But the goal is still the same— to get you back on the drug, and get those dollars flowing back into their companies. For them, that's the bottom line. Cable TV producers don't care what kind of trash they're offering. They don't care how raunchy it is, or how many kids are watching. All they want are those bucks. Do you think those companies are serving God? If not, then whom are they serving? Think about it.

Another thing you can do is spend less time on the Internet. Now, the Internet is like TV, but without any boundaries. The garbage you see on TV is nothing compared to the sewage available on the Internet. In some ways, the Internet offers more fantasy than television. With a Facebook account, you can have instant celebrity status. Now you can present yourself to the world. And you can write your own "résumé" as a human being. What can be more wonderful? From what I've heard, you can meet new people and make new friends with a Facebook account. But it's worth asking a question: Is it real? Are you really "meeting" people? Are you really making friends? Or is it all basically an electronic illusion? How much *reality* are we getting from our computers?

If you've been using drugs or alcohol to feel good, by now you've probably realized they're not the answer. No drug is going to bring you reality, any more than that TV or computer is reality. If you have to go to rehab, it's worth it.

Another thing is attitude. I've mentioned negativity before. You've got to stay self-aware. You can't let negativity creep too far into your thinking. It can drag you down farther and faster than almost anything else.

FINDING GOD — THE GREATEST TRUTH OF ALL

There's one thing we have to understand: Many of the people around us are just as isolated and confused as we are. (Or were.) A lot of people don't spend any time at all thinking about the truth. Some are so immersed in the electronic fantasy universe, they don't even care.

When you're looking for God, and for truth, you cannot depend much on others to help you find answers. You've got to maintain your own focus and stay on course. You need to identify those things that hold you back. Then you have to modify your life to break away from those things. You've got to free yourself from the chains that drag you down. But just eliminating those chains isn't enough.

Try looking at life as an ocean. Even if nothing is dragging you down to the bottom, you can still be bobbing on the surface like a cork, with the truth nothing but a distant island. That island is the goal. In this vast ocean we call life, we want to be standing on solid ground.

The greatest step is realizing God is there. The next step is far easier. You have to open up communications to Him. God's not going to force you to find Him. But He's not going to ignore you, either. Once you start communicating with God— praying to Him— He *will* be listening to you. And this is an astounding thing. Our own words, coming from the heart, actually cut through the clouds and rise far above the sky.

Once you realize that God is there, you possess a whole new universe of reality. You know there's a God who will hear you, a God who will listen to you, *a God who will help you.* There is simply no other step greater than prayer. Maybe it sounds like a cliché; but with prayer, you have a weapon more powerful than all the illusions this world can throw at you. And this weapon will work in *your favor.*

The moments we spend praying every day are extremely important to our growth. Not only does prayer center our mind on God, but it helps to clear our minds of all the things that drag us down. And once we're communicating with Him, we can begin to see how He responds in our lives.

In everyday life, we've got to realize two things. First, the world is full of illusions and false distractions. But secondly, the truth is actually out there.

WHERE TO LOOK

Truth is an interesting thing. We don't see huge amounts of it in this world. But when someone sees the truth, they'll usually recognize it. It's important to use common sense. You have to realize that this world is not geared toward truth. If you look at what the media has to offer, you will find tons of propaganda. (For a memory refresher, you can just do a quick re-read of Chapter 2.)

Another thing can save you years of wasted time. Both Judaism and Christianity recognize that a Messiah from God will save mankind. Christians accept Jesus as the Messiah, and there have been innumerable miracles to prove it. We have a solid, reliable record of His actions in the Gospels of the New Testament. They aren't biographies in the modern sense, but they were written by eyewitnesses and they tell us a lot. We have to remember, Jesus never sat down and wrote out the New Testament. What He did do, was establish a Church.

Christianity is a faith characterized by communities. Christians have been meeting together in groups since Christ was preaching in Judea. The historical record shows that some modern churches are directly descended from those original groups. And the meaning of this is clear. At least some of the churches we see nowadays still have the Spirit that Christ originally gave to His people. The Son of God didn't bring that, just to let it vanish from the Earth. {Matthew 28:20}

If you are looking for the truth, I'd say the best thing you can do is to attend church. You might even try a number of different churches. (That's what I did, after the discovery of God's existence demolished my agnosticism.)

You should keep something in mind: You're not an idiot. God gave you a brain, and a mind to go with it. In time, you'll be able to see what's wrong about a church— or what's right about it.

A VERY COMMON OBSTACLE

Going to church for the first time is something like the first day of school. It's not like waking up every day in the same room, and walking through the familiar surroundings of your home. A new environment— by its very definition— is not going to be part of your "comfort zone." So, whether we want to admit it or not, there's going to be a little bit of apprehension, a little bit of fear. It's natural, understandable and excusable.

I'd say the greatest danger is pride. Americans are saturated from birth with the notion that we are self-reliant individuals. We're supposed to be able to take on any adversity, deal with any enemy, prevail over any challenge. We're not supposed to need any help for any of this. We're all tough, strong and ornery.

Of course, the truth is that that's a lot of bull. But that's how many people think of themselves. I'm not totally immune. Pride is a drug that we've all sampled. Before we actually find the courage to walk into church, we've got to overcome the self-destructive notion that we don't need it. The more isolated we are from others, the more we need to make contact with them. Not just socially but emotionally as well. Those TV shows and computer games just aren't going to fill the void for us. We really do need to associate with people.

Now, there are clubs and societies, fraternities and sororities. There are any number of places where we can socialize with people. But how many places can bring God into the picture? If we're attending meetings of a veterans organization, are we there to enjoy drinking ourselves under the table? If we're attending meetings of a philatelic society, are we going just to share in the veneration of postage stamps? How much good are other organizations actually doing for us? How much are they actually contributing to our emotional and spiritual growth?

Don't forget, once you've discovered that God is there, you have to know that He is the cornerstone of our existence. Everything good comes from Him. And the better we get to know Him and what He wants for us, the better off we are for all eternity.

One of the great challenges of life is living up to our ideals. One of the greatest goals in life is being the kind of person we really want to be. And this is where the truth becomes critical for us. Our minds and our souls hunger for it. Without it, we're living a life that lacks meaning and purpose. Without it, we're living a lie.

Once we realize that God does exist, then we have to acknowledge that He is the greatest truth. Not only as creator but as intercessor in the world's workings, God *has* to be the ultimate truth and the ultimate meaning of life itself. If He isn't, then what is? Our own goals and desires? Our own appetites? Our own whims?

We might view the human mind as a collection of thoughts and ideas, built on a framework of primitive instincts which have been, as they say, "hard-wired" into our brains for millions of years. Sometimes those instincts can control us. But the strength we derive from God changes everything. Once we have His help— once we've freed ourselves from the chains that drag us down— we can be the type of person that we really want to be.

The challenge is not in finding the truth, but in keeping after it. The challenge is in breaking loose from the chains we've forged in our lives, and not letting them drag us down again. Pride and fear can be the strongest of chains. But when you think about it, what is there to fear? By going to a church of your choice, won't you be pleasing God? He's going to reward you for it!

Will your friends laugh at you for going to church? If they did, would they actually be your friends? Or is it possible that we'll harm our own self-image? By going to church, will we be admitting to ourselves we're not the most important person in our universe? Will it be a sign of "weakness?" Would it be an admission that we actually need help? Is it something we might want to keep from our friends?

Just where is the greatest weakness in that kind of thinking? Having those petty fears in the first place (we all have them), or in letting them control us? Only someone with courage tries to climb a mountain. It takes a lot more strength to look for God— carrying all our human failings with us— than to avoid Him.

Don't focus on the things that hold you back. Focus on the strengths that you'll be developing. Focus on the courage, the intelligence of your decision, and the countless rewards. Going to church may take an hour or so of your time each week. But the emotional and spiritual rewards will be now. And the other rewards will be forever.

Chapter 19

A QUESTION OF PROOF

The Scientific Age — the child of the age of the Enlightenment — this is the era we live in. This is the ethos which has provided us with countless modern conveniences, vastly improved our medical standards, and enabled us to enjoy longer life spans. We are living now in a world that our ancestors could only dream of.

Our modern world has, in a way, conditioned us to put our faith in the seemingly boundless capacities of the human mind. Samuel Morse, Alexander Graham Bell and Thomas Edison brought us into the electronic age. Henry Ford "put the nation on wheels." Albert Einstein opened up the mysteries of the atom. In a sense, we're living in an age of miracles. But the miracles we see around us every day are man-made. Where are the miracles we would expect to see from God?

For anyone who has the honesty to look past the blinders, they are there.

It's a funny thing about those blinders. Some people cling to them as if they were the most important thing in the world. Some people are afraid to even talk about genuine God-made miracles. They'll refuse to look at one, even if it's shoved under their nose.

Let's be honest about this: What can be more self-defeating, than stubbornly shutting out anything which contradicts our own preconceived notions? What can be more self-limiting, than putting our own mind in shackles and chains?

People who close their minds to God are denying themselves the chance of drinking from a well of infinite depth. By telling themselves there's no such thing, they're building the framework for a fantasy universe which conforms to their own tunnel vision. They are imprisoning themselves in chains of disbelief which sink them into an ocean of ignorance. Far worse, they're locking their life's compass onto a heading which can drag them down to Hell.

"But a fantasy universe without any God— if it suits our purposes and fulfills our earthly needs— must be just as good as His universe, right? After all, if we're making ourselves into our own god, how can we be wrong?" Ultimately, each of us will find out the answer to that question. No amount of denial can prevent anyone from ultimately meeting their Maker face to face. You might as well try to deny the existence of the IRS in order to avoid paying taxes.

Fortunately, most people have enough common sense to take a look at serious proof. (That's what makes the jury system possible.) There will never be enough cynicism, or enough propaganda in our culture to get the majority of Americans to shackle themselves with blinders. Narrow-mindedness may indeed be rampant in our society; but, thank God, most people know it when they see it.

THE THING ABOUT PROOF

Some of us living in the 21st century may be a little smug about such modern concepts as "proof." Some people tend to think that everyone who lived in earlier generations were intellectual Neanderthals. However, the idea of concrete, verifiable evidence was not invented yesterday.

The hunger for proof of God's reality has been with mankind from the beginning. In the medieval era in Europe, the popularity of relics and other miraculous objects reached a level which many of us moderns would call superstition.

Jesus Himself remarked on this hunger for proof of God. He was disgusted with the worldliness and complacency of the religious establishment of His time. Even while He was teaching around the region and working miracles left and right, some people in power wanted more. They demanded a spectacular "sign from God" to prove that the Messiah had appeared.

Jesus had nothing but contempt for that "evil and unfaithful age," where hypocrisy and cynicism ruled. He said no such sign would be given them— except the sign of Jonah. (Jonah was the ancient prophet who had survived for three days in the belly of a whale.) Christ was referring, of course, to His own impending death on the Cross, and the days preceding His Resurrection. {Matthew 12:38-40}

Thank God, three hundred years of persecutions in the Roman Empire forged a Church filled with people who had faith enough to put their lives on the line for God. By our current standards of material progress, the centuries we call the Dark Ages and medieval period may have been backward. But measured by the yardstick of faith, they were a vast improvement over what had preceded them.

Instead of a pagan world which delighted in watching men slaughter each other in the arena, there was a Christian society which trusted in God— even when a "nobody" like Joan of Arc showed up to save her country. I would definitely call that an improvement. In other words, the evil and unfaithful age in which Jesus appeared had been transformed. It had become a world where true faith exists in a true God. It had become a world where God *is willing* to give us great signs.

A COUPLE OF OTHER BLINDERS TO DISCARD

There's another blinder which too many people wear. It's been discussed already. This is the idea that since the Bible was written, God has somehow wandered off to take a spectator's seat for the events of this world. In other words, the deistic way of thinking. Unfortunately, there are a lot of people— good, faithful Christians among them— who cling to the notion that "if it's not found in the Bible, it can't/didn't/never will happen." This is a terrible error, and a type of constricted thinking which no believer should stumble into.

The Bible itself makes this clear. In the very last paragraph of the Gospel of John, it's stated that if everything Jesus did could be written down, it's doubtful that there would be enough room in the world to hold all the books! *The New Testament itself is telling us that no single book could record it all.* And if the Bible doesn't tell us everything done by the Son of God over three years, how can it possibly describe the totality of God the Father? Right here in this passage, we're told that there is infinitely more. And this makes sense. How could the God who created mankind— along with the entire universe— be summed up in the pages of *any* book? How could anyone comprehend it all, much less reduce it to writing?

Yet there are some Christians who will deliberately *ignore* miraculous events which have taken place in recent times. Some of them will actually scoff at the idea that God has worked such miracles. This last blinder I'm referring to here, is that most treasured commodity called religious bigotry. Some people value it highly; and I admit, I'm not totally immune.

One reason I became a Catholic is because the modern Catholic Church is directly descended from the original Church founded by Christ. This isn't a statement of religious fervor. It's simply a fact of history. I'm not going to go into some spiel about all the reasons I'm glad I'm Catholic; I'm only going to write one book here. But I'm fully aware that there are some people who actually build their faith— even their Christian faith— at least partly on their animosity toward the Catholic Church. This is tragic, because hatred between Christians violates just about everything Christ taught. He stated that He wanted His followers to be one. But hatred is evidently such a basic human need, that this particular aspect of Christ's teaching is sometimes disregarded.

However, if you actually want proof of God and His existence, you might consider suspending any such bigoted thinking at least long enough to read this chapter. Because— like it or not— some of the strongest proofs we have are found in the annals of the Roman Catholic Church.

FATIMA

The astounding events at Fatima, Portugal, have already been discussed briefly in Chapter 12. Over the last 100 years, no modern supernatural phenomenon has received more attention than Fatima.

With accuracy, one can say that much of 20th century history was laid out in advance for those three shepherd children. The Virgin didn't just show them a vision of Hell. She told those kids that the First World War was going to end. (It did the following year.) She told them that if people didn't turn away from their crimes, a worse war would follow. (Most of us have heard about World War II.) And— most astonishingly— she warned the children of the danger that Russia would "spread her errors throughout the world, causing wars and persecutions of the Church." These warnings were given on July 13, 1917, almost four months *before* the Bolsheviks seized power in Russia. [11:179]

That wasn't all. Of the three children to whom she appeared, the Virgin said that two of them would die in the near future and go to Heaven. [11:194] Both Jacinta and Francisco Marto, the two who were named, died a few years later. (The oldest child, Lucia dos Santos, lived until 2005.)

Perhaps the most stunning aspect of the Fatima apparitions was the public miracle which the Virgin had promised in advance of her last appearance. [11:178] It was on that occasion— October 13, 1917— that something happened which no one had foreseen. Thousands of people present reported the same thing: The sun, now turned silver, was described as bright as ever, but it could be observed directly without harm to the eyes. [30:148] Then it began to "dance" in the sky, darting from one location to another at "sickening speed," giving off numerous bright streams of colored light, astounding and terrifying those who were present. A great number of people— including many who'd been skeptical— spontaneously fell on their knees and began praying.

Finally the sun appeared to plunge earthward, toward the crowd. Witnesses reported that the air became warmer, and they expected everything on the ground to burst into flames. Many in the crowd thought it was literally the end of the world. All this continued for perhaps ten minutes, before it returned to its usual place in the sky and resumed its normal appearance.

Left to right: Lucia dos Santos, Francisco and Jacinta Marto, c. 1917

This was the type of "sign" that the Jewish leaders never received from Jesus. But nearly nineteen centuries later, His mother fulfilled her promise given in July. With her hosting the event, God gave the world a miracle that would never be forgotten.

The event was reported in the Portuguese press. With Europe engulfed in war, the rest of the world took little notice. *But there it is— a publicly attested miracle with many thousands of eyewitnesses.*

The miracle of the sun, the prophecies regarding Russia and World War II— these are well-documented events that defy all cynicism. The Virgin also predicted a strange light in the sky, which would be a warning if a new war was to come. [11:179] And in fact, an astonishing aurora borealis appeared over Europe on the night of January 25, 1938. The night sky was so bright red that firemen from England to Switzerland were rushing to put out non-existent fires. [21:693] Hitler seized Austria just weeks later, and invaded Poland the following year.

Spectacular as it was, the miracle in Portugal is not unique in history. The God of Creation has worked amazing miracles on other occasions as well— miracles for all the world to see.

LOURDES

The miracle of Lourdes is almost in a class by itself. It's a phenomenon that we might compare to the Moon landings of the 1960s and '70s. It was (and is) an event so sensational, so well-documented, so huge in its scope and in its constancy, that its tremendous meaning has been almost obliterated by its own fame. The original miracle of Lourdes, and the miracles that continue to be generated from that source, are so well-known that many people simply read about them and yawn. It's like saying, "Yes, men landed on the Moon. What's the big deal?" For many, it's just as easy to say, "Sure, miracles happen all the time at Lourdes. So what?"

But being jaded isn't the same as being wise. For those of us who aren't so wrapped up in our own "coolness," it's worth a few minutes to look at Lourdes— and what this ongoing miracle means for the world.

A CHILD OF POVERTY IN RURAL FRANCE

Marie Bernarde Soubirous (known to everyone as Bernadette) was an unremarkable 14 year-old girl living in the village of Lourdes, in the foothills of the Pyrenees Mountains of southern France. Her family was dirt poor. Her father was often unemployed. After being evicted from their rented lodgings, they were given a place to stay in a former jail, by a cousin who had leased the building. The Soubirous family occupied a dingy room which overlooked an area filled with trash and poultry droppings. [8:44-45]

On Thursday, February 11, 1858, while by a river gathering animal bones to sell, accompanied by one of her sisters and a friend, she heard a loud rustling near a local grotto. The sounds were coming from a hedge, and when Bernadette looked up she saw a white form, in the shape of a "young girl." Taken by surprise, Bernadette knelt down and spontaneously began to pray. The mysterious lady smiled at her, then "disappeared" into the grotto. At that moment, her two companions appeared on the other side of the river. When asked by Bernadette, they said they hadn't seen anything.

After church the following Sunday, Bernadette returned to the grotto and again saw the mysterious lady. She was later described as being about the same age as Bernadette. A newspaper quoted Bernadette as saying the Lady was attired in a white dress with a blue sash, wearing yellow shoes. [8:52] On her arm she carried a rosary. On this second occasion (February 14) Bernadette said she intended to ask the Lady if she was there "on behalf of God or on behalf of the devil," but the apparition vanished before she could question her.

Bernadette, of course, could not keep these unusual events to herself. Confiding at first to her family, she was told that it must have been a "dream," or an illusion. When she later told some of the nuns at the local hospice of her encounter, they also called it an illusion. [8:47-48] But word began to get around.

On Thursday the 18th, Bernadette returned again to the grotto, accompanied by a local Lourdes resident, a Madame Millet, and the latter's assistant. This time, the Lady of the apparition instructed Bernadette to return every morning for the next two weeks. Bernadette followed her request to the letter. Soon she was being accompanied on her visits to the grotto by crowds of more than five hundred people. By this time it was being speculated by many that the mysterious figure in white could be the Holy Virgin herself— the Lady of the Rosary. The Lady also requested that a chapel be built where all this was taking place.

The crowds grew, and so did the curiosity of the populace. One of the local priests instructed Bernadette to ask the mysterious Lady her name. He also asked for a minor public miracle— that a rose bush be made to bloom. When the girl put these requests to the Lady, she only smiled.

Many of the people observing these events were awed by the composure of Bernadette while she was communicating with the apparition. She appeared to enter a condition of ecstasy, her body not moving as her gaze was fastened on the Lady in white. When she did move, as in making the sign of the Cross, she was described as doing so "with vivacity or grace." [8:50]

On the visit of February 25th, something unique happened. During the apparition, Bernadette was observed crawling on her hands and knees to the back of the grotto. While there, she dug into the ground with her hands. Uncovering some water, she drank some of it and put more on her face. The water was muddy, but the girl seemed to take no notice. Bernadette later explained that the Lady had instructed her to dig there, and to drink the water she would find. That same day, some people dug further in that spot and uncovered a spring. They collected some bottles of water and took them home. Within a week, miraculous cures were being reported from the waters of the spring.

By March 4th, the last day of the stipulated fortnight, Bernadette was accompanied by a crowd which was estimated to be anywhere from five to twenty thousand people. Reporters were present from major newspapers. The crowds were reported to be unruly and some of the people impatient and even hostile. One notable event occurred on March 4. On leaving the grotto, Bernadette spontaneously embraced a young girl named Eugenie Troy, who was from the town of Bareges. The girl was partially blind. After the hug from Bernadette, it was reported that the girl's sight had been restored.

This, and claims of other miraculous healings, brought a stream of people to the Soubirous household. Many thought that Bernadette was a living saint and wanted to speak to her, and ask her to touch their rosaries. Someone accused the Soubirous family of charging each visitor fifteen centimes for the privilege of speaking with their daughter. Bernadette denied every such accusation. Nothing, she said, had been accepted from any of the visitors.

Before long the events of Lourdes became national news throughout France and were being reported elsewhere in Europe. The spring uncovered in the grotto was an established fact, and the many cures being reported were impossible to ignore. But one question had not been answered, and it was the most critical of all: Who was the mysterious Lady of the apparition? In spite of everything that had happened— in spite of every speculation— her identity had not been established. This was a type of unanswered question which could cause confusion in people's minds.

On March 25th, that question was answered. It was a Catholic holy day, the Feast of the Annunciation. Bernadette Soubirous returned to the grotto. It was very early in the morning and so relatively few people were present, around twenty or less. Bernadette knelt and gazed ahead. The Lady was there to greet her. Afterward, the girl reported what had taken place. She had asked the Lady several times, to have the kindness to tell her who she was. At first, the Lady in white only smiled as before. Then she opened her hands, clasped them to herself and said, "I am the Immaculate Conception." Bernadette was not familiar with the term. She had to keep repeating it to herself in order to memorize it.

The phrase, of course, refers to the Catholic doctrine that Christ's mother was given the unique grace of being conceived without any stain of original sin. This is actually an article of faith in the Church which had been officially defined just three years earlier by Pope Pius IX— an event of which Bernadette was apparently unaware.

Bernadette Soubirous, c. 1858

MIRACLES WITHOUT END

The great significance of Lourdes is not that another appearance of the Virgin Mary took place. The true meaning of Lourdes is found in the countless reports of miracles— of people being healed by the waters of the grotto. Some of these have been substantiated by expert medical testimony.

To this day, huge numbers of people travel to Lourdes to seek healing. Not everyone comes away with their health restored. But many do. Once, when I attended Mass at a church in northern California, a visiting Lourdes priest invited anyone in need of healing to line up outside for a blessing. At the time, I had a painful protrusion on the outside of my right foot. I lined up outside the church for the blessing. Within three weeks the pain left. It has never hurt like that again.

This is the type of proof that many people ask for— then often ignore— when questioning the existence of God. An event took place in modern times, an event which is well-documented and attested by huge numbers of witnesses. The spring discovered by Bernadette still exists, offering hope and healing to thousands. Even today, uncounted miracles occur there every year. Many are well documented. All anyone has to do for proof is open their eyes and have the guts to see.

An episcopal commission was established to investigate the events of Lourdes. This was not unusual, as many apparitions are reported which are later shown to be false. Bernadette testified twice before the commission. On January 18, 1862, the local bishop published a letter declaring the Lourdes apparitions to be worthy of attention by the Catholic faithful. Four years after this, Bernadette Soubirous entered a religious order and lived there the remainder of her life. [8:66] She died in 1879 at the age of 35. On December 8, 1933, she was canonized as a saint by the Roman Catholic Church.

There's one thing more to say. For those who scoff at religion and miracles and the idea of saints, I would recommend taking a look at the contemporary photo of Bernadette Soubirous which is shown in this chapter. In this photograph, taken in the late 1850s, we see the face of a girl who was born and raised in crushing poverty. But in her eyes is a look which shows an extreme disregard for this world and everything in it. In her eyes is a look of strength approaching steel.

Her entire family was living in poverty. They had known no other life. Still, she was selected by God to hear the messages transmitted by the mother of His Son. Not only that, she was His instrument to bring a literal fountain of miracles to those who believe.

Even for someone skeptical of saints, Bernadette Soubirous can be a splash of reality. When we see this photo of that young girl who lived so long ago, it can tell us more than any chapter of any book. We can actually see the face of someone who has been there. It's as if— once she had spoken with the Mother of God— nothing in this world was of any further importance. Looking into her eyes in this photograph, anyone can see it.

In a world hungering for "signs," it's not surprising that one of the priests at Lourdes would ask for a miracle. When she heard of his request for a rose bush to bloom, the Virgin simply smiled. But perhaps that was because she had no wish to repeat the same miracle a second time.

GUADALUPE

In Chapter 6, we glimpsed the Aztec Empire of human sacrifice and its downfall. But what happened afterward was far more momentous. Because, while the fall of the Aztec Empire was a storm of death and destruction, what followed was like the morning of the Resurrection.

The year was 1531. Just ten years earlier the empire of Montezuma had experienced the final convulsions of its death agony, as Spanish forces took Tenochtitlan. During the following decade Mexico underwent a transformation— from a blood-soaked empire ruled by Aztec tyranny into a Spanish province ruled by European tyranny. That first decade was especially difficult. A powerful governing official, Don Nune de Guzman, dominated the country. He had no compassion for the Indians, regarding them as sub-human beings without souls, which justified every form of exploitation. The new rulers thought nothing of using torture and murder to keep the people subjugated. [46:21]

But there were also forces for good at work in Mexico. Being a devoutly Catholic monarch, the Spanish king (who was also Holy Roman Emperor Charles V) had sent over many missionaries. Under the first Bishop of Mexico, Juan Zumarraga, schools were set up to teach the native people European styles of farming. Great efforts were made, as well, to free them from the bonds of the old pagan religion.

Bishop Zumarraga and the tyrant Guzman were natural enemies. The former wanted to help the Indians with spiritual and educational development. The latter wanted only to keep them in their miserable and degraded state, which made it easier to exploit them. The more Zumarraga protested, the more Guzman would harass churchmen throughout the province. Friars were assaulted, and the Bishop himself was threatened. Finally Bishop Zumarraga managed to smuggle a letter out of Mexico, which was delivered to Charles V. The Emperor responded quickly. Guzman was to be replaced, as soon as his successor could get his business affairs in order and cross the Atlantic.

But this was not to be the salvation of Mexico. The millions of native peoples living there would not be rescued from their misery by political means, but by a miracle which was unimaginable.

The heathen religion of their ancestors was filled with stone idols— gods of blood and death. But the people living with that religion had known nothing else. They believed what their parents and grandparents had taught them. The altars of human sacrifice had been destroyed. The idols had been overthrown. Christian churches were built over the ruins of the sacrificial temples. But in spite of all this, relatively few Indians in Mexico were converting to Christianity. It was as if the native population was gripped by a kind of spiritual numbness— some lingering shock after-effect from the Conquest. The country was, as in the words of the [23]poet,

> Wandering between two worlds— one dead,
> The other powerless to be born.

It was only in December of 1531 that Mexico's rebirth would truly begin.

THE MIRACLE THAT TRANSFORMED MILLIONS

To the people in the hill country surrounding the village of Tolpetlac, the political tensions between bishop and governor may have been unknown. One of the residents there was an Aztec man named Juan Diego. His original name had been Cuauhtlatohuac.[31:15] A humble farmer, 57 years of age, Juan Diego was one of the earliest converts to Christianity among his people. His wife had died just two years earlier and now he was living alone, growing corn and beans and supplementing his diet with venison. A devout Catholic, he regularly made the 9-mile trip to the nearest church in Tlaltololco.

On Saturday, December 9, as he was making his way toward Tlaltololco, something unexpected happened. Standing on the side of a hill called Tepeyac, he could hear incredibly beautiful music which seemed to come from the top of the hill— a hill situated miles from any village. Looking upward toward the summit, he was astonished to see a glowing white cloud, from which dazzling rays of light were streaming. Then, from the mist at the top of the hill, he heard a sweet feminine voice calling his name. Juan Diego immediately made his way up the 130-foot rise. There he found the source of the beautiful voice.

There was a Lady standing there, who was as beautiful as her voice. She appeared to be young, around 14 years of age. Her beauty went far beyond earthly standards. Her clothing "shone

---
[23] The phrase is from a poem by Matthew Arnold, titled "The Grande Chartreuse."

like the sun," with the light radiating from her illuminating everything in the area— the rocks, mesquite bushes and cactus plants. Their surroundings resembled the interior of a cathedral, as if everything was bathed by the light of stained-glass windows.

The Lady spoke directly to him. Speaking in that same sweet voice, she let him know immediately who she was. In the most loving and intimate tones, she said, "Know for certain, dearest of my sons, that I am the perfect and perpetual Virgin Mary, Mother of the True God, through whom everything lives, the Lord of all things..." [46:26]

Compared to most other appearances of the Virgin, this self-identification was unusually prompt and specific. Not only did she state her given name, Mary, but she identified herself in a way that outlined the fullest context of Church teachings in regard to her. Perhaps this directness was in consideration of Juan Diego's simplicity, as well as his status as a convert to Christianity. She chose to let him know exactly who she was, without any room for confusion. (This is in contrast to the way she identified herself to the seers at Fatima and Lourdes, all of whom had been steeped in Church teachings since birth.)

The Virgin had some requests for Juan Diego. First, she told him of her wish that a house of worship be built on the hill where they stood. Then she advised him to travel to Mexico City, and transmit her words directly to Bishop Zumarraga. Juan Diego immediately agreed. Mexico City was not far away. The next morning he presented himself at the bishop's offices.

Naturally, the servants of the bishop were reluctant to introduce a rude-appearing Indian peasant from the countryside to the most prominent religious leader in the Western Hemisphere. But we have to remember that this was still an age of faith. After some delay, Juan Diego was allowed to speak with the bishop.

He told Zumarraga everything that had happened. The bishop was perplexed by it all. Although a man of great faith himself, he had trouble believing that the Mother of God had actually spoken with this backwoods peasant. However, after some questioning, the bishop could see that the man was a sincere Christian. He treated Juan Diego with kindness, and assured him that he would reflect on all he'd said.

Diego could see that the bishop was unconvinced. He returned to the hill of Tepeyac, and the radiant lady was there waiting for him. After he confided his disappointment to her, she told him to return to the bishop and repeat her requests.

When Juan Diego arrived at the bishop's office the second time, he was greeted with obvious impatience. The servants didn't want to deal with him. He was kept waiting for hours in the cold courtyard. Finally, Bishop Zumarraga spoke with him. Juan Diego was filled with emotion by all that was happening, and tears welled up in his eyes. The bishop spoke reassuringly to him, and began asking questions. He asked for details about the Lady on the hill. Finally, Bishop Zumarraga asked Juan to request that she provide a miraculous sign, to prove the truth of her presence. Diego promised that he would ask her.

Events transpired which would complicate things. Juan Diego's closest living relative, his uncle, was stricken with a fever— or (according to another account) wounded by an arrow. [46:32] After some difficulties, he was finally in the presence of the Virgin again on the hill of Tepeyac. The bishop had asked for a sign, and now she would provide it. First, she assured Juan Diego that his uncle was healed that very moment. Then she gave him an unusual errand. She told him to gather some flowers that he would find at the top of the hill, and take them to the bishop.

Now, this was in the month of December. Neither Juan Diego nor anyone else was going to expect to find flowers growing in the frozen ground! Nevertheless, Juan followed her instructions and went to the top of the hill. He was astonished to find a multitude of flowers blooming there, including Castilian roses. He took his *tilma*, or cloak, and gathered as many blooms into it as he could. Then he set out again for Mexico City.

Once again, he was met by impatient and irritated servants. They refused at first to admit him into the compound. Then they noticed he was carrying something in his *tilma*. A minor ruckus ensued, with the servants trying to look into the folds of the garment, and then attempting to snatch some of the blooms. As they reached into it, the flowers seemed to melt away, appearing as if they were embroidered onto the inside of the *tilma*.

The bishop had been unaware of the commotion outside his office. One of the servants told the churchman what was going on, and he ordered the man to be brought into his office immediately. Juan Diego related the details of everything that had happened. He told the bishop about the field of flowers growing on the frozen summit of Tepeyac Hill. Exclaiming with joy that the requested sign had been granted, Diego opened his *tilma* and poured the flowers out onto the floor in front of the bishop and several other officials who were present.

Bishop Zumarraga and the others gaped with amazement. The servants in the room were just as stunned. However, it wasn't the flowers that had captured their attention. As they stared at the open *tilma*, they beheld something far more astonishing. The inside surface of the garment had been transformed. It was covered by an image in brilliant colors, which depicted the Holy Virgin herself, dressed in a magnificent robe, covered by a dark turquoise-blue cloak studded with stars. She was shown with her hands together in prayer, her head bowed slightly forward, with an expression which radiated love tinged with compassion. Most interestingly, her complexion appeared somewhat dark, resembling that of the native people of the country. And, not the least of the details, she was standing on a dark crescent form, which was supported by an angel portrayed as an infant with wings.

Everyone in the room fell to their knees. Here was a sign from God which no one could have dreamed of. Not a sign in the sky which vanishes within an hour— but a physical creation which could be seen and touched.

Bishop Zumarraga apologized to Juan Diego, begging forgiveness for having doubted him. The prelate ordered that a chapel be erected on Tepeyac Hill, in accordance with the

Virgin's wishes. This would honor her request until a proper church could be built.

Needless to say, word of these events spread like wildfire. On the 26th of that same December, a procession of priests and parishioners followed the miraculous image as it was carried to the temporary chapel on Tepeyac Hill. And once this was done, a far greater miracle took place.

MILLIONS LIBERATED— FROM A RELIGION BASED ON DEATH

As noted, following the fall of the Aztec Empire a decade earlier, most conversions of the native people of Mexico had been infant baptisms. Relatively few adult Indians were ready to abandon the old pagan religion. The ancient fears were still deeply ingrained.

But the image brought by the Virgin actually had the power to conquer those fears. It portrayed her as one of their own— with the same appearance as the people of Mexico. And the crescent under her feet was their symbol of the Aztec deity Quetzalcoatl. The image, in effect, showed the Virgin wearing a turquoise blue cloak— a garment of Aztec royalty— while surmounting the power of the great Quetzalcoatl. It was saying to the people that the Mother of God was one of them. It was saying that the old gods were now beaten and their power destroyed. It was saying that there was no more reason for fearing them.

The very name given by the apparition has tremendous significance. It was recorded that she told Juan Diego that she was to be known as "The Ever Virgin, Holy Mary of Guadalupe." [46:45] However, this was a name of a shrine which already existed in Spain. Generations later, scholars realized that the translator who took this information from Juan Diego must have mispronounced the original Nahuatl word she used, which would actually be *"coatlaxopeuh."* This translates as, "she who breaks, stamps or crushes the serpent"— another allusion to the serpent god Quetzalcoatl. [46:48]

The symbolism in the portrait had an enormous impact on the native people of Mexico, who were familiar with pictographic symbols. It has been estimated that— within seventeen years following the apparitions— approximately *nine million* native inhabitants of Mexico were converted to Christianity, due to the power of this miraculous image. [31:104] Within a generation, the dark empire of the Aztecs and their blood-soaked gods had been transformed into a sunlit region devoted to Christ and His salvation.

THE CONTINUING MIRACLE

Nothing could equal the millions of souls lifted out of pagan darkness and fear. Still, the miracle of the image has continued over time to astonish those who have the courage to see.

The small chapel was expanded into a church, and in 1709 a great basilica was finally opened on the same site. After centuries of settling in the soft soil the building began to tilt, and it was superseded in 1976 by a new basilica erected nearby. Through it all— vast building programs, emergencies and natural disasters— the image has remained for all to see. The Virgin's face is still there as when Juan Diego first unfurled it, radiating its beauty and compassion.

The *tilma* itself is woven from *ayate* fiber, taken from the maguey cactus. It is a type of fabric which usually rots within twenty years. But after nearly five centuries this *tilma* still survives virtually intact. [46:116-117] In 1791 some nitric acid was accidentally spilled on it during the cleaning of the frame. It left only a minor watermark. In 1921 an anonymous terrorist set off a bomb underneath the frame during a Mass, intending to destroy the image forever. Windows in the basilica were shattered and a large bronze crucifix was bent in half by the blast. But incredibly, not even the glass covering the image was broken, and not one of the many worshipers present was harmed.[31:109]

Modern scientific examinations of the image have brought fascinating results. In 1979 Dr. Philip Callahan, a research biophysicist from the University of Florida, photographed the tilma using infrared light. He found that some minor features on the image had been touched up with paint over the centuries. However, regarding the major elements— including the entire portrait and form of the Virgin— the actual creation of the image was beyond scientific explanation. [31:100-101]

In 1955, the most startling discovery of all was announced to the world. On close inspection of the image, it was found that on the pupils of the eyes there were several tiny faces— showing as they would appear in the pupils of a living person's eyes. [46:122-131] The images in the eyes are extremely small (they hadn't been noticed for four centuries), but photographic enlargements show them clearly. When compared to a portrait of Juan Diego painted in the 16th century, it can be seen that the most prominent face is his.

Those reflections in the eyes of the image are an amazing testimony to the miraculous nature of the picture. Along with the astonishing history of the relic, they provide further proof of its authenticity.

As might be expected, the image of the Virgin of Guadalupe has produced controversy. And— just as with any miracle— it has its detractors. The cynics love to focus on the spots where paint was used for touch-up work. This, they say, must prove that the entire image is a fraud. But somehow, they never want to discuss those tiny faces in the eyes.

WHAT DOES IT ALL MEAN?

Prophecies outlining the future history of the 20th century. A miracle witnessed by thousands, where the sun "danced" and appeared to plummet toward Earth. A spring in a grotto, which gives rise to countless cures for countless medical ailments. A supernatural image on a fragile garment which has survived through the centuries— an image whose origin, history and characteristics are clearly miraculous. What does it all mean?

The meaning is simple. For those who aren't afraid to look, we have concrete proof that God exists. It is also proof that God takes an active role in this world, intervening on occasions of His choosing.

This chapter covers just three of the countless miracles recorded over time. And they're only covered here briefly. Many books have been devoted to this subject. One chapter could never do it justice, and I don't pretend to do so here. But I've tried to open the curtain just a bit.

Proof is a funny thing. We have to understand that for some people, there can never be any proof. Their minds are so locked into the mental straitjacket of atheism— so hostile to the very concept of God and His existence— that the idea of proof does not enter into their thinking. (Or rather, their lack of thinking.) The more obvious it is, the greater will be their effort to disregard or dismiss it.

Thankfully, for the vast majority of humanity, the brain is still a functioning entity. Most people are willing to open their eyes and look at evidence. And many aren't afraid to acknowledge proof when they see it.

Perhaps the greatest comfort is for those who already believe. Even in this modern age, we can see that God hasn't left the world to keep guessing over whether He is real. For anyone with the courage to open their eyes, the proof is right in front of us.

Chapter 20

THE TOUGHEST HURDLE

There are definitely obstacles in life. I'm not going to be the one to tell you that once you've decided to get closer to God, everything's going to be easy for you. Then I'd be just another salesman, like the ones you see on TV. ("Buy our product, then life will be perfect.") It just doesn't work like that. Things won't automatically get easier. In fact, they might get harder. I don't like saying this, but I'm not going to lie.

Throwing off the blinders is the first hurdle. By getting rid of the false notions that were keeping your mind in chains, you're a great deal freer than you were before. Now you can take the steps that you never dared take before.

I can remember when I first began to realize that God is real. It was an amazing thing to me— He showed me in a thousand little ways that He's there. Not with any big "special-effects" miracles, like you'll see in movies. He showed me with a multitude of little miracles. And there's no doubt in my mind that He will do the same for anyone who seeks Him. Don't forget the promise made by Christ: "Seek and you will find." That promise is always going to be good. But finding out that God is real is still just the first step.

It's not enough to simply know that God is there. The devil knows that, but he's still God's enemy. Just knowing it isn't enough to save anyone. Remember, this is a radical life-change that we're talking about.

One of the toughest things for me was going to church. In all my childhood years, I'd only been to church a few times. As mentioned in Chapter 3, once in a while my great-grandparents would bring me with them. In my early 20s, I had visited a few churches. Usually a friend from college would invite me. But I just never found one that worked for me. Finally, I started going regularly to a Catholic Church.

This was the situation. I was twenty-five years old. I had never before attended any church regularly. I doubt that I'd even been to church a total of ten times in my life. But there I was, trying to go every Sunday. Everything seemed strange to me. I wasn't used to sitting in pews with others. I was totally unfamiliar with the Mass. But I just did as well as I could, using the missal (the Mass book) to try and follow along. When everybody stood up, I stood. When everybody sat down, I sat.

And, as I said in Chapter 7, I noticed one thing new. I just had the feeling that *everything was going to be all right.* There's just no other way to describe it. At the time, I couldn't understand it. Of course, it was just part of the inner peace that Jesus had promised. I didn't know it at the time. And I couldn't maintain it throughout the week. But for the first time in my life, I was feeling some of that inner peace. To tell you the honest truth, that alone is worth going to church. Of course, there are a lot more reasons. But there are also a few things we should be on guard for.

Sometimes we really are our own worst enemy. As we've seen, pride can be a powerful force in the human psyche. It can give a certain amount of strength to those who live by it. But that same strength can turn into brittleness. Pride can sometimes be self-destructive.

There is such a thing as self-respect. As I've said already, there's nothing wrong with being assertive when the occasion calls for it. No one's saying we should be doormats for others to walk over. (There are some people who— if given the chance— will do just that.) Sometimes other peoples' pride will be turned on us. For example, there are those who will sneer at anyone who goes to church. They'll call it a weakness— only for those who "need" it.

Anyone can see the flaws in that logic. Once we've found that God is real, we know that He is the only One who's supreme. When people boast about themselves, their boasting is empty. And when they use their sneers to put down others for having faith, they're actually doing the work of the devil. The scariest part of it is, *they don't even have a clue.*

Ignore such people. Once you've discovered that God is real, you know what life's real priorities are. You know that there's such a thing as salvation. Nothing is more important than that. Don't pay attention to the sneers of others, and don't let your own fears— or pride— hold you back. What's to be afraid of in going to church? Kids go. Little old ladies go. You'll find people of all types and all ages in most churches. If they're not afraid, why should you be?

Of course the people you see in church are strangers. Everyone is, until they get to know each other. Some things are worth the time they take. I'd say that salvation is at the top of the list.

THERE WILL BE DIFFICULTIES

This is the point where the highly-rationalized, "sophisticated" thinkers will burst into their usual knee-jerk spasms of laughter. This is the threshold where we must decide whether to cling to those comfortable blinders, or step forward into the not-so-comfortable realm of the supernatural. Not the earthbound, "paranormal" stuff of ghosts and séances. I mean the *real* supernatural domain of good and evil. And yes, that includes angels and demons.

We must know this: Once we realize that God is there, we have to admit the likelihood that a lot of other things are true as well. If anything as tremendous as God can exist, then an entire universe of spiritual realities can exist right along with Him. And— trust me on this— it does.

Unfortunately, the devil is one of those realities; he really exists. (As shown in Chapter 13, I found that out first-hand.) And one thing you have to know, is that he *will* try to stop you. The devil wants your soul almost as much as God does. The devil does take an interest in you. But unlike God, the devil does not love you. We have to remember: Satan is trying to fill Hell with as many victims as possible. That's what he's all about.

They say that one of the devil's greatest advantages is in getting people to think he doesn't exist. And that's undoubtedly true. After all, how many people who disbelieve Satan's existence are going to be on guard against him? Certainly, the devil prefers to work with subtlety whenever he can. The possession thing that he tried on me is probably not his standard type of attack. Usually he uses more ordinary means to distract us, to tempt us— to discourage us in any way he can, from staying on the path to salvation. He wants us to give up. (That's the only way he has any chance of winning.)

But that's no cause for fear. There's a magnificent prayer to St. Michael the Archangel, that's worth praying every day. Copies of it should be available at any Catholic church. It calls on the great Archangel to defend us against the devil, and to cast him into Hell where he belongs. I'd recommend the St. Michael prayer to anyone seeking God— in fact, to anyone, period.

Don't ever forget: God is infinitely more powerful than any angel, including the devil. Once you're moving on a trajectory toward God, Satan can't stop you. Once you know that God is real, you know that His power is greater than anything else. Greater than this world. Far greater than the devil, or any number of devils.

THERE'S MORE THAN THE DEVIL TO WATCH OUT FOR

If Satan were the only thing dragging people down, everyone we know would probably be saints already. The devil is the easiest thing to reject. He is a single entity. He hides whenever he can, usually working behind the scenes; but his workings can be seen, and occasionally his presence can be identified. There's a lot more to the perils of this world than one damn devil. One thing we have to reckon with is the world itself. And that's not a comfortable thought. After all, let's face it— *the world?*

It's not a pleasant thing to wrap our minds around. But from the perspective of a spiritual, God-seeking person, the world is *not our friend*. This is one of those reality checks that make life so interesting, challenging, and at times unsettling. What is it about the world we live in? What is it that makes it not-our-friend?

First of all, let's examine the idea itself. Do you view the world as friendly? I don't. I like to read a lot. Also, I spend hours watching movies and favorite TV shows on videodiscs, just to get my mind off the world. As I mentioned earlier, entertainment (that is, escapism) is a multi-billion dollar industry. It seems that *lots* of us like to get our minds off the world and its hassles. And most Americans are willing to spend money to do so. There are huge amounts of time when people don't even want to *think* about life's troubles— much less *deal* with them. And there's a reason for that. The world tends to drag people down. In the slang of the recent past, "it can be a real drag."

It can be more than that. It can destroy people. We live in a society which has one of the highest— if not *the* highest— per-capita prison populations of any developed country on Earth. We have drug dealers in cities and towns, trying to make a dishonest buck by getting kids hooked on crack. We have credit card companies trying to make an honest buck by getting people hooked on high interest payments. We have an entertainment media that throws slanted news, "retouched" history and brain-sucking sitcoms at us in an effort to demolish what's left of our minds. (They want us to get hooked on cable.) These examples are only the tip of the iceberg. Some of the hazards of everyday life were mentioned in Chapter 1. Anyone who takes a serious look can see the truth of the situation: The world just really isn't a friendly place.

And this is one of the recurring themes found in the Bible. Very clearly, the New Testament warns against trying to be "friends with this world." {James 4:4} And Jesus Himself described the devil as the *prince of this world.* In other words, right here— the world we live in— is one of the places where Satan's power is strongest. And all you have to do to see it, is to open your eyes and look around.

God created the world— a world that was good, even if it was primordial. Then man abused his gift of free will and it's been a minefield ever since. This is *our world* I'm talking about. It's this beautiful world of beaches and bikinis, alpine vistas and avalanches, gleaming skyscrapers and suicide bombers. This is the world where Satan spreads his glitter, lays his snares, and harvests souls for Hell.

I knew a fellow at work not too many years ago. Another employee, a good friend of mine, said he used to give this guy a lift home after work. My friend complained that the other guy never had money to give him for gas. But he always had money for the state lottery. Without fail, he would buy at least five dollars worth of lottery tickets every week.

The lottery guy came down with cancer. I approached him once, and asked him if he'd like to go to church with me. I wasn't sounding preachy about it. He replied that his family was coming over to visit him, and said that at this point in his life, seeing them was more important to him than church. I'm not passing any judgment on this guy. This is all I know about him. He finally got too weak to work any more. Not long after that, he died.

Maybe he was the most faithful individual in the world. A lot of people like to play the lottery; that doesn't make anyone evil. But the question for each of us is this: Is there a point where we let something like the lottery become an object of idolatry? Is there a point where we put our faith in something like that, instead of in God? Is there a point where we catch ourselves putting our faith in *anything* besides God?

This world is always trying to sell us something. If you have five preset stations on your dashboard radio, most of the time three or four of them will be belting out commercials. If you're paying forty or fifty bucks a month (or more) for cable, you're paying for those wonderful ads that try to entice more money out of you. You're paying for everything— *including* the commercials.

That's how the world works. You are part of the crop. And it wants to harvest from you all that it can. It wants your money; it wants to take over your life— it wants your very soul.

The world is geared for taking. If it can't destroy you on the outside, it will try to ensnare your heart and mind and destroy you on the inside. God is the One who wants to give. And when it comes to real salvation, He's the only one who *can* give.

AND THEN THERE'S HUMAN NATURE

It's a funny thing. But sometimes the people we care about most can be the very things that hold us back. We can usually accept the notion that we belong to our families. After all, we need family. Without my kids in my life, I know that I'd feel like almost nothing. And I can remember what my life was like without them. Even though they're grown now and pursuing their own lives, they are essential to my own.

And many people feel the same toward their friends. In a way, this is healthy. It's good to have close friends, people we know and trust. But there are times when the very people who count most in our lives can be a negative force. And nowhere is this more obvious than when we start drawing closer to God. Friends are often brought together by mutual interests. If someone senses that your interest in seeking God threatens his or her own personal interests, that person might just turn into an obstacle. They might just try to discourage you from going forward. Maybe it's not even intentional.

Is going to church once a week going to jeopardize someone's social schedule? Could it be an obstacle to an important fishing trip? How about old drinking buddies? If you start "acting religious," would it get in the way of those weekend sports events? Or force you to pick another time for workouts at the gym?

Is there a friend who needs you so much as a crutch, that he or she resents any new change in your life? Even if it's for your own good? You'd be surprised, how many reasons some people might find to view your spiritual path as a threat to their own comfortable world.

Friends are friends, right? But when are friends *not* friends? It's simple. They're not being your friend if they try to hold you back from finding God. In such a situation they're not thinking about you, but only about themselves.

BE ON GUARD AGAINST NEGATIVE FORCES

Perhaps the toughest single hurdle is to view the world— and everything in it— from the right perspective. You have to remember that God is supreme, and He is also the greatest thing in your favor.

A lot of people in this world are out of touch with that reality. And the further out of touch anyone is with God, the more vulnerable they are to the wiles and snares of the devil. That's a mind-bending thought. But there are various references in the New Testament to the devil's power in the world, and over many of the people in it. {Acts 10:38} Also: {1 John 3:10}

This isn't to say that people intentionally choose to do evil. Far from it. Nearly everyone tries to do what he *thinks* is good. The power of the devil is not in converting people to the cause of evil. His power is in deceiving people into seeing destructive things as "good." There are a few outright Satan worshipers in our society. But the vast majority of people on the wrong path are there because they actually think it's a good path.

Just look at what the world teaches, and see for yourself. {1 John 4:5} You won't see many rock singers or sitcoms warning about the *consequences* of casual sex. But they will sing about it, brag about it, joke about it, and build it up as one of the greatest things in life— and they'll make millions doing so. They make the money, and countless young people taken in by such propaganda pay the price. Falling into mindless, dead-end relationships has ruined more lives than anyone can count. And who knows how many young people, while "experimenting" with sex (or drugs), have been dealt a fatal hand of AIDS?

That's just one example of how many can be deceived into thinking something self-destructive is "good." Of course, that doesn't mean sex itself is bad. On the contrary, it's a precious gift from God— it strengthens married love, and makes possible God's gift of children. It's only the way selfish people have twisted it into something else, that turns it into a type of quicksand for so many.

It's the same with wealth, material goods and individual freedom. None of these things are evil in themselves. If they're put in the right perspective as gifts from God— and not allowed to become objects of idolatry— there's nothing wrong with any of that. It's only what some people have done with them that make them self-destructive.

But the destructiveness is real. The line is there, which can destroy us once it's crossed. Just as God is real, just as Heaven is real, so is everything else.

THE GREATEST CHALLENGE

The greatest challenge is not in seeing that there's a right direction. It's not even that difficult to find it. The greatest challenge— by far— is *finding that direction and staying on course*. The obstacles will always be there. The greatest challenge is in not allowing those obstacles (or the one who lays the snares) to divert us.

It's amazing how little it sometimes takes, to make us forget that. The sneering laughter of a "friend;" the scathing comments of an adversary; the momentary humiliation of losing an argument that seems important— all these binding cords of pride compressing our mind— all these things and many others can threaten to turn us away from God, if we let them. And all we have to do is look to the world around us, to see it trying to do the same.

I don't have all the answers, and I don't pretend to. But the answers are there.

Each of us must search for God the best way he can. Anyone who dares will find hurdles along the way. But the hurdles can be overcome. All we have to do is open our minds and look for Him. Life is the journey, and we have to strengthen ourselves for it— not cling to things that drag us down.

Tear off the blinders. Break loose from the chains of pride and skepticism. Keep rationality, but keep it in its proper place, after faith. Common sense should tell you that faith is more important, because some people are so "rational" that their labyrinthine thinking drags them further away from God. Realize— and be courageous enough to admit— that He is in charge, and everything else is secondary. There are many rewards possible in life. But salvation is the *only* reward we can keep forever.

You've got to remember that God is there, and that He's for you and not against you. He really is a loving Father— patient, generous and even indulgent, knowing our flaws and weaknesses. He will forgive our mistakes and help us to put them behind us. He will lift us up from the depths of self-doubt or self-loathing, and give us a soul that can withstand anything the world throws at us.

Don't panic and start running from a God like that. You should run towards Him. Run as hard, and as fast, and as steadily as you can. And once you start in His direction, even if you stumble once in a while, never let yourself forget the goal— because everything depends on it.

As the Man said, what good is it to gain the whole world, if it costs you your soul? {Matthew 16:26} It was a rhetorical question, of course.

But it's a question worth repeating.

GLOSSARY

AD — This is an abbreviation for the Latin words *Anno Domini*, or "year of our Lord." It is the basis for our modern calendar. In this system the year 1 AD is counted as the birth year of Jesus Christ. The year was calculated in the 6th century by a monk (or abbot) named Dionysius Exiguus (Denis the Little). Although it's now known that Christ was born several years earlier than the date calculated, because of its widespread usage and convenience the year calculated by Dionysius has been kept as the basis for the calendar. [9:Vol. 4:109]

australopithecine apes — Various fossil species of extinct apes which walked erect. The first to be identified (by Professor Raymond Dart in 1925) was *Australopithecus africanus* ("southern ape of Africa").

Bab edh-Dhra and Numeira — Some Carbon-14 dates obtained from Numeira since 2003 have given an earlier destruction date for that site, indicating a time frame of c2600 BC. This data may require further study. In a video documentary titled "Sodom and Gomorrah," produced in 2001 (an episode of the "History's Mysteries" series), the late Dr. Walter E. Rast— one of the primary archaeologists on both sites— stated confidently that, "Bab edh-Dhra was finished as a city at the same time as Numeira. That is according to our Carbon-14 dates, and also the pottery and artifacts, and our general historical picture. So these two sites are— have reached their end at the same time." If the newer Carbon-14 data proves to be accurate, it could mean that Numeira was destroyed some 250 years before Bab edh-Dhra. However, these new Carbon-14 results might simply reflect an earlier burning of the city, after which it was rebuilt. It may take some years of further study to determine the final destruction date of Numeira beyond any doubt.

BC — The abbreviation for "before Christ." Going by the calculations of Dionysius Exiguus (see listing for "AD" above), these are the dates counted backward in time from the birth of Jesus. For this reason, BC dates run in reverse from AD dates. For instance, the year 100 BC came before 50 BC. If a monarch ruled during those dates, his reign would be shown as "100 – 50 BC."

St. Catherine of Siena — Catholic saint (1347-1380) born in Siena, Italy. She was a religious mystic and strong activist in the affairs of the Catholic Church. A literary giant of her time, she was named a Doctor of the Church by Pope Saint Paul VI in 1970.

cihuacoatl — The highest official in the Aztec Empire, after the *tlatoani* (the emperor) himself. [5:104] Some historians have described him as a sort of "prime minister." Although not a full-time military leader, at the Battle of Otumba he was serving as general-in-chief, no doubt because the objective of annihilating the Spanish was so critical at that point.

Croesus — The last king of Lydia, a kingdom of Asia Minor (modern Turkey). He lived in the 6th century BC, and was renowned for his vast wealth.

cuneiform — A type of writing which originated in ancient Mesopotamia. The word is from the Latin language, and means "wedge shaped." Usually written with a stylus on tablets (or other items) made of clay, the object was then baked in a kiln, making it hard as stone. Consequently, many thousands of cuneiform writings have survived in the soil of the Middle East, for archaeologists to unearth and philologists to translate.

Dark Ages — A dark age is any era in which a civilization declines, and suffers a break with its more civilized past. Historically, during such times fewer records have survived to tell us what was going on. The last dark age of Europe officially began with the fall of the western Roman Empire in 476 AD, and effectively ended with the establishment of the Holy Roman Empire under Charlemagne in the year 800. During that time Europe was largely in chaos, with the only real stabilizing force being the Catholic Church.

Evolution — (Also known as Natural Selection) A scientific theory proposed in the late 1850s by Charles Robert Darwin and Alfred Russel Wallace, two British naturalists. The theory asserts that many species change, or evolve, through natural selection. It further proposes that the main dynamic for natural selection is a process described as the "survival of the fittest." This theory is used to explain the many variations shown in the fossil record over vast expanses of time.

fuhrer — German word for "leader." This was a new title assumed by Adolf Hitler (1889-1945) after the death of President Paul von Hindenburg in August 1934. Prior to that, Hitler had held only the office of chancellor. [9:Vol. 5:933-934]

Hessians — Mercenary troops from several German states, which were used by Great Britain to augment British forces during the American War of Independence. Since George III was (by virtue of his family dynasty) also the Elector of the German state of Hanover, he had close ties to many other German princes. As a large proportion of those German mercenaries were from the landgraviate (county) of Hesse-Cassel, they all were usually referred to as Hessians. [9:Vol. 5:194]

hippies — This term originated in the 1960s, to describe individuals who reject traditional social standards. The word "hippie" was originally meant to imply that such people were "hip," or wise, to what was going on in society. (Before that, the term "hipster" was sometimes used.) In 1966 the news media started focusing on these colorful people who had "dropped out"— people who were going to events called "happenings" and getting "high on life." Actually, they were getting high on drugs like LSD (which was also getting a lot of media attention). Soon, young people from coast to coast were mimicking these hippies who were being glamorized by the news media, and the counterculture was effectively launched. Following the Woodstock rock festival of 1969, some journalists romanticized the movement even further, referring to the new drug subculture as the "Woodstock Nation."

indulgences — Special dispensations available to faithful Catholics, to free them from the penalties of sin. In the medieval period, there developed in some dioceses a practice of granting indulgences for a fee. Greed had crept into the workings of some churchmen. This was one of the chief complaints of Martin Luther when he launched the Protestant Reformation.

jihadist — A modern-day Muslim extremist, who believes that his cause justifies the massacre of civilians. The Arabic word *jihad* refers to "holy war."

Judeo-Christianity — A term to describe the entire scope of Judaism and Christianity. Since Jesus Christ is accepted by Christians as the Jewish Messiah, the two theologies are inextricably linked— both by Christian teachings and by history. Often the term *Judeo-Christian* is used to describe the religious and cultural foundation of Western civilization itself.

Mother of God — One of the titles of the Blessed Virgin Mary. Since she was chosen by God to be the mother of His Son, and since Jesus Christ is God the Son (one person of the Trinity), she is thus given credit for being the mother of God the Son. The title, therefore, is more a recognition of His status than of hers.

"mother goddess" worship — A modern, fabricated religion which became popular in the 20th century. Similarly to Wicca, it caters to the feminist ideology by offering a belief system which is designed to oppose such "patriarchal" religions as Christianity. Mother goddess devotees like to claim their theology was predominant in the distant past, before invading Indo-Europeans imposed male sky-gods on the early populations of Europe. Sometimes they assert that the Sumerians worshiped a great mother goddess called "Innin." This Innin, however, was actually the Sumerian goddess of sex and war, and her name is usually transliterated as "Inanna." (The Sumerians did have a mother goddess figure named Ninhursag, but this deity was only one among a number of secondary figures in the pantheon.) As noted in Chapter 5, the paramount Sumerian god was called Enlil, a male sky-god who was credited with creating their civilization. [13:91-92]

New Kingdom period of Egypt — The last great flowering of Egyptian civilization, lasting from the start of the 18th Dynasty (about 1550 BC) to the end of the 20th Dynasty (about 1070 BC).

pantheon — A group of recognized gods linked in the same mythology. Also, the term applies to any building devoted to honoring the official gods of a nation.

Paspaheghs — One of the Indian tribes of the Powhatan Confederation in Virginia. The Paspaheghs were centered about ten miles northwest of the original Jamestown colony, across the Chickahominy River. [33:39]

Pax Romana — The "Roman Peace." The period of internal tranquility following the establishment of the Roman Empire by Augustus. Despite occasional *coups de etat,* the Empire itself enjoyed general peace and stability from the victory of Octavian (Augustus) in the last civil war of the Republic (31 BC) until the death of the emperor Marcus Aurelius in 180 AD.

pinnace — In the 17th century, this was a small vessel (rigged like a schooner, with two masts), which was often used as a scout vessel, or ship's tender. Nowadays, the term "pinnace" often describes a six or eight-oared boat of the type carried by a warship, or is loosely used to identify any ship's boat.

prefect — *(praefectus).* In the Roman Empire, a title used for various offices. In Egypt, and early in Judea, the governor was a prefect of knightly rank (the noble class of the *equites*). Later in the province of Judea, the governor was raised to the rank of procurator. [36:340]

Sea of Reeds — This was the body of water where God miraculously parted the waters, for the Hebrews to cross during the Exodus. The name was also used to describe parts of the Red Sea, and is translated this way in many English language Bibles. [18:272-274]

stele — A slab or tablet of stone or some other durable material, set upright. Such monuments were covered with inscriptions to honor rulers and record events. Also spelled "stela."

Sumerians — An ancient people who lived in southern Mesopotamia (part of modern Iraq). Although some very ancient Egyptian hieroglyphic signs have recently been found on small ivory labels, the Sumerians are most often credited with the invention of writing (about 3200-3000 BC). Sumerian civilization was so ancient that it was virtually forgotten by the time the Old Testament was being written, and it was only rediscovered when Sumerian cuneiform tablets were unearthed in the last half of the 19th century. The language of the tablets proves that they were not an Indo-European people. Due to their (non-Indo-European) origins, modern "mother goddess" devotees often try to claim that the Sumerians had such a goddess as their main deity— simply one more attempt to re-write history.

Vestal Virgins — In ancient Rome, a group of priestesses responsible for tending the sacred fire of Vesta, the goddess of the hearth. They were required to take vows of virginity for a duration of thirty years. By ancient custom, any Vestal Virgin who broke her vow was subject to the punishment of being buried alive. [9:Vol. 12:337-338]

Wallace, Alfred Russel — (1823-1913) British naturalist who arrived at his own theory of Natural Selection independently of Charles Darwin. [9:Vol. 12:466-467]

Wicca — Another modern prefab religion based on the theory that "the witches of western Europe were the lingering adherents of a once general pagan religion that has been displaced, though not completely, by Christianity." [10:Vol. 25:95] This (now debunked) theory was touted in the first half of the 20th century by two British citizens, Margaret Murray and Gerald Gardner. Murray proposed a number of ridiculous ideas to support her theory, including the notion that Joan of Arc was actually a witch. (Joan of Arc's trial records prove that she was a staunch Christian and completely faithful Catholic.)

BIBLIOGRAPHY

1. *New American Bible*, Sponsored by the Bishops' Committee of the Confraternity of Christian Doctrine. Published by Catholic Bible Publishers, Wichita, Kansas, in 1985.
2. *Ancient America*, by Jonathan Norton Leonard. Published by Time-Life Books, New York, in 1967.
3. *The Annals of Imperial Rome*, by Publius (or Gaius) Cornelius Tacitus. English translation by Michael Grant. Published by Penguin Books in 1956. Reprinted 1987, in Aylesbury, Bucks, U.K.
4. *The Archives of Ebla*, by Giovanni Pettinato, Ph.D. Published by Doubleday & Co., Inc., Garden City, New York, in 1981.
5. *The Aztec Empire — The Toltec Resurgence*, by Nigel Davies. Published by the University of Oklahoma Press, Norman, Oklahoma, in 1987.
6. *Don't Know Much About American History*, by Kenneth C. Davis. Published by HarperCollins, New York, in 2003.
7. *The Early History of the Ancient Near East — 9000-2000 B.C.*, by Hans J. Nissen. Published by the University of Chicago Press, Chicago, in 1983.
8. *Encountering Mary*, by Sandra L. Zimdars-Swartz. Published by Avon Books, New York, in 1991.
9. *Encyclopedia Britannica*, Fifteenth Edition, Micropaedia. Published in 1990.
10. *Encyclopedia Britannica*, Fifteenth Edition, Macropaedia. Published in 1990.
11. *Fatima in Lucia's Own Words*, edited by Fr. Louis Kondor, SVD. 18th Edition. Published by *Secretariado Dos Pastorinhos*, Fatima, Portugal, in 2011.

12. *The Harper Encyclopedia of Military Biography,* by Trevor N. Dupuy, Curt Johnson, and David L. Bongard. Published by Castle Books, Edison, New Jersey, in 1995.
13. *History Begins at Sumer,* by Samuel Noah Kramer, Ph.D. Published by the University of Pennsylvania Press, in 1981.
14. *How Did It Really Happen?,* Reader's Digest Books. Published by the Reader's Digest Association, Inc., in 2000.
15. *Indian Wars,* by Robert M. Utley and Wilcomb E. Washburn. Published by Houghton Mifflin Company, Boston, in 1987.
16. *Joshua's Altar — The Dig at Mount Ebal,* by Milt Machlin. Published by William Morrow and Company, Inc., New York, in 1991.
17. *Life in Ancient Rome,* by F.R. Cowell. Published by G.P. Putnam's Sons, New York, in 1980.
18. *The Lion Encyclopedia of the Bible,* edited by Pat Alexander. Published by the Reader's Digest Association, Inc., in 1987.
19. *Mesopotamia and the Ancient Near East,* by Michael Roaf. Published by Stonehenge Press, (a division of Time-Life, Inc.), in 1990.
20. *Moments in Time,* (video documentary). Episode: "Jamestown: Against All Odds," by Discovery Education, 2003.
21. *National Geographic Magazine,* November 1947 issue. Article: "Unlocking Secrets of the Northern Lights," by Carl W. Gartlein.
22. *National Geographic* Magazine, May 1974 issue. Article: "Tanna Awaits the Coming of John Frum," by Kal Muller, Ph.D.
23. *National Geographic* Magazine, December 1978 issue. Article: "EBLA — Splendor of an Unknown Empire," by Howard La Fay.
24. *National Geographic* Magazine, December 1980 issue. Article: "The Aztecs," by Bart McDowell.

25. *National Geographic* Magazine, February 1997 issue. Article: "Sons of Genghis — the Great Khans," by Mike Edwards.
26. *National Geographic* Magazine, December 2008 issue. Article: "Herod — the Holy Land's Visionary Builder," by Tom Mueller.
27. *Nature* Magazine, December 22, 1983 issue. Article: "Dating the Crucifixion," by Colin J. Humphreys and W.G. Waddington.
28. News article (Associated Press) — "Satan lives in fact, not fantasy — church". Published in the *Progress Bulletin* newspaper, Pomona, California, on June 28, 1975.
29. *Old Testament Times,* by R.K. Harrison, Ph.D. Published by the William B. Eerdmans Publishing Company, Grand Rapids, Michigan, in 1970.
30. *Our Lady of Fatima,* by William Thomas Walsh. Published by the MacMillan Company, New York, in 1951.
31. *Our Lady of Guadalupe And the Conquest of Darkness,* by Warren H. Carroll, Ph.D. Published by Christendom Press, Front Royal, Virginia, in 1983.
32. *The Oxford Dictionary of Popes,* by J.N.D. Kelly. Published by Oxford University Press, Bungay, Suffolk, England, in 1986.
33. *Pocahontas,* by Grace Steele Woodward. Published by the University of Oklahoma Press, Norman, Oklahoma, in 1969. Reprinted in 1976.
34. *RAMESES — Wrath of God or Man?* (video documentary). Produced by Atlantic Productions for the Discovery Channel, in 2004.
35. *Reader's Digest* Magazine, January 1980 issue. Article: "The Mysterious Bonds of Twins," by Edward Ziegler.
36. *The Roman Emperors,* by Michael Grant. Published by Charles Scribner's Sons, New York, in 1985.
37. *The Southeastern Dead Sea Plain Expedition: An Interim Report of the 1977 Season,* edited by Walter E. Rast and R. Thomas Schaub. Published by American Schools of

Oriental Research, Cambridge, Massachusetts, in 1981. (Volume 46 of *The Annual of the American Schools of Oriental Research.*)

38. *The Spirit of 'Seventy-Six*, edited by Henry Steele Commager and Richard B. Morris. Published by Bonanza Books, New York, in 1983.
39. *Tenochtitlan*, by Samuel Willard Crompton. Published by Chelsea House Publishers, Philadelphia, in 2002.
40. *Thomas Jefferson Word For Word*, edited by Maureen Harrison and Steve Gilbert. Published by Excellent Books, La Jolla, California, in 1993.
41. *Through the Wormhole with Morgan Freeman* (video science presentation). Episode: "Is There a Creator?," by Discovery Communications, 2010.
42. *The War of the American Revolution,* by Robert W. Coakley and Stetson Conn. Published by the Center of Military History of the United States Army, U.S. Government Printing Office, Washington, D.C., in 1975.
43. *What Happened When,* by Gorton Carruth. Published by Signet, New York, in 1991.
44. *What If?*, edited by Robert Cowley. Published by Penguin Putnam, Inc., New York, in 1999.
45. *When Weather Changed History,* (video documentary). Episode: "[George] Washington's Weather," broadcast by the Weather Channel, in 2009.
46. *The Wonder of Guadalupe*, by Francis Johnston. Published by TAN Books and Publishers, Inc., Rockford, Illinois, in 1981.

www.ingramcontent.com/pod-product-compliance
Lightning Source LLC
LaVergne TN
LVHW091535060526
838200LV00036B/612